Crossings 26

Othello

Othello

As Interpreted by Luigi Lo Cascio

Translated and edited by
Gloria Pastorino

BORDIGHERA PRESS

© 2012, Mesogea by Sabir srl, Messina
© 2020, Translation and Introduction by Gloria Pastorino

Cover art by Jojo Karlin based on an original photograph by Antonio Parrinello.

Library of Congress Control Number: 2019956478

Printed in the United States.

Published by
BORDIGHERA PRESS
John D. Calandra Italian American Institute
25 W. 43rd Street, 17th Floor
New York, NY 10036

CROSSINGS 26
ISBN 978–1–59954–158–7

CONTENTS

A Ugo e Diego

CRIMES OF PASSION: LO CASCIO'S *OTELLO*
A SICILIAN SHAKESPEAREAN MOOR

Italian actor Luigi Lo Cascio is best known for his remarkable career in film, which began in 2000 with Marco Tullio Giordana's biopic of Peppino Impastato, a lone mafia fighter in the small town of Cinisi, in *The Hundred Steps*. His passionate and nuanced portrayal of a tormented and courageous soul proved him an effective film actor, able to "pierce the screen" with the strength of his expressiveness. However, Lo Cascio is a graduate of the National Academy of Dramatic Arts "Silvio D'Amico" and his passion for acting began in the theatre, a medium that pushes actors to find a physical as well as a verbal language to express themselves. In several interviews, Lo Cascio has commented on how, per force, film flattens expression and uses a more quotidian language that takes poetry away from actors in order to leave it to directors and cinematographers. After having played several Shakespearean characters on stage, in 2014 he decided to adapt Shakespeare's *Othello* in Sicilian dialect, writing an original play, which he also directed and acted in as Iago. The adaptation is motivated by an understandable desire to make the classic text speak to a twenty-first-century audience, while the choice of a language that few understand is determined by its rawness and intrinsic poetry. As he explains in the introduction to the published version of his adaptation, for a Sicilian the dialect is needed when "it is necessary to state one's sense of belonging [...] to a language considered unequalled for shrewdness and wit" (7). More importantly, the use of Sicilian is the abandonment of the "mask" (7) of standard Italian, a language not nearly as expressive, colorful, immediate, or close to one's deepest emotions and thoughts as the dialect is. Any Italian dialect is more tied to one's essence, if assimilated when growing up: a dialect is a mother tongue, a shorthand, an oral familiar way of expressing oneself, far from the official Italian learnt in books. Lo Cascio has remarked that when he tried to adapt *Othello* into Italian his language was stilted, artificial, literary — i.e., the farthest thing from what works on stage. Therefore, he got the idea of using the Sicilian he heard growing up in the occidental part of the island, in hepta- and hendeca-syllable verse to enhance the language's intrinsic melody. The rhythm of his poetry when heard in the theatre is truly mesmerizing: even though the language he uses is quite far from Italian (both in terms of lexicon and syntax), after a while the translation provided by super-titles can be ignored, in favor of a more instinctive and melodic, albeit less precise, understanding of the terms used. Unlike other masters of dialectal theatre (Gilberto Govi or Eduardo De Filippo, for instance), Lo Cascio does not simplify his language to make it more comprehensible to a non-Sicilian audience; yet, his gamble pays off.

Lo Cascio uses only four characters in his free adaptation: Othello, Iago, Desdemona, and a nameless soldier, who functions as *raconteur* and commentator. This is not an original choice *per se*: for instance, in 2008 in *Othello, Bye Bye* the Dutch company Dood Paard had a cast of three male actors: two on stage playing most of the main parts (using props or garments as signifiers of a different character) and one off, serving as stage manager who would like to participate in the acting but is literally and figuratively marginalized by his job and color (the two main actors are white, acting in makeshift blackface, while he is either black or Arab, or whatever is perceived as the "other" in the culture where the play is staged). In 2012 Toni Morrison's *Desdemona* envisioned an all-female cast recounting the unfortunate protagonist's story with words and music, as she spoke from the grave to her nursemaid Barbary (mentioned in *Othello*, IV.3.24–31) in a class-erasing meeting of minds. Peter Sellars directed this heartfelt rendition of womanhood, in which issues of gender, race, motherhood, war, and love as an all-conquering force were discussed by the two women (Malian singer-songwriter Rokia Traoré interpreted an array of Desdemona's interlocutors). What is original about Lo Cascio's *Othello* is that the three male characters speak Sicilian, while Desdemona speaks standard Italian. This immediately establishes two important ideas for the audience: this is not a play about jealousy and race, but rather about class and gender, and incomprehension between genders is deepened by the fact that they speak a different language. That also explains how Iago is able to convince Othello of his wife's infidelity so quickly and with such flimsy, inconclusive proofs: as comrades in arms, they share a language (and so do the soldier and Lodovico, briefly played by the same actor who plays the soldier). Desdemona is patrician, too highly educated for her own good, and the real "different" character in the play, no matter how hard she tries to adapt her life to her husband's culture.

Lo Cascio's *Othello* can be divided into sixteen major scenes that benefit from his experience in cinema, since the montage of new scenes and rewritten ones from Shakespeare's original play alternate, creating filmic narrative and temporal structures. A prologue and a coda frame fourteen scenes: Othello's humiliation of Desdemona in front of Iago and her cousin Lodovico, Venetian ambassador to Cyprus (corresponding to Shakespeare's act four, scene one); a very cinematographic "jump cut" to a monologue from the condemned and soon-to-be-tortured Iago, who explains the beauty and power of hatred; the soldier's explanation of the background story; an exchange of courtship letters (two each) between Desdemona and Othello, interspersed with comments from the soldier on the nature of their love; the scene in which Iago first insinuates the idea of jealousy and questions Desdemona's demeanor with Cassio, ending with Othello's monologue on marriage (corresponding to act three, scene three); the soldier's narration; a monologue in which Desdemona laments that Othello did not give her an extra day to live (a flash-forward to a non-existing post-mortem scene in Shakespeare); the pivotal scene between Othello and Iago, in which the general is progressively more and more convinced of his wife's betrayal to the point that he faints in an epileptic fit (conflating acts three, scene three and act four, scene one); the soldier's comment; the scene between Iago, Othello, and eventually Cassio, only perceived as a shadow (corresponding to act four, scene one); Othello's direct and escalating accusations to Desdemona (conflating act three, scene four and act four, scene two); the soldier's comment; a modern, twentieth-century Iago explaining the psychological motives of his misogyny; Othello's killing of Desdemona (corresponding to act five, scene two); and the soldier's dream, which concludes the play. From this quick list it is clear that Lo Cascio uses pivotal scenes in Shakespeare's play to shape his own play about human sentiments and gender incomprehension, adding quite a bit of original material. The alternance between Shakespearean scenes and dialogues and lyrical monologues or fairy-tale like dreams creates a poetical play where flashbacks and flash-forwards help the audience get a more in-depth insight into the characters' psyche.

The play's prologue and the first two scenes already set the tone of this deconstructed new *Othello,* by focusing on key aspects of the well-known story extrapolated from the original text and expanded into a non-linear representation, placing the thematic crux of the play first. The prologue is taken from Othello's tale of the handkerchief he gave to Desdemona as a gift (III.4.54–67), which was, in turn, given to his mother by an Egyptian charmer, who warned her of its magical properties: "... while she kept it / 'Twould make her amiable and subdue my father / Entirely to her love — but if she lost it, / Or made a gift of it, / my father's eye / Should hold her loathèd, and his spirits should hunt / After new fancies" (III.4.57–62). To scare Desdemona further, Shakespeare's Othello probably invents the story of a two-hundred-year-old Sybil who sewed it from silk bred by "hallowed worms" "dyed in mummy, which the skilful / Conserved of maidens' hearts" (III.4.73–74). In Lo Cascio's adaptation, in the obscurity of the theatre, we see a dark-blue-hued video of something that eventually looks like silk worms spinning a thread that turns into fabric with embroidered strawberries on it. As the mysterious and eerily magical video captures the audience's attention, Othello's voice, in Sicilian, asks to borrow the handkerchief he gave her, the one imbued with magic, whose silk came from sacred worms of an ancient Sybil and whose pale red color came from the embalmed hearts of virgin women prematurely taken by death. The adaptation is faithful to Shakespeare's story, although it adds different nuances to the text in the language used: while Shakespeare's woman would be "amiable" and "subdue [Othello's] father to her love," Lo Cascio's woman's "beauty will always be the charm that binds a man tightly to the chain" (biddizza resta sempre 'ncantu / ca teni strittu l'omu a la catina, 15) and losing the handkerchief would not simply make her "loathèd" and push the man to pursue new loves, but cause "the light in [her] husband's eyes / in an instant [to] die out," as the "time / of contempt, indifference, / and the hunt after new fancies / for all the other women in the world" comes (a luci intra all'occhi 'i to' maritu / nt'un attimu s'astuta e veni u tempu / di lu disprezzu, di l'indiffirenza, / e di la caccia a novi fantasie / pi tutti l'autri fimmini d'u munnu, 15). The language is stronger, more charged with hatred and mistrust; the curse for losing the gift "pollutes and poisons love and life" ('ntossica e avvilena amuri e vita, 15).

The first scene, still in the same dark hue, sees Othello seated with his back to the audience, during Desdemona's cousin Lodovico's visit from Venice. It is Act IV, scene one in Shakespeare's play. The tense interaction between Othello and Desdemona, witnessed by Lodovico and Iago, follows closely the original, even though this Othello is more spiteful in his words and his slap to Desdemona catches the audience by surprise because not built up by a whole act of Iago's accusations planted in Othello's ears. What is missing is Lodovico's reaction after Othello humiliates Desdemona showing her at his beck and call, respond like a trained monkey: Lo Cascio is not concerned with Othello's reputation in Venice but with the building incomprehension in the married couple. The audience is immediately confronted with an unreasonable Othello, violent, unyielding, displaying excessive and seemingly unjustified anger. Lo Cascio conflates the rest of the scene with scene two in Shakespeare's act four, when Othello repeatedly calls Desdemona, in private, a strumpet and a whore. In this interpretation the accusation is public and the shame is beyond repair. The whole scene feels like a witch trial where Desdemona is wrongly accused on the basis of hearsay and has no right to any defence. Only woman on stage, she never has anyone stand up for her, no one to help her explain herself especially when the virulence of the attacks stuns her into silence. In Shakespeare's original play at least she has Emilia, unwitting accomplice of her husband Iago's machinations when she delivers the handkerchief to him, and relentless advocate and witness to Desdemona's fidelity and devotion, to the point of losing her own life to defend her mistress.

The second scene shows Iago approaching the stage from somewhere in the orchestra, harnessed and bound by ropes, as he reaches his place of torture and eventual death. In Shakespeare Iago's fate is sealed in Act V scene two by Lodovico's final words after Othello has stabbed himself and

Cassio has been put in charge: "to you, lord governor, / Remains the censure of this hellish villain / —The time, the place, the torture, O enforce it" (V.2.366–68). In Lo Cascio's interpretation Iago is dialoguing with the audience, as he walks to his punishment. The spectacle is not for their benefit: it is not meant to be a satisfying moment of justice being done. His death is a common destiny, his evil actions are not just his but part of the human condition. Man is like a cancer that goes crazy, following no laws, and his madness multiplies, destroying life. He revels in the upcoming torture, because pain is part of life and it actually glorifies it. Human laws, when one's mind incites criminal acts, are just a piece of paper, powerless against human will. Iago does not reveal the reason for his actions: even under torture, he remains a mystery because, he says, "I am not what I am" (iu nun sugnu chiddu chi sugno, 25). In saying this he mirrors Shakespeare (I.1.65), somewhat obscurely admitting that he is playing a role and that we cannot get to know the man behind it. Iago maintains the right to keep private his own thoughts, motives, and actions throughout the play, not just with the pawn of his scheming, Roderigo, but with Othello himself, when he refuses to disclose what he is thinking, claiming that even slaves are masters of their thoughts (III.3.137–45). Gone are the character's histrionics that made Shakespeare write Iago's role for the best comic actor in the King's Men: much like *Romeo and Juliet,* his *Othello* has a comic structure upon which tragedy develops irreparably and lethally. As Peter Ackroyd states in his biography of Shakespeare: "Iago, customarily seen as the epitome of evil in modern productions, was initially played by the company's resident clown and fool, Robert Armin. Iago was in the comic mode, and spoke to the audience in his confidential soliloquies" (431). Indeed, Lo Cascio's Iago has no direct interactions with Desdemona, no lewd banter (only obscene insinuations for Othello's ears only), no asides to the audience to get them to appreciate his cleverness, no displays of wit that would have made audiences admire his intellect in spite of themselves. This Iago speaks directly to the audience not to get them in on the cruel joke that he is playing on Roderigo, Brabantio, Cassio, Desdemona, and Othello, as he does in Shakespeare, but rather to encourage them to look into their souls and recognize that hatred is a more powerful sentiment than love. Even the constant references to Iago's honesty, which perfectly exemplify dramatic irony in Shakespeare, are gone here and the few times Othello describes him as honest the effect on the audience is bitterness rather than irony and comedic repetition.

As in a *noir* film from the '40s (such as *D.O.A.* or *Double Indemnity*), the audience enters the story at its climax: the crime and punishment of Desdemona, Othello, and Iago. What follows is the appearance of the soldier, who first interacts with Iago as his executioner and then takes on the role of *raconteur,* of our Virgil in this hellish tale of love and death, telling us the backstory, what happened to lead to this dark and violent outcome. It is a *noir*: the whole play is a dark murder mystery of sorts with an unredeemable anti-hero. The set, the lights, and the costumes reflect the darkness of the story: there is no airiness, no moment of lightness to accompany Othello and Desdemona's love story, not even in the letters that make them fall for one another in Lo Cascio's interpretation. In Shakespeare's play we know in act one how they fell in love because Othello, accused of kidnapping Desdemona, needs to justify her flight to her father, Brabantio, the Duke, and the whole court. Lo Cascio, instead, has the two lovers write letters to each other, on handkerchiefs, which serve the diegetic function of fooling her father's watchfulness (since less conspicuous than paper) and the role of signifiers of illicit love affairs: through handkerchiefs she betrays her father's trust and because of one she is accused of unfaithfulness. They also establish a deeper level of intimacy, since a handkerchief is used to wipe bodily fluids and is kept close to the body (bosom, sleeves), especially in women's clothing in the seventeenth century where, if a pocket existed at all, it would be under one's petticoat and not meant for handkerchiefs. In her letters Desdemona says that she learns about herself through Othello's words: "For me 'foreigner' has the familiar ring / of something of myself I did not know" (Per me straniero ha il suono familiar / di qualcosa di me che non sapevo, 33); she addresses him with the familiar "tu" (thou) in Italian to shorten the distance between them but promises to keep a respectful "voi" (you) in public; she asks him to turn her into an obedient soldier, who knows "sacrifice and submission" (38), and confesses that his victories and successes, but mostly his pains and sorrows, made her fall for him. She begs him to take her to battle with him, perhaps to die together, because for her "there is no sweeter death / than falling by [his] side" (Non c'è per me fine più dolce / che quella di cadere fianco a fianco, 39). In his replies he tells her about his noble origins, his bewilderment at her perfection, how she fills all of his thoughts, and how his heart had turned into stone until he met her, from the day his brother had been killed in front of him and his revenge had brought no solace. The ineffectiveness of revenge as consolation is, thus, already expressed by Othello regarding the loss of a dearly beloved person (non-existent in Shakespeare, who is not concerned with giving his audience psychological explanations of his characters' actions). The letters are read on different sides of the stage, in cones of light, that only further emphasize the darkness that surrounds these two solitary lovers. Before telling the story the soldier remarks on Othello's aloneness, who hasn't got a single friend (mancu 'n amicu, 29), and, before Desdemona's death scene, on her aloneness: "Alone you walk, towards disaster" (sula camini, 'ncontru a la ruina, 91). In Shakespeare they are alone as well, surrounded by false friends (Iago and his wife Emilia, who gives the handkerchief to her husband to try to ingratiate him to her) and devoted subjects who are used to create tension (Cassio), but usually people do not take into account the lack of true confidants as a reason for the lovers' demise. Othello is a foreigner and Desdemona is as good as orphaned, since her father disowns her when she chooses her husband over him. That is why Othello ends up trusting a false friend and all his interactions with his wife, from the moment Iago insinuates the idea of betrayal, are at cross purposes: Othello takes everything Desdemona says as a sign of duplicity, while she answers to the best of her abilities, reiterating her love and devotion. In Lo Cascio's version she goes so far as wanting to be Othello's secret weapon against enemies, like a hidden dagger, but ends up unwittingly cutting him and causing his death and damnation.

The soldier tells us that he witnessed parts of the story and the rest comes from reliable sources. There is something of Coleridge's ancient mariner in this soldier: the story is too well known where he is from and tinted with people's assumptions about race and gender roles, but "when [he] leave[s] for a trip / and meet[s] a stranger / who knows nothing / about Othello and poor Desdemona / [he] want[s] to tell him about a general and nothing more" (Ma quannu mi nni vaju pi quarchi viaggiu / e 'ncocciu quarchi cristianu furisteru / ca 'un sapi propriu nenti / d'Otello e di Desdemona piatusa / iu ci vogghiu cuntari d'un ginirali e basta, 31). He feels compelled to tell the story and to set the record straight: it is wrong to think of Othello as black. When one thinks of historical characters (Brutus, Cassio, Coriolanus, the Prince of Denmark, King Lear — all Shakespearean characters, not necessarily historical figures), their passion, feelings, cruelty, and doubts, are the topic of discussion, not their skin color. It is wrong, he argues, to think that the difference between Othello and Desdemona is that "one is white / with sweet rosy lips and the other one dark / with the mouth of a primitive / and savage black" (una è janca / chi labbruzza di rosa e l'autru scuru / c'a funciazza di niuru primitive / e sarbaggiu, 31): the difference between the two is that one is a man and the other a woman. Between Iago's misogyny and Othello's insecurity (both widely played up in Shakespeare), Desdemona doesn't have a prayer: insofar as woman, she is guilty. Lo Cascio's Iago's winning argument is not the circumstantial, fabricated evidence or the fact that her betrayal of her father's trust is used against her both by her father and Iago in Shakespeare's version: the very fact that she falls for Othello proves that she is depraved. He tells Othello: "when she pretended to fear / your awesome looks / the fever to be possessed by you / mounted in her flesh" (quannu si mustrava timurusa / d'u vostru aspettu d'omu colossali / dintri la carni ci crescìa la frevi / d'essiri di voscenza possiduta, 61). If, so young, she proved to be such a good actress, what else could be expected? Refusing the courtship of her young, rich, and strapping compatriots shows a desire that goes against nature: "And doesn't this indicate / a depraved heart / lewd flesh, / thoughts that know no blush / tinted with lechery and lust?" ("E chistu 'un fa pinzari / a cori depravatu / e carni purcariusa, / pinzeri ca 'un canusciunu russuri / 'nchiappati di libìdini e lussuria?, 62). Desdemona is a woman, oversexed and promiscuous, as all women are believed to be from Greek classical literature to the nineteenth century: her job is to keep quiet and dissimulate her unbridled desires. The soldier comments on how for Iago it must have seemed truly unnatural that Desdemona would sleep with an older and foreign man; surely, like all women, she must be a whore. Later on, Iago suggests to Othello to act like a man, because "the number of cuckolds in the world is endless" (Ntù munnu nun si cuntano i cornuti, 81). In one of the final scenes, a beginning-of-twentieth-century Iago explains the Freudian origins of his misogyny: his own mother, whom he loved dearly, slept with another man in her conjugal bed: the only possible conclusion is that "all women are whores" (i fimmini su' tutti buttani, 94). There is no possible salvation: with such a premise, all the love Othello has for Desdemona cannot hide the fact that she must be false, like all women. Iago plays on Othello's insecurities to provoke his fury, but also feeds a strong seed that is already inherent in the culture. No woman is satisfied with just one man.

The language she speaks acts as a further barrier between her and Othello. As already mentioned, all male characters speak Sicilian while she speaks Italian. This highlights her isolation both in terms of class — she is more refined, more cultured, better with words — and of gender: men speak a different language that corresponds to a different code of conduct. How else could Iago convince a man in love, who has opened himself up to Desdemona so thoroughly, to renege on his feelings at the first slanderous comment? Lo Cascio's Othello may try to make a warrior of Desdemona, at her request, but she cannot be a soldier, she cannot share the camaraderie and the lingo that ties all soldiers together. The idea to turn Desdemona into a woman who wants to learn to fight and be by her husband's side in love and war comes from Othello's greeting in Shakespeare's act two, scene one when, finally arriving in Cyprus after defeating the Turks, he addresses his wife as "O, my fair warrior!" (II.1.177). Her battle has been for their love, defending her choice of husband in front of her father, the Duke, and the whole Venetian council, and begging to be allowed to go with her husband not to be "a moth of peace [while] he go[es] to war" (I.3.254). Lo Cascio makes her want to learn the art of war from Othello, as she says in her second letter: Othello's story to the Duke ("she loved me for the dangers I had passed, / and I loved her that she did pity them" I.3.167–68) here is told by her: "It were the victories, the successes, / but mostly the torments, the pains, / that have touched thy heart / to make me fall for you ..." (Sono state le vittorie, i successi, / ma soprattutto i tormenti, le pene, / che ti hanno intaccato il cuore / a farmi innamorare ..., 39). This Desdemona wants to fulfil her childhood dream to ride horses astride, as she dismembered dolls and felt the coldness of a sword's blade, she wants to live the adventures Othello has recounted, one day fight side by side with him, and perhaps become his secret weapon to protect his life and their love.

The distance between Othello and Desdemona is enhanced by the fact that they use a different linguistic register and, therefore, they will never be able to understand each other fully. Convinced that she is unfaithful and false, he asks her who she is, translating his question into Italian — a nuance totally lost in English translation, that reinforces the fact that the distance between them is beyond repair: "Who art thou, in truth? / "Who art thou?" to be clearer / I will translate my question in your parlance. / "Who are you? What are you? Answer!" (Cu' sì tu pi ddaveru? / "Che cosa sei tu?" pi essiri cchiù charu / ntà to' parrata a dumanna traduce. / "Che cosa sei?"! Nzoccu sì tu? Rispunni!, 87). Of course, she answers that she is his faithful and devoted wife. She cannot understand his jealousy, since she gave him no cause for it. However, his comrades do understand his code of conduct, even if they know that it is misguided. As the soldier comments: "The world is as we read it / Our general read / Iago's words / passing them through the funnel / of a predisposed mind" (U munnu è comu nautri lu liggemu. / I palori di Iago / u nostru ginirali li liggìu / facennuli passari ntà lu 'mbutu / di na menti cu na certa 'nclinazioni, 66). It is Othello's principles that make him vulnerable, "as clear crystal / a spit and it breaks" (comu [...] limpidu cristallu: / basta nu sputu e subitu si rumpi, 66). Indeed, this Othello does break: in an unforgettable feat of physical acting by Lo Cascio's co-star Vincenzo Pirrotta, the verbalization of Othello's fears and suspicions that leads to his fainting in act four scene one in Shakespeare is turned here into a fall into an abysmal delirium that can only provoke a breakdown, both mental and physical. Othello is seized by an almost epileptic fit in which words take over the body's gestures completely, leaving him, finally, exhausted and spent on the floor, lifeless. He has reached the point of no return: his principles and his love make him weak. As Iago says when he first appears in the soldier's tale, "stronger than love is hatred" (cchiù forti di l'amuri è l'odiu, 51), and when love is killed in Othello, hatred takes over and for ever. Calling Othello and Desdemona cretins for believing in a fantasy, he says that "love is the illusion / of having a mouthful of infinity / for a few pennies" (l'amuri è l'illusiuni / d'aviri nu vuccuni d'infinitu / pagatu cu du' liri, 52), while "hatred, instead, is infinity for real, / it is never satisfied nor satiated" (L'odiu 'nveci è 'nfinitu pi ddaveru, / mai si sudisfa e mancu si sazìa, 52). Iago's hatred is his endless source of pleasure: his schemes to destroy feeds his insatiable desire.

Iago also delivers lines that sound particularly Sicilian in the philosophy they express, whether they are totally original or present in Shakespeare as well, but with a slightly different nuance. For instance, Lodovico's question in Act four scene one "How does Lieutenant Cassio?" is answered by Iago with "Lives, sir" (IV.1.216–17); in the adaptation it turns into: "Right now? He lives" (A stu minutu? Campa, 17), which implies that Cassio's days are numbered. It is the kind of answer one would expect in a mafia movie, especially when delivered by a character who seems to know and imply more than his words say. In Act III, scene 3, Shakespeare's Iago twice refuses to share his thoughts about Cassio with Othello, asserting that there are limits to a soldier's service: "Good my lord, pardon me: / Though I am bound to every act of duty, / I am not bound to that all slaves are free to —" (III.3.137–39). In the adaptation he maintains twice that "my thoughts know no master" (Lu me' pinzeru 'un canusci patruni, 57) and "I am master of my thoughts" (sugnu patruni di li me' pinzeri, 58): a similar concept that reinforces the idea of being one's own master, of being in control, but also reasserts his pride. Lastly, without resorting to a *Cavalleria rusticana* Sicilian stereotypical scenario of love, passion, and death, Iago's comment that the world is full of cuckolds sounds particularly Sicilian: take a man's life, but not his honor. For this reason in Lo Cascio's version his description of Desdemona's presumed infidelity is particularly detailed: When Othello asks for proof that his wife is unfaithful, Iago wonders how can that be done and asks: "Would you the supervisor grossly gape on? / Behold her tupped?" (III.3. 397–98); Lo Cascio adds a simile "as a young man takes and tups her / and as a horse mounts her" (mentri un picciottu 'a pigghia e la pussedi / e comu nu cavaddu s'accavadda, 72). Iago also adds that he "think[s] it very difficult / to catch them as Cassio / plays in [Othello's] bed / the part of a ram and has his fun" (Mi pare assai difficili / 'ncoccialli mentri Cassio / ntù vostru lettu joca / la parti d'u muntuni e s'addiverti, 73). Shakespeare has Othello think of "unauthorized kiss[es]" (IV.1.2), but Lo Cascio adds "embraces and kisses far from prying eyes / In some secret hideout" (abbrazzi e vasi luntani dill'occhi / dintr'a quarchi ricoviru sigretu) and "being naked with her friend / together in bed" (starisi alla nuda cull'amico / 'nsemmula stinnicchiati 'ncapu ô lettu, 77). He does not just say that Cassio lay "with her, on her; what you will" (IV.1.44), he adds that Cassio got "into [his] lady [...] in her, on her, everywhere" (dintr'a vostra signura [...] Dintr'a idda, supr'a idda, unn'egghiè, 78) torturing Othello to the point of causing him to faint. Lo Cascio also uses expressions that are peculiarly Italian: for instance, Iago calls to defend him "Jesus' heart and all the saints in heaven" (cori di Gèsu e tutti Santi 'ncelu, 71), a much more Catholic invocation than Shakespeare's "O grace! O heaven forgive me! (III.3.375); Othello's "'Swounds!" becomes "Holy Mother of God!" He also uses literary references that no Italian would miss. Othello's initial reaction when Iago's insinuations have seeped through his defences and have planted a strong seed of doubt is a series of good-byes to carefree times and the "peaceful" moments of war, now gone to leave room to a much more destructive internal war; the series of good-byes calls to mind Lucia Mondella's famous, lyrical good-bye to her mountains in nineteenth-century realist writer Alessandro Manzoni's most famous novel *The Betrothed* (*I promessi sposi*). Iago's invocation of torture as "hygiene of the mind" recalls Tommaso Marinetti's *Manifesto of Futurism,* which claims that war is the only hygiene of the world (guerra sola igiene del mondo). Othello's description of killing the captain responsible for his brother's death by cutting him in two recalls Emilio Salgari's in-mid-air gutting of a tiger in *Sandokan.*

After Othello kills Desdemona, the rest of the world ceases to exist in Lo Cascio's adaptation. He decides to end his play not by showing Othello's suicide and the administration of justice, but with a dream that the soldier has. It is a fantasy ending that reasserts the author's signature on the adaptation, but that also shows a third-millennium philosophy rather than a sixteenth/seventeenth-century one (*Othello* was first performed in November 1604). The soldier and Othello go on the moon, where all the things that are lost on earth can be found, to look for the handkerchief, in a scene reminiscent of Astolfo's voyage on the moon in Ariosto's *Orlando furioso,* whose first edition appeared in 1516, almost a century before Shakespeare's *Othello.* Therefore, a fantastic voyage aboard a hyppogriph would not be so far-fetched for Othello: Astolfo is sent by god to the moon with Saint John Evangelist as a guide to recover Orlando's sanity that, lost on earth, is preserved there in a vial. Lost mental sanity is not all one can find there: "lovers' tears and sighs [...] what you ever lost down here, / you will find going up there" (le lacrime e i sospiri degli amanti [...] ciò che in somma qua giù perdesti mai, / là su salendo ritrovar potrai,

XXXIV.75). Lo Cascio's Othello goes with the soldier, who acts as his guide, aboard a hyppogriph as well, and he finds first a vial with Desdemona's "tears and sighs" (l'ampolla di li lacrimi e de li suspiri di Desdemona, 106) and then the handkerchief. He has ulterior motives for going on the moon, though: he has heard that the souls of all women killed on earth end up there and he wants to find Desdemona to ask her to forgive him for having killed her without a reason. The soldier points out that forgiveness should be asked for killing women even with a reason: in this, Lo Cascio's sensitivity is in line with a twenty-first-century preoccupation with feminicide. Othello's problem, according to the soldier, was to put Desdemona on a pedestal, not realizing that, like the moon, she was imperfect and beautiful because of it. With this ending, Lo Cascio is saying that in our world, where the most-frail sentiments and values are constantly under threat, embracing each other's imperfections is the true meaning of love. His ending, which at first sight seems oddly naïve and off kilter, both fits a sixteenth-century imagination and a twenty-first-century need to take a stand against gratuitous violence on women. Respect for life is what emerges from the soldier's dream. Othello wants to build an altar for his dead wife, keeping the vial with sighs and tears and the handkerchiefs as relics to be venerated. However, women need to be respected when they are alive, not when they are dead. Othello seems lost and childish in the soldier's dream, and the only way to calm him down is by showing him the immensity of the universe, seen from the moon. From Virgil to Ancient Mariner compelled to retell his cautionary tale, to Saint John guiding him on the moon's uneven surface to understand terrestrial problems, the soldier finally seems to turn into a Sancho Panza, who tries to rein in his wayward Quijote as he fights his demons when it is too late. It is an uplifting, if bitter-sweet, ending for a senseless tragedy in which Iago's hatred is the predominant sentiment from the beginning and obfuscates even Othello and Desdemona's great love.

WORKS CITED

Ackroyd, Peter. *Shakespeare. The Biography.* New York: Anchor Books, 2006.
Ariosto, Ludovico. *Orlando furioso.* Torino: Einaudi, 2015.
Lo Cascio, Luigi. *Otello.* Messina: Mesogea, 2015.
Shakespeare, William. *Othello.* London: Oxford UP, 2006.

TRANSLATOR'S NOTE

Luigi Lo Cascio published the text of his adaptation with Mesogea, a Sicilian publisher. In his introductory note he explains his transliteration choices, since there is no single Sicilian dialect, nor a single way to write it, even when it comes from the same area—Palermo in this case. My journey into his language, as a Milanese in love with the musicality I heard in the performance of his text, has been two-fold: first I had to teach myself his Sicilian and then translate it both into Italian and into English, in order to have a full grasp of how the nuances worked across these three languages. Lo Cascio used an Italian translation of Shakespeare's text to write the parts of his adaptation close to the original, so I went back to the bard's text and provided the original wording alongside my English translation where Lo Cascio diverges significantly from the bard. In his interpretation, stage directions and Desdemona's words are in Italian, while the soldiers and other characters speak in Sicilian.

I did not try to keep the metre of either play in my translations because this *Othello* should only be performed in Sicilian and translations are for content, not for poetry. Same reason why I chose not to try to find an English dialect to show the difference in parlance between soldiers and Desdemona: an equivalent one simply does not exist and it would not be intelligible everywhere in the English-speaking world. I kept Lo Cascio's word repetitions, as well as the habit to begin sentences with the conjunction "and," since they give an idea of the way spoken, discursive Sicilian sounds. My main goal was to make the play available to Anglophone audiences.

I would like to thank Luigi Lo Cascio and Vincenzo Pirrotta for their kindness and availability. Heartfelt thanks to Anthony Tamburri and the editors at Bordighera Press for believing in this project; Martin Donoff for being my first reader, editor, and sympathetic critic; Renato Ventura for being my first teacher of the beautiful Sicilian language, and his Syracusan friends for helping me learn words so far from my northern sensitivity; Davide Sisia for unlocking the last mysteries; and Federica Zibordi for introducing me to my new love, Palermo.

Othello

SICILIAN-ITALIAN-ENGLISH TRILINGUAL EDITION

As Interpreted by Luigi Lo Cascio

Translated and edited by
Gloria Pastorino

Buio in sala. Il suono sotterraneo di una nota, che ha cominciato a scavare nell'ascolto degli spettatori già da qualche minuto, crescendo poco a poco di volume, sembra pretendere che adesso finalmente si apra il sipario. L'oscurità cancella la profondità presunta del palcoscenico. E quando la luce progressivamente invade lo spazio ci accorgiamo della presenza di un enorme panno bianco che scende dall'alto e vela tutto quello che forse si prepara alle sue spalle. La prima immagine di un proiettore che comincia a funzionare coincide perfettamente con la fisionomia del tessuto così che adesso supporto e apparizione si perdono l'uno nell'altra.

Dopo qualche secondo d'immobilità, l'immagine inizia a impegnarsi in una sequenza impulsiva e ormai decisamente incontenibile di fughe e di trasformazioni senza sosta.

Si tratta della storia del fazzoletto che Otello ha regalato a Desdemona. Ne seguiremo il percorso dalla lontana, remota origine magica via via lungo tutto il tragitto di scambi illimitati di mano in mano secondo logiche di slittamento che non riescono a trovare compimento in un approdo definitivo: paesaggi obbligati, doni sostituzioni, transiti cadute e incroci, furti, inversioni e smarrimenti. E soprattutto l'impossibilità che il fazzoletto, già molto difficile da raccogliere e impugnare, riesca a restare saldo dentro i confini di un unico dominio.

Darkness in the house. The underlying sound of a note that has begun to insinuate itself in the audience's ears for some time now seems to indicate that the curtain will open. Darkness erases the stage's perceived depth. When light progressively invades the space we notice a large white cloth hanging from above and hiding everything that happens behind it. The image of a film leader overlaps with the texture of the cloth so that canvas and action melt into each other.

After a few seconds of stillness the image begins to turn into a jerky, now unstoppable sequence of images and transformations.

It is the story of the handkerchief that Othello gave to Desdemona. We follow its journey from its remote magical origin through the endless exchanges from hand to hand according to sliding logical patterns that can't find a way to end in a definitive way: fixed exchanges, gifts, substitutions, transits, falls, crossings, thefts, changes of direction, losses. But mostly, the impossibility that the handkerchief, already difficult to pick up and hold, could be confined to a sole owner.

VOCE DI OTELLO: M'u mpresti u
      fazzulettu, pi faùri?
Chiddu ca iu ti desi
como pignu d'amuri.
'Un vogghiu chistu, no.
Unn'è la stissa cosa.
U fazzulettu chi ora t'addumannu
ci havi 'n tissutu pregnu di magia.
A sita veni di li vermi sacri
di na sibilla antica e pussiduta
ntù mentri c'u facia di gran fururi.
U russu ca pigghiò
pi tinciri u ricamu
è lu culuri pallidu sprimutu
d'u cori 'mbalsamatu
di fimmini 'llibati
ch'a morti si pigghiò prima d'u tempu.
'Un vogghio un fazzulettu senza storia.
Vogghiu chiddu chi a mmia lassò me'
      matri.
Na maga dill'Egittu
l'avìa rialatu a idda
pi farici all'amuri un sortilegiu.
Putenti era sta maga fattucchiera:
sapìa nzirtari ô scuru li pinzeri,
liggìa u distinu scrittu ntà li manu
e tutti li sigreti canuscìa
pi mòviri li stiddi a so' piaciri.
Mentri ci dava 'n manu u fazzulettu
cu vuci di l'abbissu a maga dissi
propriu dintra l'aricchi di me' matri:
"Fin'a quannu tu sarbi u fazzulettu
a to' biddizza resta sempri 'ncantu
ca teni strittu l'omu a la catina.
Ma s'iddu tu lu perdi pi svintura
o si ti nni sbarazzi o l'arriali,
a luci dintra all'occhi 'i to' maritu
nt'un attimu s'astuta e veni u tempu

VOCE DI OTELLO: Mi presti il fazzoletto,
      per favore?
Quello che io ti diedi
come pegno d'amore.
Non voglio questo, no.
Non è la stessa cosa.
Il fazzoletto che ora ti chiedo
ha un tessuto pieno di magia.
La seta viene dai vermi sacri
Di una sibilla antica e posseduta
mentre lo faceva di gran furia.
Il rosso che prese
per tingere il ricamo
è il colore pallido spremuto
dal cuore imbalsamato di donne
      illibate
che la morte si prese prima del tempo.
Non voglio un fazzoletto senza storia.
Voglio quello che mi lasciò mia
      madre.
Una maga dell'Egitto
glielo aveva regalato
per fare un incantesimo d'amore.
Era potente questa maga fattucchiera:
sapeva indovinare nell'oscurità i
pensieri, leggeva il destino scritto sulla
      mano
e conosceva tutti i segreti
per muovere le stelle a suo piacere.
Mentre le dava in mano il fazzoletto
con voce profonda la maga disse
proprio nelle orecchie di mia madre:
"Fin quando serberai il fazzoletto
la tua bellezza rimarrà sempre
      l'incanto
che tiene stretto l'uomo alla catena.
Ma se per sventura lo perdi
O se te ne sbarazzi o lo regali,
la luce negli occhi di tuo marito
in un attimo si spegne e viene il
      tempo

OTHELLO'S VOICE: Would you lend me thy handkerchief, please?
That which I gave you
as a love token.
I don't want this one, no.
'Tis not the same thing.
the handkerchief I am asking for now
has magic in the web of it.
The silk was bred by hallowed worms
of an old Sybil, possessed
by prophetic fury when she sewed it.
The red she used
to dye the embroidery
is the pale colour squeezed
from the mummified hearts
of maidens
whose life was prematurely taken.
I don't want a handkerchief without history.
I want the one my mother left me.
An Egyptian charmer
to her did give
for a love spell.
She was powerful this charmer witch
could guess thoughts in darkness,
could read one's destiny written
on hands and knew all secrets
to move stars at will.
While she handed her the handkerchief
with deep voice the charmer said
in my mother's ears:
"While you keep it
your beauty will always be the charm
that binds a man tightly to the chain.
But if by ill luck you lose it
or give it away or make a gift of it,
the light in your husband's eyes
in an instant dies out and comes the time

di lu disprezzu, di l'indiffirenza,
e di la caccia a novi fantasie
pi tutti l'autri fimmini d'u munno."
Chistu ci dissi a maga a la cunsigna.
Chistu murennu mi cuntò me' matri.
E 'nfini mi lassò cu la prumisa,
si u tempu fussi juntu
pi mmia d'u matrimoniu,
di dari u fazzulettu a me' mugghieri.
Ora ca s'avviraru sti palòri
sempri lu donu ha' tèniri preziusu
picchì si 'u perdi è gran malidizioni
ca 'ntossica e avvilena amuri e vita.

del disprezzo, dell'indifferenza,
e della caccia a nuove fantasie
per tutte le altre donne del mondo."
Questo disse la maga nel darglielo.
Questo, morendo, mi raccontò mia madre.
E infine mi lasciò con la promessa,
se fosse giunto il tempo
per me del matrimonio,
di dare il fazzoletto a mia moglie.
Ora che si sono avverate queste parole
Sempre devi tenere prezioso il dono
Perché se lo perdi è gran maledizione
Che intossica e avvelena amore e vita.

La tela immacolata collassa a terra e assume la sua reale consistenza di lenzuolo. Qualcosa, da dietro le quinte, trascina via lo schermo improvvisato. Il buio che stava alle spalle del panno bianco a poco a poco mostra la sua profondità di palco e appaiono, immobili come bassorilievi scolpiti nella pietra di un antico tempio, alcune figure sempre più nitide, d'implacabile rigidità, come soggette a un incantesimo che bloccando il tempo ha reso impossibile qualunque movimento. E nonostante tutto, per quanto siano distribuite nello spazio in maniera talmente composta da sembrare irreali, sono presenze vive e come accese da un interno furore. La condizione di paralisi rende ormai quasi insostenibile l'eccesso di tensione. Non solo la rabbia, anche lo smarrimento e il timore scalpitano dentro una gabbia d'incandescenza trattenuta.

of contempt, indifference,
and the hunt after new fancies
for all the other women in the world."
This the charmer said in giving it to her.
This, dying, my mother told me.
And finally she bid me,
when my fate
would have me wived,
to give it her.
Now that these words came true
take heed on this gift
to lose't were such perdition
that pollutes and poisons love and life.

The immaculate cloth falls to the ground and reveals its real texture as a sheet. A hook from behind the wings drags away the makeshift screen. The darkness behind the white cloth slowly reveals the stage's depth and some figures appear as still as bas reliefs sculpted in the stone of an ancient temple, implacably rigid as if under a spell that made time stand still and prevented any movement. Even though they are fixed in space in such a choreographed way to seem unreal, they are live presences almost animated by an inner fire. This stasis makes the exceeding tension almost unbearable. Not just rage, but also dismay and fear are barely contained in a cage of controlled incandescence.

Quasi in proscenio, seduto di spalle, c'è Otello. Ogni tanto lo scopriremo di profilo, ma per lo più, in questa prima scena, non vedremo il suo volto. A destra, di tre quarti, un po' più in profondità, scorgiamo Lodovico. Desdemona è a sinistra, sul fondo defilata, col corpo rivolto verso il pubblico. Accanto al generale, attento e silenzioso, c'è Iago. Sarebbe molto conveniente all'esatta composizione della scena se potessero unirsi altre presenze, forse figure dipinte, testimoni muti di questa prima atrocità di Otello.

Un suono prolungato e potente. La rigidità iniziale che imbalamava i personaggi si allenta senza mai totalmente scomparire.

OTELLO: Chi veni a diri stu sonu putenti?

IAGO: Vor diri annunziu d'arrivu 'mpurtanti..
Ecco ca vi sta 'nnanzi
l'amicu Lodovico…

OTELLO: Cu'?

IAGO: L'amicu Lodovico,
stimatu ambasciaturi,
cucinu caru d'a vostra cunsorti.

LODOVICO: V'accumpagnassi sempri lu Signuri
e sempri V'aiutassi, ginirali.

OTELLO: Cu tutt'u cori! Amicu Lodovico…

LODOVICO: Lassu ntì manu di vostra eccillenza
a littra ca mi detteru ô Sinatu
pi cunsignalla alla vostra attinzioni.

OTELLO E iu fideli vasu lu strumentu
Ca porta fin'a 'ccà lu gran cumannu.

OTELLO: Cosa vuol dire questo suono potente?

IAGO: Annuncia l'arrivo di qualcuno importante.
Ecco che vi sta davanti
l'amico Lodovico…

OTELLO: Chi?

IAGO: L'amico Lodovico,
stimato ambasciatore,
cugino caro di vostra moglie.

LODOVICO: Che sempre Vi accompagni il Signore
e sempre Vi aiuti, Generale.

OTELLO: Con tutto il cuore! Amico Lodovico…

LODOVICO: Lascio nelle mani di Vostra Eccellenza
la lettera che mi diede il Senato
perché la consegnassi alla Vostra attenzione.

OTELLO E io, fedele, bacio lo strumento
che porta fin qua il gran comando.

Almost on the proscenium, sitting with his back to the audience, is Othello. At times we are able to see his profile, but in this first scene we mostly won't see his face. Stage right, askew, a bit farther away we see Lodovico. Desdemona is stage left, upstage, with her body facing the audience and her head looking at Othello. Silent and attentive, Iago is by his side. It would be good if for this first scene other presences, perhaps painted figures, could be added, mute witnesses to this first atrocity of Othello.

A prolonged and powerful sound. The initial rigidity that made the characters standstill relaxes without ever completely disappearing.

OTHELLO: What is the meaning of this powerful sound?   **What trumpet is that same?**

IAGO: It warrants the arrival of someone important.
    'Tis in front of you
    Lodovico, our friend.

OTHELLO: Who?

IAGO: Our friend Lodovico
    esteemed ambassador
    your wife's dear cousin.

LODOVICO: God save you, worthy general,
    and always help you.

OTHELLO: With all my heart, friend Lodovico…

LODOVICO: I leave in Your Excellency's hands
    the letter that the Senate gave me
    to bring to your attention.

OTHELLO: And I, faithfully, kiss the instrument
    that brings their orders here.

Otello sembra sprofondare nella lettura

LODOVICO: Sugnu tuttu contentu 'i stari
ccà.
Vuatri stati bonu?
Comu s'a passa Cassio,
amicu e gran surdatu
chi sempri s'ha' distintu
ntù campu di battagghia?

IAGO: A stu minutu? Campa.

DESDEMONA: Carissimo cugino,
tra Cassio e mio marito
è sorto da non molto
un piccolo contrasto.
So che la vostra voce
saprà trovare il modo
per fare ritornare il loro accordo.
E questo per l'amore
che porto al nostro Cassio.

OTELLO: Surfuru e focu!

DESDEMONA: Che dite, mio signore?

OTELLO: Chi fa'? Niscisti foddi?

DESDEMONA: Non vi capisco proprio,
mio signore.
Siete sconvolto. Sembrate irritato…

OTELLO: Criatura d'u dimoniu.

Otello colpisce Desdemona brutalmente.

DESDEMONA (*dopo qualche secondo di
gemiti e silenzio*):
Che ho fatto io di male
adesso per subire
la vostra prepotenza?

LODOVICO: Sono molto contento di
essere qui.
Voi state bene?
Come sta Cassio,
amico e gran soldato
che sempre si è distinto
nel campo di battaglia?

IAGO: In questo istante? Vive.

DESDEMONA: Carissimo cugino,
tra Cassio e mio marito
è sorto da non molto
un piccolo contrasto.
So che la vostra voce
saprà trovare il modo
per fare ritornare il loro accordo.
E questo per l'amore
che porto al nostro Cassio.

OTELLO: Zolfo e fuoco!

DESDEMONA: Che dite, mio signore?

OTELLO: Che fai? Sei uscita di senno?

DESDEMONA: Non vi capisco proprio,
mio signore.
Siete sconvolto. Sembrate irritato…

OTELLO: Creatura del demonio.

DESDEMONA (*dopo qualche secondo di
gemiti e silenzio*):
Che ho fatto io di male
adesso per subire
la vostra prepotenza?

Othello seems immersed in the letter

LODOVICO: I am very glad to be here.
    How are you?
    How does Lieutenant Cassio,
    friend and great soldier,
    who always shone in battle?

IAGO: At the moment? Lives.

DESDEMONA: Dearest cousin,
    There's fallen
    between Cassio and my lord
    an unkind breach.
    I know that your voice
    will find the way
    t'atone them.
    And this for the love
    I bear to Cassio.

OTHELLO: Fire and brimstone!

DESDEMONA: My lord?

OTHELLO: What are you doing? Are you wise?

DESDEMONA: I don't understand you, my lord.
    You seem upset. You seem irritated…

OTHELLO: Devil's spawn.

Otello strikes Desdemona brutally.

DESDEMONA (*after a few seconds of moans and silence*):
    What did I do
    now to suffer
    your wrath?

LODOVICO: Sta cosa 'un si pò crìdiri
  nemmenu
  si la cuntassi sutta giuramentu
  d'avilla vista: quann'è troppu è troppu.
  Addumannatici pirdonu: chianci
  e trema e p'a viogna si dispera.

OTELLO: Dimonio! Gran terribili
  dimonio!
  Si u campu si facessi 'ngravidare
  di lacrimi nisciuti
  di l'occhi d'ogni fimmina,
  ntà terra si scavassi
  'n orribili pantanu
  càrricu 'i cucutrigghi.
  Ma cerca d'jiritinni a gghiri ddà!
  Va' levat'i davanti gran buttana!

DESDEMONA: Certo non resto se vi
  pare offesa.

LODOVICO: Sta cosa non si potrebbe
  credere nemmeno
  se raccontassi sotto giuramento
  d'averla vista: quando è troppo è
  troppo.
  Domandatele perdono: piange
  e trema e per
  la vergogna si dispera.

OTELLO: Demonio! Gran terribile
  demonio!
  Se la campagna si facesse ingravidare
  dalle lacrime nate
  dagli occhi d'ogni femmina,
  nella terra si scaverebbe
  un orribile pantano
  pieno di coccodrilli.
  Ma cerca di andartene via di qua!
  Levati d'innanzi, gran puttana!

DESDEMONA: Certo non resto se vi pare
  offesa.

Desdemona, molto lentamente, comincia ad allontanarsi.

LODOVICO: Che fimmina divota!
  Vi supplicu signuri
  di falla riturnari.

OTELLO (*con tono di scherno*):
  Signorina… pupetta…
  frastocchia… bambolina…
  Amicu me', sapiti: pò turnari
  e turnari, jirisinni e riturnari.

LODOVICO: Che donna devota!
  Vi supplico signore
  di farla ritornare.

OTELLO (*con tono di scherno*):
  Signorina… pupetta…
  bugiardella… bambolina…
  Amico mio, sappiate: può tornare
  e tornare, andarsene e ritornare.

LODOVICO: This would not be believed
    though I should swear
    I saw't: 'Tis very much —
    Make her amends: she weeps
    and trembles and, ashamed despairs.

OTHELLO: Devil! Great terrible devil!
    If that the earth could teem
    with tears
    from each woman's eyes,
    each drop she falls would dig
    a horrible swamp
    full of crocodiles.
    Try to get thee away!
    Out of my sight, thou whore!

DESDEMONA: I will not stay to offend you.

Desdemona, very slowly, starts to leave.

LODOVICO: Truly, an obedient lady.
    I do beseech your lordship
    call her back.

OTHELLO (*mockingly*):
    Miss… doll…
    little liar… puppet…
    Know, my friend: she can turn
    and turn, and turn, and yet go on
    and turn again.

Otello comincia a dare ordini come se Desdemona fosse un triste animale ammaestrato. La giovane donna, a testa bassa per la vergogna, ubbidisce a tutti i comandi. Ha qualcosa dell'automa o della marionetta.

OTELLO: Ehi, scimia! Veni ccà! Aràciu!
    Aràciu!
  Votati! Cancia strata! Ora firrìa!
  Mòviti! Ferma! Allèstiti ti dissi!
  Chi fa', ti riss'aràciu! Statti ferma!
  E bravu l'armaluzzu rispittusu…

OTELLO: Ehi, scimmia! Vieni qua!
    Adagio! Adagio!
  Voltati! Cambia strada! Ora gira!
  Muoviti! Ferma! Muoviti ti ho detto!
  Che fai, ti ho detto adagio! Stai ferma!
  E bravo l'animaletto rispettoso…

Adesso si avverte il suono del pianto sommesso di Desdemona.

OTELLO: Ma chi fa', chianci?
  S'a fira puru a chianciri, vediti?
  Comu chianci bonu… chi
    grann'attrici…
  (fingendo commozione)
  Ma iu 'un ti pozzu abbiriri chi chianci…
  Sì accussì brava ca macari chianciu
  puru iu…
  (recitando il pianto)
  'u vi', 'u vi', mi fai chianciri…
  *(interrompendo di colpo i singhiozzi e
  perlustrandole il viso molto da vicino)*
  Famm'abbiriri bonu… chi facisti?
  Ma ti mittisti u truccu? Ti 'mpupasti?
  Ma vero graziosa sei… buttanella…
  Va' ddà, spirisci e chiuiti ntà to' stanza.

OTELLO: Ma che fai, piangi?
  È capace pure di piangere, vedete?
  Come piangi bene… che grande
    attrice…
  (fingendo commozione)
  Ma io non ti posso vedere che
    piangi…
  Sei così brava che magari piango
  pure io…
  (recitando il pianto)
  lo vedi, lo vedi, mi fai piangere…
  *(interrompendo di colpo i singhiozzi e
  perlustrandole il viso molto da vicino)*
  Fammi vedere bene… che hai fatto?
  Ma ti sei messa il trucco? Ti sei
    impiastricciata?
  Ma sei graziosa davvero…
    puttanella…
  Vai via, sparisci e chiuditi nella tua
    stanza.

Othello begins to give orders as if Desdemona were a sad trained animal. The young woman, head bent in shame, obeys all commands. She looks like an automaton or a puppet.

OTHELLO: Hey, monkey! Come over! Slowly! Slowly!
    Turn around! Change course! Now turn!
    Move! Stop! I said move!
    What are you doing? Slowly I said! Stand still!
    Good respectful little pet…

Desdemona's soft crying can be heard now.

OTHELLO: Proceed you in your tears?
    She can even cry, you see?
    How well thou criest… what a great actress…   **O well-painted passion!**
    (*feigning emotion*)
    I can't watch thee cry…
    Thou art so good that I may cry too…
    (*pretending to cry*)
    thou seest, thou seest, thou mak'st me cry…
    (*stopping his sobs abruptly and looking at her face up close*)
    Let me see… what didst thou do?
    Didst thou powder up? Paint thy face?
    Thou art really pretty… little whore…
    Get thee away, disappear and lock thyself in thy room.
                              Get you away and lock yourself in your room.

Desdemona si avvia lentamente verso l'uscita. Subito dopo escono Lodovico e Iago. Otello resta solo.

OTELLO: 'Un ti fari truvari 'n quarchi
  agnuni
  iccata 'nterra a fari purcarìe.
  Va curcati ntù lettu c'ora arrivu.
  Vidi chi sugnu sulu…
  (rivolto a Desdemona lontana)
  Fussi pi ttia…
  vulissi tutt'a 'ntera guarnigioni
  ntù lettu sdivacata ncap'a ttia.
  E c'amu a ffari: se una è troia, è troia.
  Carissimi amici, sugnu filici.
  V'aspetto tutti quanti pi manciari
  quannu fa scuru e acchiana lu pitittu.
  Nni videmu cchiù tardu, ora jitivinni.

OTELLO: Non ti far trovare in qualche
  angolo
  ficcata in terra a fare porcherie.
  Vai a coricarti a letto che ora arrivo.
  Vedi che sono solo…
  (rivolto a Desdemona lontana)
  Se fosse per te…
  Vorresti tutta la guarnigione
  nel letto stravaccata addosso a te.
  Che ci dobbiamo fare: se una è troia
   è troia.
  Carissimi amici, sono felice.
  Vi aspetto tutti quanti per mangiare
  quando fa scuro e vien voglia.
  Ci vediamo più tardi, ora andatevene.

Otello, che fino ad ora è stato per lo più con le spalle al pubblico, si gira verso la platea. È una maschera di dolore.

OTELLO *(non si capisce se si rivolge alle persone appena uscite o agli spettatori)*:
  Scimie e capruni… Scimie e capruni…

OTELLO *(non si capisce se si rivolge alle persone appena uscite o agli spettatori)*:
  Scimmie e caproni… Scimmie e
  caproni…

Desdemona slowly gets to the exit. Lodovico and Iago exit after her. Othello remains alone.

OTHELLO: Don't let me find thee hiding in some corner
    doing the dirty on the ground.
    Get thee to bed and I'll follow.
    Thou seest I'm alone…
    (*talking to Desdemona now far*)
    If it were up to thee…
    Thou wouldst want the whole garrison
    sprawled in bed on top of thee.
    What's to be done: if she's a trollop she's a trollop.
    Dear friends, I am glad.
    I do entreat that we may sup together
    when it gets dark and hunger strikes.
    Till then, go now.

Othello, who until now has mostly given his back to the audience, turns towards it. He is a mask of pain.

OTHELLO (*it is unclear if he is addressing the people who just left or the audience*): Goats and monkeys… Goats and monkeys…

Dal fondo della platea, tenuto per il collo da una lunga fune, fa il suo ingresso Iago. Cammina molto lentamente. A un certo punto salirà per mezzo di uno scivolo alla destra del palcoscenico.

IAGO: Chi ci taliati?
    'Un sugnu ccà pi darivi spittaculu.
    'Unn'è pi vuatri stu tiatru. 'Unn'è p'u
        vostru saziu.
    Ddocu, ntù parcu d'u suppliziu, iu ci
        acchianu
    sulu pi mmia. Sulu pi mmia ci acchianu.
    E vuatri stati ccà bell'assittati,
    filici e chini di sudisfazioni
    di vìdiri com'è ca mori 'n omu
    perfidu, diabbolicu e malignu,
    com'è ca mori Iago
    doppu na pocu di turturi,
    doppu na pocu d'afflizioni.
    Ammazzannu a mmia
    vi pari ca lu cancru
    veni abbruciatu e cchiù la carni
    'un vi pò muzzicari.
    Pinzati ca vi salva a me' ruina.
    E 'nveci 'un cancia nenti:
    a dannazioni è comuni distinu.
    Stu cancru 'un si nni va,
    'ncoddu v'arresta, 'ncoddu attaccato,
    picchì stu cancru 'unn'è cosa luntana,
    è a cosa cchiù vicina chi ci aviti,
    siti vuatri stissi u cancru,
    semu nuatri, razza umana,
    razza chi nasci già diginirata…
    È cancru pi natura, l'omu,
    cancru e fangu.
    Cancru senza liggi.
    È pezzu di corpu ca 'mpazzisci
    e s'accumincia a spartiri, a multiplicari…
    Havi manìe di grannizza stu pizziddu
        i carni…
    Veni pigghiatu d'u disìu di curriri,
    stu pezzu di tissutu, ma 'un si sapi
        dunni.

IAGO: Che guardate?
    Non sono qua per darvi spettacolo.
    Non è per voialtri questo teatro. Non
        è per vostro godimento.
    Là, nel palco del supplizio, io ci salgo
    solo per me stesso. Solo per me ci salgo.
    E voialtri state qui belli seduti,
    felici e pieni di soddisfazioni
    di vedere come muore un uomo
    perfido, diabolico e maligno,
    com'è che muore Iago
    dopo un po' di tortura,
    dopo un po' di afflizioni.
    Ammazzando me
    vi pare che il cancro
    venga bruciato e più la carne
    non vi possa mordere.
    Pensate che la mia rovina vi salvi.
    E invece non cambia niente:
    la dannazione è un destino comune.
    Sto cancro non se ne va,
    vi resta addosso, attaccato addosso,
    perché sto cancro non è una cosa
        lontana,
    è la cosa più vicina che avete,
    siete voi stessi il cancro,
    siamo noialtri, la razza umana,
    razza che nasce già degenerata…
    È un cancro per natura, l'uomo,
    cancro e fango.
    Cancro senza leggi.
    È un pezzo di corpo che impazzisce
    e comincia a dividersi, a
        moltiplicarsi…
    Ha manie di grandezza sto pezzettino
        di carne…
    Viene preso da un desiderio di
        correre,
    sto pezzo di tessuto, ma non sa dove.

From the back of the parterre, with a noose around his neck and a long rope, comes Iago. He walks very slowly. Finally he gets on stage using an incline on the right.

IAGO: What are you looking at?
  I'm not here to be turned into a spectacle.
  This show is not for you. It's not for your entertainment.
  Up there, on the torture stage, I go
  for me alone. Only for my sake I go up there.
  And you, you just sit there,
  happy and satisfied
  to see how a man,
  wicked, diabolical, and evil,
  dies; how Iago dies
  after a little torture,
  after a little pain.
  By killing me
  it seems to you that the cancer
  is excised and it no longer
  can bite your flesh.
  You think that my ruin will save you,
  instead, nothing changes:
  damnation is a common destiny.
  This cancer doesn't leave,
  it stays on you, glued on,
  because this cancer is not a remote thing,
  it's the nearest thing you have,
  you are the cancer yourselves,
  it's us, the human race,
  degenerate race from birth…
  Man, by nature is a cancer,
  cancer and mud.
  Cancer with no laws.
  It's a piece of the body that goes crazy
  and starts to spit and multiply…
  It has delusions of grandeur, this little piece of flesh…
  It gets seized by the desire to run,
  this piece of tissue, but it doesn't know where.

Curriri pi curriri, pi sbattiri cchiù forti,
p'addivintari cosa ca si schianta,
cosa ca poi ritorna pezzi pezzi,
munseddu d'ossa e doppu cìnniri
    cunfusa,
e doppu purviri ca s'assuttigghia
e doppu finarmenti arreri nenti,
ddu nenti ca ntà vita
cu mascari, custumi e pantumimi,
avìamu fattu finta di scurdari…
E cu ll'occhi attuppati di chiddu chi
    c'è fora
stu dintra ca nni mancia 'unn'u videmu.
Pi mmia dunca allisteru
sta seggia di turtura.
Spiramu ca u programma è minuziosu:
cuteddi e pinzi, marteddi e tinagghi,
ogghiu ca vugghi e abbrucia li firiti,
vrazza e jammi frantumati,
lassati pinnuliari di lu troncu
    abbannunati,
e 'nfini, doppu li denti scippati e la
    lingua 'nchiuvata,
o quattru o sei cavaddi per squartàrimi
    di vivu e vivu
mentri ca isànnu l'ascia
lu boia cafudda 'n corpu
e fa satari a testa di lu coddu.
Sintìti…
mmenzu a rumuri e strepitu i firragghia,
sintìti la granni milodia di la turtura
mentri ca s'addiventa
tuttu na cosa sula cu duluri,
cu tuttu lu duluri di lu munnu,
tuttu sintutu mpressu ntà la carni,
ntà la carni urlanti,
ntà la carni siviziata e marturiata…
E vuatri siti ccà tutti riuniti
pi ddari applicazioni
a la liggi chi punisci lu dilittu

Correre per correre, per battere più
    forte,
per diventare una cosa che si schianta,
cosa che poi ritorna pezzo a pezzo,
mucchietto di ossa e dopo cenere
    confusa,
e dopo polvere che si assottiglia
e dopo finalmente di nuovo niente,
del niente che nella vita
con maschere, costumi e pantomime,
avevamo fatto finta di scordare…
E con gli occhi otturati da quello che
    c'è fuori
sto dentro che ci mangia non lo
    vediamo.
Per me dunque allestirono
sta sedia di tortura.
Speriamo che il programma sia
    preciso:
coltelli e pinze, martelli e tenaglie,
olio che bolle e brucia le ferite,
braccia e gambe frantumate,
lasciate penzolare dal tronco,
    abbandonate,
e infine, dopo aver rotto i denti e
    inchiodato la lingua,
o quattro o sei cavalli per squartarmi
    da vivo a vivo
mentre qua issando l'ascia
il boia dà un colpo
e fa saltare la testa dal collo.
Sentite…
in mezzo al rumore e allo strepito
    della ferraglia,
sentite la grande melodia della tortura
mentre qui si diventa
tutta una cosa sola col dolore,
con tutto il dolore del mondo,
tutto sentito impresso nella carne,
nella carne urlante,
nella carne seviziata e martoriata…
E voialtri siete qua tutti riuniti
per applicare
la legge che punisce il delitto

Run for the sake of running, to beat faster,
to become something that breaks,
something that gets back piece by piece,
heap of bones and then mixed-up ashes,
and then dust that thins out
and then once again nothing,
that nothing that, while living,
with masks and pantomimes,
we had pretended to forget…
with our eyes confounded by what's out there
we can't see what's eating us inside.
So they set up for me
this torture chair.
Let's hope the program is well planned:
knives and pliers, hammers and pincers,
boiling oil that burns wounds,
arms and legs shattered,
hanging from the torso, let go,
and, finally, after breaking teeth and nailing the tongue,
four or six horses to tear me apart alive
while raising the axe
the executioner strikes a blow
and makes the head pop away from the neck.
Listen…
amidst the noise and clanging of iron
listen to the great melody of torture
while here you become
one with pain,
with all the pain in the world,
all firmly lodged in the flesh,
in the screaming flesh,
in the tormented and tortured flesh.
And you are all gathered here
to enforce
the law that punishes a crime

purtannu u criminali a lu supplizziu
atruci ed esemplari…
Ma unn'è sta liggi?
Mentri lu corpu annagghia la menti
e la menti spinci lu corpu all'attu
    criminali
a liggi è fogghiu 'i carta e 'un vali nenti.
E iu, chiddu chi fici, fici.
'Un c'è liggi, turtura o patimentu
ca m'avissiru pututu scuraggiari.
Io 'un canusciu a nuddu,
'un canusciu mancu a mmia…
E sta seggia di turtura,
stu tempu didicatu allu supplizziu
'un mi dispiaci.
In prìmisi picchì cu me' duluri
s'accrisci a quantità di straziu dintra u
    munnu.
Tutto è straziu, tuttu è lamentu,
tuttu ntù munnu è patimentu.
Puru si 'n omu ridi
è picchí nautru sta chiancennu…
In secùnnisi a turtura è gloria
triunfu e vantu
di lu corpu che ripigghia ntù capistru
u scettru e a signuria
supra lu granni usurpaturi:
l'inutili pinzeru di la menti.
Ah turtura, turtura!
Turtura igieni di la menti!
Ora ci pigghiò a a Cassio
— ca ntù mentri addivintò guvirnaturi —
a Graziano e Lodovico
— ziu e cuginu di bonanima la nostra
    signura —
di sapiri u picchì.
Picchì ci cumminavu stu gran dannu?
Picchì tutta sta furia di vinnitta?
Picchì tutta sta gran macchinazioni

portando il criminale al supplizio
atroce ed esemplare…
Ma dov'è sta legge?
Mentre il corpo afferra la mente
e la mente spinge il corpo all'atto
    criminale
la legge è un foglio di carta e non vale
    niente.
E io, quello che feci, feci.
Non c'è legge, tortura o sofferenza
che mi avrebbe potuto scoraggiare.
Io non conosco nessuno,
non conosco nemmeno me stesso…
E questa sedia di tortura,
questo tempo dedicato al supplizio
non mi dispiace.
Primo, perché col mio dolore
cresce la quantità di strazio nel
    mondo.
Tutto è strazio, tutto è lamento,
tutto nel mondo è patimento.
Anche se un uomo ride
è perché un altro sta piangendo…
Secondo, la tortura è gloria
trionfo e vanto
del corpo che riprende nel capestro
lo scettro e il potere
sul grande usurpatore:
l'inutile pensiero della mente.
Ah tortura, tortura!
Tortura igiene della mente!
Ora prese brama a Cassio
— che nel frattempo è diventato
    governatore —
a Graziano e Lodovico
— zio e cugino della buon'anima
    nostra signora —
di sapere il perché.
Perché combinai questo gran danno?
Perché tutta sta voglia di vendetta?
Perché tutta sta grande macchinazione

by taking the criminal to torture
atrocious and exemplary…
but where is the law?
As the body takes over the mind
and the mind pushes it to a criminal act
the law is a piece of paper and it counts for nothing.
And I did what I did.
There is no law, torture, or suffering
that could have discouraged me.
I don't know anybody,
I don't even know myself…
And this torture chair,
this time devoted to torment
does not upset me.
Firstly, because with my pain
the amount of pain in the world rises.
All is pain, all is wailing,
all in the world is suffering.
Even when a man laughs
it is because another one is crying…
Secondly, torture is glory,
triumph and merit
of the body that regains in the noose
the sceptre and the power
over the great usurper:
the useless thinking mind.
Ah torture, torture!
Torture, hygiene of the mind!
Now the desire overwhelmed Cassio
— who in the meantime became governor —
Graziano and Lodovico
— uncle and cousin of our dearly departed Lady —
to know why.
Why did I make this mess?
Why all this need for revenge?
Why this whole machination

ca fici sprufunnari ntà l'abissu
Otello e poi Desdemona ed Emilia?
Picchì? Picchì sta sproporzioni
tra chiddu chi pativu
— l'odiu contru Otello
ca fici locotinenti Cassio ô postu miu
e u fattu ca iddi dui, a turnu si capisci,
si curcaru cu Emilia, me' mugghieri —
picchì sta diffirenza smisurata
tra dannu ricivutu
e chiddu ca ci desi 'n puniziuni?
Ci rispunnivu allura
a cu' m'addumannava:
"Di stu mumentu
di mia cchiù na palora
nuddu mi pò scippari.
Nzoccu sapiti sapiti,
chiddu ch'arresta è silenziu."
E ora ci pari ca sutta turtura
a lingua m'addiventa modda,
si sciogghi e fa parrari
ddu focu ca li visciri m'abbrucia
comu vampa c'acchiana da lu 'nfernu
pi purtari unn'egghiè morti e ruina.
Pi vuatri arrestu sempri un gran
    misteru…
Picchì iu nun sugnu chiddu chi sugnu.
Nun penzu ntù locu dunni sugnu
e sugnu dunni manca lu pinzeru.

che fece sprofondare nell'abisso
Otello e poi Desdemona ed Emilia?
Perché? Perché sta sproporzione
tra quello che pativo
— l'odio contro Otello
che fece luogotenente Cassio al posto
    mio
e il fatto che loro due, non insieme
    ovviamente,
si coricarono con Emilia, mia moglie —
perché sta differenza smisurata
tra il danno ricevuto
e quello che gli diedi come punizione?
Rispondevo allora
a chi mi domandava:
"Da questo momento
da me più una parola
nessuno mi può cavare.
Ciò che sapete sapete,
quello che resta è il silenzio."
E ora pensano che sotto tortura
la lingua mi diventi molle,
si sciolga e faccia parlare
di quel fuoco che mi brucia le viscere
come vampa che sale dall'inferno
per portare dov'è morte e rovina.
Per voi resto sempre un gran
    mistero…
Perché io non sono quello che sono.
Non penso nel posto in cui sono
e sono dove manca il pensiero.

that plunged into the abyss
Othello and then Desdemona and Emilia?
Why? Why this disproportion
between what I suffered
— hatred against Othello
who made Cassio lieutenant in my stead
and the fact that the two of them, not together of course,
lay with Emilia, my wife —
why this boundless difference
between the damage I received
and what I gave him as punishment?
I answered then
to those who asked:
"From this moment on
no one can get a word
out of me   **Demand me nothing:**
What you know, you know,
what is left is silence."   **from this time forth I will never speak word**
And now they think that under torture
my tongue will be loosen'd,
untied, and will make me voice
that fire that burns my guts
like a flame rising from hell
to go where is death and destruction.
For you I am still a mystery…
Because I am not what I am.
I don't think where I am
and I am where thought is absent.

Durante le ultime frasi di Iago, senza farsi notare troppo, prende posto sulla destra un soldato. È lui che impugna la lunga corda del prigioniero. Nell'altra mano tiene un grande secchio di metallo.

SOLDATO: 'Unn'haiu 'ntinzioni
    di sèntiri ancora
    sta gran camurrìa.
    Si 'un ti zitti, ti pigghiu a càuci 'mmucca.

IAGO: Appena m'arriva u peri 'mmucca
    m'u manciu e m'agghiuttu sanu sanu.
    E doppu a digistioni
    'u sai nzoccu addiventa lu to' peri?
    Statt'accura ca sugnu cannìbbalo…

SOLDATO: Tantu a n'atra nticchia
    'a finisci di babbiari…

IAGO: Pi mmia finju lu jocu.
    M'abbasta ca fineru
    comu fineru ddì cristiani,
    specialmenti u ginirali.
    Otello mi stava ccà
    ntì cannarozza. 'Unn'u putiva agghiuttiri
    'U putiva sulu sputari.
    E 'u sgraccavu a gghiri ddà, luntanu…

SOLDATO: Mancu di mortu ci porti
    rispettu.

IAGO: Fin'a quannu d'Otello
    resta ricordu, immagini, cuncettu,
    l'odiu m'imponi vilenu e disprezzu.
    E ora aspettu sulu
    c'u tempu nni scancella la memoria
    comu s'unn'avissi mai nasciuto.

SOLDATO: Sia biniditta sta seggia di
    turtura…

IAGO: Sugnu d'accordu.
    Megghiu sta seggia
    cchiuttostu di turnari
    â casa unni na fimmina t'aspetta.

SOLDATO: Non ho intenzione
    di sentire ancora
    sto gran trambusto.
    Se non stai zitto ti piglio a calci in
      bocca.

IAGO: Appena mi arriva il piede in bocca
    me lo mangio e inghiotto sano sano.
    E dopo la digestione
    lo sai cosa diventa il tuo piede?
    Stai attento che sono cannibale…

SOLDATO: Tanto, un altro po'
    e la finisci di scherzare…

IAGO: Per me è finito il gioco.
    Mi basta finire
    come finirono quelle persone,
    specialmente il generale.
    Otello mi stava qui
    sul gozzo. Non lo potevo mandare
      giù.
    Lo potevo solo sputare.
    E lo scaracchiai laggiù, lontano…

SOLDATO: Manco da morto gli porti
    rispetto.

IAGO: Fin quando di Otello
    resta il ricordo, l'immagine, il
      concetto,
    l'odio mi impone veleno e disprezzo.
    E ora aspetto solo
    che il tempo ne cancelli la memoria
    come se non fosse mai nato.

SOLDATO: Sia benedetta questa sedia di
    tortura…

IAGO: Sono d'accordo.
    Meglio sta sedia
    piuttosto che tornare
    a una casa dove ti aspetta una donna.

During Iago's last phrases, without being noticed much, a soldier appears on the right. He is the one holding the prisoner's long rope. In the other hand he holds a big metal bucket.

SOLDIER: I have no wish
  to keep listening
  to this rant.
  If you don't shut up I'll kick you in the mouth.

IAGO: As soon as the foot gets to my mouth
  I'll eat it and swallow it whole.
  You know what your foot becomes
  once digested?
  Watch out for I am a cannibal…

SOLDIER: Oh, in a bit
  you'll stop kidding…

IAGO: For me the game is over.
  I'll be happy ending up
  as those people did
  especially the general.
  I couldn't stand Othello.
  I couldn't swallow him.
  I could only spit him.
  And I spat him all the way there…

SOLDIER: Not even dead you respect him.

IAGO: As long as Othello's
  memory, image, concept remains,
  hatred compels my poison and contempt.
  Now I just wait
  for time to erase his memory
  as if he were never born.

SOLDIER: God bless this torture chair…

IAGO: I agree.
  Better this chair
  than returning
  to a home where a woman is waiting.

Iago sale i gradini della macchina della tortura. Dopo le sue ultime parole lo vedremo scomparire lì dentro, in fondo.

IAGO: 'Un c'è cosa cchiù gravi e dulurusa
  d'aviri u ciatu ncoddu di la spusa.

IAGO: Non c'è cosa più grave e dolorosa
  di avere addosso il fiato della consorte.

Il soldato raggiunge Iago e gli porge il secchio che teneva in mano.

SOLDATO: Appena 'n minutu. Pòrtati stu catu.

SOLDATO: Appena un minuto. Portati sto secchio.

IAGO (*prendendo con diffidenza il secchio*):
  E chistu chi è? Nzoccu n'haiu a ffari?

IAGO (*prendendo con diffidenza il secchio*):
  E questo cos'è? Cosa ne devo fare?

SOLDATO: U catinu p'a testa quannu cadi.

SOLDATO: È il catino per la testa quando cade.

IAGO: Accura a quannu mori
  ca si finisci ô 'nfernu
  arreri trovi a mmia e nun ti cunveni…

IAGO: Attento che quando muori
  se finisci all'inferno
  mi ritrovi e non ti conviene…

SOLDATO: E chi sapemu? Ancora 'un si pò diri:
  macari u 'nfernu ti fa bonu
  e addiventi nu bravu cristianu…

SOLDATO: E che ne sappiamo? Ancora non si può dire:
  magari l'inferno ti rende buono
  e diventi un brav'uomo…

IAGO: Puru ddà ssuta, sempri a mmia assumigghiu.
  E vistu ca ntà terra
  finìu pi mmia lu tempu 'i fari dannu
  ora allu 'nfernu ci portu scumpigghiu.

IAGO: Anche là sotto, sempre a me assomiglierò.
  E visto che sulla terra
  è finito per me il tempo di fare danno
  ora porto scompiglio all'inferno.

Iago si allontana fino a perdersi tra gli ingranaggi del suo luogo di supplizio. Il soldato si rivolge al pubblico.

Iago climbs the steps of the torture chamber. After his last words we see him disappear inside.

IAGO: There isn't a heavier and more painful thing
than having a spouse breathing down one's neck.

The soldier joins Iago and hands him the bucket he was holding.

SOLDIER: Hold on a minute. Take this bucket.

IAGO (*grabbing the bucket suspiciously*):
What is this? What am I supposed to do with this?

SOLDIER: It's the basin for your head when it falls.

IAGO: Watch out, when you die
if you end up in hell
you'll find me and it won't be pretty…

SOLDIER: What do we know? Too soon to tell:
perhaps hell will do you good
and you'll become a good man…

IAGO: Even down there, I'll still be myself.
And since on earth
my time to do damage is over
now I'll reap havoc in hell.

Iago moves away until he disappears in the maze of his torture place at the back of the stage. The soldier addresses the audience.

SOLDATO: Disertu.

    Disertu e morti.

    Morti, abbannunu e ruina.

    Chistu purtò ntù munnu ddu flagellu

    ca tutti li cristiani

    chiamavano di sempri: "Onestu Iago".

    Ma comu succirìu?

    Ma comu fu possibili

    ch'a vita a lu 'mpruvisu

    addivintò tragedia?

    Comu potti essiri? U ginirali…

    cristianu eccellentissimu, squisitu…

    chi ogni vota chi parrava

    parìa ca ci niscevanu d'a vucca

    Pàgini di 'n libbru chinu d'avventuri.

    Ma comu potti essiri?

    Com'è ca si pirdìu

    dintr'a stu gran dilirio

    di furia e di vinnitta

    tantu ca jiu a distruggiri

    a cosa ca ntù cori avìa cchiù cara?

    Ma chi fa m'u 'nsunnavu?

    Possibili mai? 'U fici pi ddaveru?

    'U fici, 'u fici.

    L'urtimi palori

    vagnati di lacrimi

    ca niscìanu a ciumi

    diciano accussì:

    "Scriviti littri

    di mannari a lu Sinatu

    chi parranu di mia pricisamenti.

    Tistimuniati ntà giusta manera

    cu' fuvu e comu fu la vita atruci

    cu mmia e suprattuttu cu me' beni.

    Parrati di mia cu versu echilibratu,

SOLDATO: Deserto.

    Deserto e morte.

    Morte, abbandono e rovina.

    Questo portò nel mondo il flagello

    che tutti gli uomini

    chiamavano sempre: "Onesto Iago".

    Ma come è successo?

    Ma come è stato possibile

    che la vita all'improvviso

    diventasse tragedia?

    Come è potuto essere? Il generale…

    uomo eccellentissimo, squisito…

    che ogni volta che parlava

    pareva che gli uscissero di bocca

    pagine di un libro pieno di avventure.

    Ma come è potuto essere?

    Com'è che si è perso

    in questo gran delirio

    di furia e di vendetta

    tanto che è andato a distruggere

    la cosa che aveva più cara nel cuore?

    Ma cos'è, me lo sono sognato?

    Possibile mai? Lo fece per davvero?

    Lo fece, lo fece.

    Le ultime parole

    bagnate di lacrime

    che sgorgavano a fiumi

    dicevano:

    "Scrivete una lettera

    da mandare al Senato

    che parli di me con precisione.

    Testimoniate nel modo giusto

    come fui e come fu la vita atroce

    con me e soprattutto col mio bene.

    Parlate di me con versi equilibrati,

SOLDIER: Desert.
    Desert and death.
    Death, abandonment, and ruin.
    This is what the scourge
    that all men always called
    "Honest Iago" brought to the world.
    How did it happen?
    How was it possible
    that all of a sudden life
    became tragedy?
    How could it be? The general…
    Excellent man, exquisite…
    Every time he spoke
    it seemed like out of his mouth
    came pages of an adventure book.
    How could it be?
    How did he get so lost
    in this delirium
    of fury and revenge
    to end up destroying
    what he held dearest to his heart?
    What is it, did I dream of it?
    Can it be? Did he really do it?
    He did it, he did it.
    His last words
    wet with tears
    flowing like rivers
    said:
    "Write a letter
    to send to the Senate
    to speak of me as I am.
    Relate accurately
    how I was and how atrocious was life
    with me and especially with my beloved.
    Speak of me with balanced words,

nenti chiossài, nenti cchiù picca, nenti
ca 'unn'assumigghia â virità cchiù vera.
Parrati di mia pi comu fuvu".
E comu putemu nuatri diri
cu' era pi ddaveru u ginirali
vistu ch'iddu stissu 'unn'u sapìa?
Mannaja a lu 'nfernu
quant'era sulu Otello…
mancu 'n amicu…
mancu 'n amicu c'era, mancu unu
pi tèniri la funebri orazioni.
Siccomu nuddu 'u potti fari tannu
e vaju sempri sintennu malevuci,
vinni u mumentu allura ch'haiu a parrari
di chiddu ca successi ntà ddì jorna.
Ora vi cuntu la storia di Otello.
Ora ci provu. Provu a sistimari
tanti cosi ca mi vannu firriannu
dintra la testa china 'i cunfusioni.
Iu stissu era prisenti
a certi accadimenti.
Autri cosi 'nveci m'i cuntaru
pirsuni di fiducia e di rispettu
ca s'eppiru a truvari
propriu ddà mmenzu
mentri chi succidìa lu pandimoniu.
E chistu parcuscenicu stasira
è comu nu palazzu spalancatu
dintra li stanzi di la me' mimoria
d'unni agghiòrnanu, d'u funnu di la
    notti,
— abissu scuru di diminticanza —
l'istanti trapassati
ca 'un ponnu cchiù turnari.
Ma i cosi s'hannu a diri onesti e boni.

niente di più, neanche un poco,
    niente
che non assomigli alla verità più vera.
Parlate di me come fui".
E come potremmo noi dire
com'era per davvero il generale
visto che egli stesso non lo sapeva?
Mannaggia all'inferno
quanto era solo Otello…
manco un amico…
manco un amico c'era, manco uno
per dire l'orazione funebre.
Siccome nessuno lo poté fare allora
e vado sempre sentendo maldicenze,
è venuto ora il momento che devo
    parlare
di quello che successe in quei giorni.
Ora vi racconto la storia di Otello.
Ora ci provo. Provo a sistemare
tante cose che mi van girando
nella testa piena di confusione.
Io stesso ero presente
a certi avvenimenti.
Altre cose, invece, me le raccontarono
persone di fiducia e di rispetto
che si trovarono
proprio lì in mezzo
mentre succedeva il pandemonio.
E questo palcoscenico stasera
è come un palazzo spalancato
nelle stanze della mia memoria
da dove affiorano, dal fondo della
    notte,
— abisso scuro di dimenticanza —
gli istanti passati
che non possono più tornare.
Ma le cose si devono dire
    onestamente e bene.

nothing more, not even a bit, nothing
that does not resemble the truest truth.
Speak of me as I was."
And how could we say
how the general really was
considering he didn't know it himself?
Goddamn it to hell
how alone Othello was…
not a friend…
not a single friend, not one
to speak the funeral oration.
Since no one could do it then
and I keep hearing malicious gossip,
the time has come for me to talk
about what happened in those days.
Now I'll tell you the story of Othello.
Now I'll try. I'll try to clarify
many things that keep swirling
in my head all confused.
I was present
at certain events.
Other things, instead, were told to me
by trusted and respectable people
who found themselves there
as all hell broke loose.
And this stage tonight
is like a palace open wide
on the rooms of memory
from which surface, from the depth of the night,
— dark abyss of oblivion —
the past moments
that cannot return.
But things must be said honestly and well.

Pi chistu u sangu è amaru e mi va 'ntesta
sintennu chiddu ca si va cuntannu
di comu ha' succidutu sta tragedia.
A storia d'u 'nfilici ginirali
addivintò u curtigghiu
d'un nivuru bistiali e assassinu
chi vosi ammazzari a so' mugghieri
picchì avìa cadutu nta la riti
di Iago satanassu e tradituri…
Ma a cosa ca 'mprissiona li cristiani
è a peddi nivura d'u nostru ginirali.
Ora iu dicu: si unu penza
a certi pirsunaggi di la storia
chi sacciu: Bruto, Cassio o Coriolano,
opuru u principi di Danimarca
o si penza a Re Lear, penza a quarcosa
d'u sentimentu d'iddi,
d'a passiuni particolari d'iddi…
na cosa quarsiasi: crudeltà, cumannu,
'ncirtizza, dubbiu, sdignu, dilusioni…
'Nveci quannu si dici Otello,
di subitu si penza ch'era niuru.
Prima ancora di passiuni o tradimentu
si penza ch'iddu avìa la peddi scura.
"Cu'? Otello? U niuru, u turcu,
    l'africanu"…
Sta cosa 'un si pò suppurtari…
U fattu chi Desdemona e Otello
'un sunnu uguali 'unn'è picchì una è
    janca
chi labbruzza di rosa e l'autru scuru
c'a funciazza di niuru primitivu
e sarbaggiu. A cosa 'mpurtanti
ca 'i fa diversi e pi sempri luntani
— l'amuri 'nfatti è l'arti
di rispittari chista luntananza —
dicìa, a differenza tra iddi dui,

Per questo il sangue è amaro e mi va
    alla testa
sentendo dire ciò che si va dicendo
su come è successa questa tragedia.
La storia dell'infelice generale
diventò il pettegolezzo
su un negro bestiale e assassino
che volle ammazzare sua moglie
perché era caduto nella rete
di Iago diavolo e traditore…
Ma la cosa che fa impressione agli
    uomini
è la pelle nera del nostro generale.
Ora io dico: se uno pensa
a certi personaggi della storia
che so: Bruto, Cassio o Coriolano,
oppure il principe di Danimarca
o se pensa a Re Lear, pensa a qualcosa
dei loro sentimenti,
della loro particolare passione…
una cosa qualsiasi: crudeltà, potere,
incertezza, dubbio, sdegno,
    delusione…
Invece quando si dice Otello,
subito si pensa che era nero.
Prima ancora della passione o del
    tradimento
si pensa che aveva la pelle scura.
"Chi? Otello? Il negro, il turco,
    l'africano"…
Sta cosa non si può sopportare…
Il fatto che Desdemona e Otello
non sono uguali non è perché una è
    bianca
con le labbrucce di rosa e l'altro scuro
con la bocca di negro primitivo
e selvaggio. La cosa importante
che li rende diversi e per sempre
    lontani
— l'amore infatti è l'arte
di rispettare questa lontananza —
dicevo, la differenza tra loro due,

That's why blood is bad and pressure mounts
hearing what they say
about how this tragedy came about.
The story of the unhappy general
became the gossip
about a bestial black assassin
who wanted to kill his wife
because he had fallen in the trap
of Iago, treasonous devil…
But what impresses men the most
is the dark skin of our general.
Now I say: if one thinks
of some characters in history
say: Brutus, Cassio or Coriolanus,
or the prince of Denmark
or if one thinks of Lear, one thinks something
about their feelings,
about their particular passion…
anything: cruelty, power,
uncertainty, doubt, disdain, disappointment…
when one says Othello, instead,
one immediately thinks that he was black.
Even before passion or betrayal
one thinks that he had dark skin.
"Who? Othello? The black, the Turk, the African"…
It is unbearable…
The fact that Desdemona and Othello
are not the same is not because one is white
with sweet rosy lips and the other one dark
with the mouth of a primitive
and savage black. The important thing
that makes them different and forever distant
— love, in fact, is the art
of respecting such distance —
I was saying, the difference between the two of them,

è ch'unu è masculu mentri l'autra è
     fimmina.
Pi chistu mi veni vogghia
d'aggrizzari u latu tortu di la storia
comu veni cuntata ntà sti jorna.
Di sti parti 'un si pò picchì si tratta
di storia troppu nota e canusciuta.
Ma quannu mi nni vaju pi quarchi
     viaggiu
e 'ncocciu quarchi cristianu furisteru
ca 'un sapi propriu nenti
d'Otello e di Desdemona piatusa
iu ci vogghiu cuntari d'un ginirali e
     basta,
senza chiariri u mantu di la peddi.
A mmia mi premi diri ca sta storia
era accussì, ntà stu modu para para,
puru si Otello avissi statu jancu.
Pi tutti vali sempri a stissa cosa:
lu sensu precisu d'a nostra pirsona
è sempri 'ncolleganza e dipinnenza
di l'intima cuistioni di l'amuri.
Ntù me' ricordu e ntù me' cuntu Otello
ci havi na peddi nova,
lucenti e janca comu luna china.
E ora accuminciamu.
Stava Otello ntù campu di battagghia.
Desdemona aspittava a la so' casa.
E accuminciava a nasciri l'amuri
ntà lu cori di li du' nnamurati,
cori ca si virsava
dintra li littri scritti
supra li fazzuletti.
Accuminciamu.
Facemula sta strata
c'aiuta stu passatu di svintura
a grapiri la porta d'u duluri
e nèsciri ddà fora

è che uno è maschio mentre l'altra è
     femmina.
Per questo mi viene voglia
di raddrizzare il lato storto della storia
come viene raccontata quest'oggi.
Da ste parti non si può perché si
     tratta
di storia troppo nota e conosciuta.
Ma quando me ne vado per qualche
     viaggio
e incontro qualche forestiero
che non sa proprio niente
di Otello e della povera Desdemona
io gli voglio raccontare di un generale
     e basta,
senza specificare il colore della pelle.
A me preme dire che questa storia
sarebbe stata così, in questo preciso
     modo,
anche se Otello fosse stato bianco.
Per tutti vale sempre la stessa cosa:
il senso preciso del nostro essere
è sempre collegato e dipendente
dall'intima questione dell'amore.
Nel mio ricordo e nel mio racconto
     Otello
ha una pelle nuova
lucente e bianca come la luna piena.
E ora incominciamo.
Stava Otello nel campo di battaglia.
Desdemona aspettava a casa sua.
E cominciava a nascere l'amore
nel cuore dei due innamorati,
cuore che si riversava
nelle lettere scritte
su fazzoletti.
Cominciamo.
Facciamola sta strada
ci aiuta questo passato di sventura
ad aprire la porta del dolore
e ad uscire fuori

is that one is male while the other is female.
That's why I feel the need
to straighten the crooked angle of the story
as it's told today.
Around here one can't because it is
a too well-known story.
But when I leave for a trip
and I meet a stranger
who knows nothing
about Othello and poor Desdemona
I want to tell him about a general and nothing more,
without specifying the colour of his skin.
I need to say that this story
would have been like this, this very same way
even if Othello had been white.
It's always the same for everyone:
our precise sense of self
is always tied to and dependent on
the intimate matter of love.
In my memory and in my tale Othello
has a new skin,
shining and white like a full moon.
Let's begin.
Othello stood in the battlefield.
Desdemona waited at home.
And love began to grow
in the hearts of the two lovers,
hearts that poured
in the letters written
on handkerchiefs.
Let's begin.
Let's walk down this road
the unfortunate past helps us
to open the door of pain
and to go out

p'addivintari cuscenza cumuni
p'addivintari riscattu e pirdonu.
Comora accuminciamu d'u cominciu
ch'ora accumincia arreri
e arreri 'un lassa mai d'accuminciari.

per diventare coscienza comune
per diventare riscatto e perdono.
Come ora incominciamo dall'inizio
che ora comincia di nuovo
e di nuovo non smette mai di
    cominciare.

Torniamo indietro ai giorni dell'innamoramento. Otello e Desdemona sono lontani. Il generale è dovuto partire e ora si trova sul campo di battaglia. Desdemona aspetta il suo ritorno. Nel frattempo i due amanti si scrivono. Per non fare scoprire questa corrispondenza al padre della ragazza, al posto della carta usano dei fazzoletti che i loro complici vanno recapitando di nascosto.

LETTERA DI DESDEMONA:

Ogni volta che ricevo
un nuovo fazzoletto
prima di aprirlo lo porto alla bocca
e assaggio con le labbra il tuo profumo
che resta intatto nonostante il viaggio
da quei luoghi remoti in cui ti trovi.
Speriamo che mio padre non si accorga
di questo nostro gioco
segreto e temerario.
Per lui straniero è come dire
contaminato, barbaro, selvaggio.
E anche se si mostra bendisposto
al fondo invece resta
l'ostilità riservata ai nemici.
Per me straniero ha il suono familiare
di qualcosa di me che non sapevo.
Tu sei la terra
in cui ora voglio mettere radici.
Oddio, scusate…
Non ho saputo trattenere il tu…
quel tu che nel mio cuore
vi rende più vicino.

LETTERA DI DESDEMONA:

Ogni volta che ricevo
un nuovo fazzoletto
prima di aprirlo lo porto alla bocca
e assaggio con le labbra il tuo
    profumo
che resta intatto nonostante il viaggio
da quei luoghi remoti in cui ti trovi.
Speriamo che mio padre non si
    accorga
di questo nostro gioco
segreto e temerario.
Per lui straniero è come dire
contaminato, barbaro, selvaggio.
E anche se si mostra ben disposto
al fondo invece resta
l'ostilità riservata ai nemici.
Per me straniero ha il suono familiare
di qualcosa di me che non sapevo.
Tu sei la terra
in cui ora voglio mettere radici.
Oddio, scusate…
Non ho saputo trattenere il tu…
quel tu che nel mio cuore
vi rende più vicino.

to become common knowledge
to become redemption and forgiveness.
As if it were now, let's begin from the start
that now begins again
and again it never ceases to begin.

Let's go back to the days of courtship. Othello and Desdemona are apart, on two separate ends of the stage in a cone of light. Othello has had to leave for battle. Desdemona is awaiting his return. In the meantime the two lovers exchange letters. In order not to get caught by the girl's father, instead of paper they use handkerchiefs that their accomplices deliver in secret.

DESDEMONA'S LETTER:
Every time I receive
a new handkerchief
before opening it I bring it to my mouth
and I taste with my lips your scent
that lingers intact notwithstanding the trip
from those remote places where you are.
Let's hope that my father won't notice
this game of ours,
secret and daring.
For him foreigner means
contaminated, barbaric, savage.
Even if he appears sympathetic
deep down the hostility reserved
to enemies remains.
For me foreigner has the familiar ring
of something of myself I did not know.
Thou art the earth
where I want to take root.
Oh god, forgive me…
I couldn't help being familiar…
that "thou," in my heart,
makes you seem closer.

Vogliate ora permettermi
di continuare in queste lettere
ad infiltrarmi in voi con questo "tu"
quasi fossi un eroe spericolato
che pieno di esplosivo si nasconde
nel vostro cuore intatto
per farlo a un tratto esplodere d'amore.
Mi serve questo tu
per farmi avvicinare
a te così lontano.
Quando sarete qui, ve lo prometto,
mi obbligherò a quel voi che meritate.
Sarà così gioiosa
la nostra vicinanza
che il voi sarà lietissima distanza.
Voglio sapere tutto, scrivi ancora.
Ogni parola che scrivi è importante
come il pane che nutre
o l'acqua che disseta.
E l'aria dentro il petto
non può tenere in vita
se non è piena della voce
che da così lontano
mi porta di continuo il tuo respiro.

LETTERA DI OTELLO:

Iu puru, cara Desdemona, ogni vota
C'arriva ntì me' manu u fazzulettu
ca tu tuccasti, m'u portu a vucca
e 'u vasu e 'u strinciu e 'u manciu a
    muzzicuni
como si fussi parti
d'a to' stissa pirsona.
E quannu 'ncampu arriva u missaggeru
e m'assicura ca pigghiò la littra
propriu direttamenti di to' manu

Vogliate ora permettermi
di continuare in queste lettere
ad infiltrarmi in voi con questo "tu"
quasi fossi un eroe spericolato
che pieno di esplosivo si nasconde
nel vostro cuore intatto
per farlo a un tratto esplodere
    d'amore.
Mi serve questo tu
per farmi avvicinare
a te così lontano.
Quando sarete qui, ve lo prometto,
mi obbligherò a quel voi che meritate.
Sarà così gioiosa
la nostra vicinanza
che il voi sarà lietissima distanza.
Voglio sapere tutto, scrivi ancora.
Ogni parola che scrivi è importante
come il pane che nutre
o l'acqua che disseta.
E l'aria dentro il petto
non può tenere in vita
se non è piena della voce
che da così lontano
mi porta di continuo il tuo respiro.

LETTERA DI OTELLO:

Io pure, cara Desdemona, ogni volta
che mi arriva nelle mani il fazzoletto
che tu toccasti, me lo porto alla bocca
e lo bacio e lo stringo e lo mangio a
    morsi
come se fosse parte
della tua stessa persona.
E quando al campo arriva il
    messaggero
e mi assicura che prese la lettera
proprio direttamente dalle tue mani

Please allow me, then,
to continue in this letters
to get inside of you with this "thou"
as if I were a daring hero
who hides, full of explosives,
in thy untouched heart
to make it suddenly explode with love.
I need this "thou"
To get closer
to thee so far away.
When thou art here, I promise,
I will stick to the "you" that thou deservest.
Our closeness
will be so joyful
that the "you" will be a happy distance.
I want to know everything, write again.
Every word thou writest is important
like bread that nourishes
or water that quenches thirst.
And the air in my chest
cannot keep me alive
if it's not filled with the voice
that from such distance
constantly brings me thy breath.

OTHELLO'S LETTER:

I too, dear Desdemona, every time
that I hold in my hands the handkerchief
that thou touched, I bring it to my mouth
and I kiss it, I hold it, eat it in small bites
as if it were part
of thy body.
And when the messenger gets to the field
and assures me that he took the letter
directly from thy hands

mi sforzu a malapena e mi trattegnu
pi 'un vasarici a frunti puru a iddu
c'havi ancora ammucciata dintra
    all'occhi
a maravigghia di la to' biddizza.
Sì lu primu pinzeru d'u matinu,
l'urtimu prima d'jirimi a curcari.
E puru mentri dormu 'nsonnu a ttia.
Mi torna a la menti ntà stu mentri
ddu jornu ca chioveva forti assai.
E iu mi scantava
ca tu 'un putivi nèsciri di casa
pi veniri nni mia
ô primu appuntamentu ca ti desi.
C'era un gran tirribili uraganu
cu trona 'i l'aria e fulmini a timpesta
ma iu 'un m'a sintìa d'abbandunari
u posto unni m'avìa mmaginatu
ca n'avissimu pututu 'ncuntrari.
Ed eccu a l'u 'mpruvisu
ti vitti spuntari darreri di 'n agnuni.
'Unn'è ca m'u 'nsunnavu, pi ddaveru
u ventu si firmò, turnò l'aria sirena,
e dunnegghiè quariavi
e alluminavi cu lu to' splinnuri.
Ti giuru ch'era tanta l'armunia,
la cueti ca purtasti a ddu minutu
ca dintr'i mia pinzavu:
"Megghiu si moru.
Megghiu si moru con ntà sta cuntintizza
picchì secunnu mia stu paraddisu
è troppu e certu nun pò cchiù turnari".

Ntà littra mi scrivisti di to' patri…
Sugnu filici di chiddu chi dici,
di comu passi supra
u fatto ca iu sugnu furasteru.

mi sforzo a malapena e mi trattengo
per non baciare sulla fronte anche lui
che ha ancora nascosta negli occhi
la meraviglia della tua bellezza.
Sei il primo pensiero del mattino,
l'ultimo prima di andare a coricarmi.
E anche mentre dormo ti sogno.
Mi torna alla mente ora
quel giorno che pioveva forte.
E io ero spaventato
che tu non potessi uscire di casa
per venire da me
al primo appuntamento che ti diedi.
C'era un grande e terribile temporale
con tuoni nell'aria e fulmini da
    tempesta
ma io non me la sentivo di lasciare
il posto dove mi ero immaginato
che ci saremmo potuti incontrare.
Ed ecco all'improvviso
ti vidi spuntare da dietro un angolo.
Non è che me lo sognassi, per davvero
il vento si fermò, tornò l'aria serena,
e ovunque stavi riscaldavi
e illuminavi tutto col tuo splendore.
Ti giuro che era tanta l'armonia,
la quiete che portasti in quel
    momento
che dentro di me pensavo:
"Meglio se muoio.
Meglio se muoio con questa
    contentezza
perché secondo me sto paradiso
è troppo e certamente non può più
    tornare".

Nella lettera mi scrivesti di tuo
    padre…
Sono felice di quello che dici,
di come passi sopra
al fatto che io sono forestiero.

I try my best and I restrain myself
not to kiss his forehead too
that still hides in its eyes
the wonder of thy beauty.
Thou art the first thought in the morning,
the last one before going to bed.
And as I sleep I dream of thee.
That day when it rained hard
comes to mind now.
And I was afraid
that thou couldst not leave the house
to come to see me
for the first date we made.
A great and awesome storm raged
with thunder in the air and bolts of tempest
but I could not leave
the place that I had pictured
for our meeting.
When all of a sudden
I saw thee appear around the corner.
I wasn't dreaming: for real
the wind ceased, the clear air returned,
and everywhere thou wert thou diffusedst warmth
and light with thy splendour.
I swear that such was the harmony,
such the tranquillity that thou hath brougth
that I thought to myself:
"Better to die.
Better to die with this happiness
because methinks this paradise
is excessive and it surely can't come back."

In the letter thou wrote about thy father…
I am happy with what thou sayest,
how thou overlookest
the fact that I'm a foreigner.

Quantu a la discinnenza…
presto veni lu jornu,
si a cosa nni pò essiri d'aiutu,
ca to' patri havi a sapiri
ca sugnu guerrieru di stirpi riali
e quantu a nascita
a nuddu mi sentu nfiriuri.
Si 'un fussi statu pi stu grann'amuri
avissi cuntinuato cu piaciri
na vita fatta sulu d'avvinture
e 'unn'avissi datu limiti e cunfini
all'infinita libertà ch'avìa.

Amuri, amuri, amuri…
Si Diu si cimintassi,
cu tutta l'intinzioni
pi fari na criatura uguali a ttia
di certo s'addannassi pi truvari
la formula sigreta
dunn'è stampata la to' pirfizioni.
Cu sta brevi canzuni ora ti lassu.
Sugnu stunatu ma sempri mi la cantu
pi farimi na 'nticchia i cumpagnia:
"Di mia stissu mi scaccia e m'alluntana
cu teni arrassu u corsu de me' strata
di l'occhi, di li manu e d'a vuccuzza
di tia ca sì pi mmia l'unica gioia,
di tia ca sì lu ciatu
chi trasi ntì purmuna
e 'nfunnu suspirannu m'arriala
lu ventu di la vita dilicatu".

SECONDA LETTERA DI DESDEMONA:
Non scrivermi mai più frasi d'amore.
Non perdere il furore
sul campo di battaglia.

Quanto alla discendenza…
presto verrà il giorno,
se la cosa ci può essere d'aiuto,
in cui tuo padre dovrà sapere
che sono guerriero di stirpe reale
e in quanto a nascita
non mi sento inferiore a nessuno.
Se non fosse stato per questo grande
        amore
mi sarebbe continuata a piacere
una vita fatta solo di avventure
e non avrei dato limiti e confini
all'infinita libertà che avevo.

Amore, amore, amore…
Se Dio si cimentasse,
con tutte le intenzioni
di fare una creatura uguale a te
di certo si dannerebbe per trovare
la formula segreta
su cui è stampata la tua perfezione.
Con questa breve canzone ora ti
        lascio.
Sono stonato ma sempre me la canto
per farmi un po' di compagnia:
"Da me stesso mi scaccia e mi
        allontana
chi tiene lontano il corso dalla mia
        strada
dagli occhi, dalle mani e dalla
        boccuccia
di te che sei per me l'unica gioia,
di te che sei il fiato
che respiro nei polmoni
e in fondo sospirando mi regala
il vento della vita delicato".

SECONDA LETTERA DI DESDEMONA:
Non scrivermi mai più frasi d'amore.
Non perdere il furore
sul campo di battaglia.

As for my descent…
soon the day will come,
if this could be of help,
when thy father will learn
that I am a warrior of noble origin
and as for my birth
I don't feel inferior to anyone.
If it hadn't been for this great love
a life filled only with adventures
would have kept being pleasing
and I wouldn't have set limits and boundaries
to the endless freedom I had.

Love, love, love…
If God tried,
with all His might
to make a creature like thee
surely He'd be hard pressed to find
the secret formula
on which your perfection is based.
I leave thee with this brief song.
I am tone deaf, but I always sing it to myself
to keep me company:
"He who steers my course away
from the eyes, the hands and the lovely mouth
of thee who art for me the only joy,
of thee who art the breath
I draw in my lungs
and deeply, by breathing, givest me
the delicate wind of life
drives and keeps me away from myself."

SECOND LETTER FROM DESDEMONA:
Don't ever write me love words again.
Don't lose thy wrath
on the battlefield.

Io sono solo
una piccola provincia
che tu hai già conquistato.
Non ti curare di adularmi.
Riprendi il tuo racconto
e affianca agli episodi
del tuo romanzo d'armi
alcuni squarci di norme, di motti,
precetti e insegnamenti
su tattiche manovre e strategie
che possano servirmi
per quell'apprendistato militare
a cui voglio arruolarmi
nelle mie stanze trasformate in
    accademia.
Lì dentro tu dovrai insegnarmi
tutto sull'obbedienza,
il sacrificio e la sottomissione.
Ti chiederai il perché
di questa mia insistenza:
ho sempre sognato di essere un soldato.
Non sai il mio dispiacere
di non potere mai montare in sella
se non a gambe sistemate
solo su un fianco del cavallo
e non come sta in groppa un cavaliere.
Quand'ero piccola sventravo bambole
che poi nessuno riparava
e il pavimento della cameretta
simulava un campo di battaglia
dove fantasticavo attacchi e assalti.
E tutte le biblioteche dei parenti
ho saccheggiato di nascosto
leggendo le avventure
dei prodi cavalieri…
Ricordo, non avevo sette anni,
la prima volta che impugnai una spada…

I am just
a small province
that thou hast already conquered.
Don't bother with flattering me.
Get back to thy tale
and add to the episodes
of thy chanson de geste
some bits of rules, of mottoes,
precepts and teachings
on tactical manoeuvres and strategies
that could be useful to me
for that military training
I wish to undertake
in my rooms, transformed in academy.
There thou wilt teach me
everything about obedience,
sacrifice and submission.
Thou wilt wonder the reasons
of my insistence:
I have always dreamt of being a soldier.
Thou dost not know the sorrow
of not being able to ride a horse
other than side straddle
rather than how a horseman mounts.
As a child, I dismembered dolls
that no one would mend
and the floor of my room
looked like a battlefield
where I imagined attacks and assaults.
I have secretly raided
all the libraries of relatives
reading the adventures
of valiant knights…
I recall, I wasn't even seven yet,
the first time I held a sword…

e ancora adesso ogni tanto mi assento,
mi chiudo nella stanza…
può bastarmi un semplice pugnale…
La lama fredda mi trasmette
il gelo della morte.
È un pensiero che scuote e innalza il
      cuore.
È un pensiero che costringe
la vita a visitarci mentre accade.
Chi conosce l'urlo e il furore di un
      combattimento
ormai per sempre ha incontrato la morte
e la tiene nascosta nel suo sangue.
Sono state le vittorie, i successi,
ma soprattutto i tormenti, le pene,
che ti hanno intaccato il cuore
a farmi innamorare…
Inoltre ti confesso
— questa è la parte più difficile da attuare
di questo desiderio
che solo tu, se vorrai, potrai esaudire —
che questi viaggi d'avventura
con cui mi hai preso il cuore
io vorrei viverli davvero.
Con te, ti prego, portami in battaglia.
Starò sempre al tuo fianco
mentre infliggi dolori
e sconfitte ai tuoi avversari.
E forse un giorno
combatteremo insieme
forse fino a morire insieme.
Non c'è per me fine più dolce
che quella di cadere fianco a fianco.
E a Dio, se rinascessi, chiederei
soltanto di poterti assomigliare.

e ancora adesso ogni tanto mi assento,
mi chiudo nella stanza…
può bastarmi un semplice pugnale…
La lama fredda mi trasmette
il gelo della morte.
È un pensiero che scuote e innalza il
      cuore.
È un pensiero che costringe
la vita a visitarci mentre accade.
Chi conosce l'urlo e il furore di un
      combattimento
ormai per sempre ha incontrato la
      morte
e la tiene nascosta nel suo sangue.
Sono state le vittorie, i successi,
ma soprattutto i tormenti, le pene,
che ti hanno intaccato il cuore
a farmi innamorare…
Inoltre ti confesso
— questa è la parte più difficile da
      attuare
di questo desiderio
che solo tu, se vorrai, potrai esaudire —
che questi viaggi d'avventura
con cui mi hai preso il cuore
io vorrei viverli davvero.
Con te, ti prego, portami in battaglia.
Starò sempre al tuo fianco
mentre infliggi dolori
e sconfitte ai tuoi avversari.
E forse un giorno
combatteremo insieme
forse fino a morire insieme.
Non c'è per me fine più dolce
che quella di cadere fianco a fianco.
E a Dio, se rinascessi, chiederei
soltanto di poterti assomigliare.

to this day sometimes I excuse myself,
lock myself in my room…
a simple dagger may be enough…
The cold blade carries
the coldness of death.
It is a thought the shakes and raises the heart.
It is a thought that forces
life to visits us, when it occurs.
Those who know the scream and fury of a fight
have now met death forever
and hide it in their blood.
It was the victories, the successes,
but mostly the torments, the pains,
that have touched thy heart
that made me fall for thee…
moreover I confess
— this is the hardest part to achieve
of this desire
that only thou, if thou wilt, couldst fulfill —
that I would like to live through
these adventurous journeys
that have captured my heart.
I beg thee, bring me to battle with thee.
I will always be by thy side
as thou inflict pain
and losses on your opponents.
And perhaps one day
we'll fight together
perhaps till we die together.
There's no sweeter death for me
than falling by thy side,
and of God, if I were born again, I'd only ask
to be like you.

SOLDATO: 'I sta pigghiannu bonu la
    passiuni…
    Taliati sti palummi nnamurati…
    Forsi l'amuri è chistu:
    unu chi scrivi,
    l'autru ch'aspetta…
    unu chi leggi
    mentri l'autru già si 'nsonna
    ca l'autru forsi già ci ha' rispunnutu…
    Forsi l'amuri è chistu:
    na littra.
    Na littra chi parti
    mentri l'autra arriva.
    Na littra ca gira mentri l'autra firrìa.
    L'amuri è littra mannata
    di na banna luntana
    a n'autra banna cchiù luntana ancora.
    E mentri l'amanti fannu
    ritratti di palori,
    sunnu iddi stissi sempri furasteri,
    sempri straneri a sti frasi d'amuri.
    Eppuru l'amuri è littra.
    È carta e 'nsemmula scrittura
    sulu di chiddu chi vulemu diri,
    di chiddu chi vulemu ca si sapi,
    di chiddu ca nui stissi
    pinzamu di sapiri.
    U restu nesci fora
    quannu finisci l'ura
    di littri ch'attraversanu a distanza…
    Quannu 'nfatti s'accurza a luntananza
    finu a spirìri e trovanu dimora
    ntù stissu locu l'amanti e l'amata,
    e pi ddaveru Amuri
    li corpi 'ntrizza e accucchia li distini,
    allura sì, accumincia tutt'u restu,

SOLDATO: Li sta pigliando per bene la
    passione…
    Guardate sti colombi innamorati…
    Forse l'amore è questo:
    uno che scrive,
    l'altro che aspetta…
    uno che legge
    mentre l'altro già sogna
    che l'altro forse gli ha già risposto…
    Forse l'amore è questo:
    una lettera.
    Una lettera che parte
    mentre l'altra arriva.
    Una lettera che gira mentre l'altra va
    in giro.
    L'amore è una lettera mandata
    da un posto lontano
    a un altro posto ancora più lontano.
    E mentre gli amanti fanno
    ritratti di parole,
    sono essi stessi sempre forestieri,
    sempre estranei a queste frasi d'amore.
    Eppure l'amore è una lettera.
    È carta e insieme scrittura
    solo di quello che vogliamo dire,
    di quello che vogliamo che si sappia,
    di quello che noi stessi
    pensiamo di sapere.
    Il resto viene fuori
    quando finisce l'ora
    delle lettere che attraversano le
    distanze…
    Quando infatti si accorcia la
    lontananza
    fino a sparire e trovano dimora
    nello stesso luogo l'amante e l'amata,
    e per davvero l'Amore
    intreccia i corpi e unisce i destini,
    allora sì, comincia tutto il resto,

SOLDIER: Passion is seizing them whole…
    Look at these two doves in love…
    Perhaps this is love:
    one who writes,
    the other one waits…
    one who reads
    while the other one dreams
    that the other has perhaps already answered…
    perhaps this is love:
    a letter.
    A letter that leaves
    as the other one arrives.
    A letter circulating as the other circulates.
    Love is a letter sent
    from a faraway place
    to another place even farther away.
    And while lovers paint
    portraits with words,
    they are themselves still strangers,
    always estranged from these words of love.
    Yet, love is a letter.
    It is paper and writing
    of just what we want to say,
    of what we want to be known,
    of what we ourselves
    think we know.
    The rest comes out
    when the time of letters
    that cross distances is over…
    in fact, when distances shorten
    to the point of disappearing and lover and beloved
    find themselves in the same place,
    and Love for real
    tangles bodies and ties destinies
    only then the rest begins,

tuttu accumincia u strepitu, u rumuri,
tutta si fa prissanti e nni cumanna
la pritinzioni d'infilare l'autru
dintr'allu 'mbutu d'u nostru disìu.
L'oggetto di lu nostru sintimentu,
'un ci su' Santi, havi pi forza
    assumigghiari
a 'nsonnu ca nuatri ni 'nsunnamu,
'nsonnu, spettru, fantasima, visioni.
Quannu l'oggetto amatu s'arribbella
e mustra, prutistannu, a so'natura
finisci u 'ncantu e accumincia u duluri.
E allura pacenza…
scrivemu ancora littri,
littri d'amuri.
L'amuri 'unn'è di casa 'ncapu ô lettu
ma joca 'i sulu e sulu
ntù jancu 'mmaculatu
d'un fogghiu ca strincemu ntà li manu.
E mentri l'amanti
'mpruvvisanu palori
cu troppa vicinanza
s'addunanu ca mmenzu ci hannu 'n
    muru
e sentunu li carni
sirrati di catini di turtura.

SECONDA LETTERA DI OTELLO:
    Amuri duci, amuri da me' vita,
    chista ch'ora ti scrivu
    è storia amara
    ch'a nuddu haiu mai cuntatu.
    Stu tristi pisodiu da me' vita
    l'haiu sempri tinutu pi mmia
    picchì sulu pinzannu a nzoccu avvinni
    mi tremanu li carni p'u duluri
    e arreri sciddicu ntù mari apertu

tutto comincia lo strepito, i rumori,
si fa tutta pressante e ci comanda
la pretesa di infilare l'altro
nell'imbuto del nostro desiderio.
L'oggetto del nostro sentimento,
non ci son santi, deve per forza
    assomigliare
al sogno che noi abbiam sognato,
sogno, spettro, fantasma, visione.
Quando l'oggetto amato si ribella
e mostra, protestando, la sua natura
finisce l'incanto e cominciano i dolori.
E allora pazienza…
scriviamo ancora lettere,
lettere d'amore.
L'amore non sta di casa dentro a un
    letto
ma gioca da solo e solo
nel bianco immacolato
di un foglio che stringiamo fra le
    mani.
E mentre gli amanti
improvvisano parole
con troppa vicinanza
si accorgono che in mezzo hanno un
    muro
e sentono le carni
serrate da catene di tortura

SECONDA LETTERA DI OTELLO:
    Amore dolce, amore della mia vita,
    questa che ora ti scrivo
    è una storia amara
    che non ho mai raccontato a nessuno.
    Questo triste episodio della mia vita
    l'ho sempre tenuto per me
    perché solo a pensare a ciò che è
    accaduto
    mi tremano le carni per il dolore
    e di nuovo scivolo nel mare aperto

everything begins: the din, the noises,
the pretence to fit the other
in the funnel of our desire
becomes all-encompassing and governs us.
The object of our feeling
there is no other way, must resemble
the dream we have dreamt:
dream, spectre, ghost, vision.
When the beloved object rebels
and shows, protesting, its nature
the spell ends and pains begin.
Then, patience…
We still write letters,
love letters.
Love doesn't live in a bed
but plays alone and only
in the immaculate white
of a paper we hold in our hands.
And while lovers
improvise words
with excessive closeness
they realize they have a wall between them
and feel their flesh
bound by chains of torture.

SECOND LETTER BY OTHELLO:
Sweet love, love of my life,
what I now write to thee
is a bitter story
that I have never told anyone.
I have always kept to myself
this sad episode of my life
because just thinking about what happened
my flesh trembles in pain
and again I slide into the abyss

di l'angoscia,
di la disperazioni.
Finu a quannu 'un canuscivu a ttia
u cori era na petra
e dintr'e vini 'un c'era sangu
ma rina abbruciata d'u suli
di nu disertu africanu.
E ddocu 'nfatti
accuminciò sta storia:
ntù disertu.
Doppu nu scontru orribili
cu li giganti d'a muntagna 'ncantata
avìa persu tutti li surdati
e suli ntà guarnigioni
avìamo arristatu iu e me' frati.
'Un ti parravu mai di me' frati
picchì già pronunciannu lu so' nomi
accumincianu li lacrimi e i singhiuzzi
e a vucca si rifiuta di parrari.
Ma mi fazzu forza
e provu a cuntariti lu stissu
di comu ntà me' vita a lu 'mpruvisu
finìu lu jocu e s'abbattìu a tragedia.
Me' frati era pi mmia lu munnu 'nteru.
A terra, u celu,
e tutto l'universu canusciutu
'un sunnu accussì granni
quant'era la so' 'mmensa 'ntelligenza.
Pi mmia ca era cchiù nicu
avìa sempri primuri e attinzioni.
E i cosi chi ora sacciu
tutti me' frati mi l'avìa 'nsignati.
E iu 'u taliava pi ddaveru
comu fussi nu Diu scinnutu 'nterra.
'Nsomma… camina camina,

dell'angoscia,
della disperazione.
Finché non ti conobbi
il cuore era una pietra
e nelle vene non c'era sangue
ma sabbia bruciata dal sole
di un deserto africano.
E là infatti
ebbe inizio questa storia:
nel deserto.
Dopo uno scontro orribile
coi giganti di una montagna incantata
avevo perso tutti i soldati
e soli nella guarnigione
eravamo rimasti io e mio fratello.
Non ti ho mai parlato di mio fratello
perché solo a pronunciare il suo nome
cominciano le lacrime e i singhiozzi
e la bocca si rifiuta di parlare.
Ma mi faccio forza
e provo a raccontarti lo stesso
di come nella mia vita all'improvviso
finì il gioco e si abbatté la tragedia.
Mio fratello era per me il mondo
    intero.
La terra, il cielo,
e tutto l'universo conosciuto
non sono così grandi
come la sua immensa intelligenza.
Per me che ero il più piccolo
aveva sempre premure e attenzioni.
E le cose che ora so
me le aveva insegnate tutte mio
    fratello.
E io lo guardavo per davvero
come se fosse un Dio sceso sulla terra.
Insomma… cammina e cammina,

of angst,
of desperation.
Until I met thee
my heart was a stone
and in my veins flowed no blood
but sand burnt by the sun
of an African desert.
In fact, it's there
that this story began:
in the desert.
After a horrible clash
with the giants of an enchanted mountain
I had lost all my soldiers
and, alone in the garrison,
my brother and I had remained.
I have never told you about my brother
because just by mentioning his name
tears and sobs flow
and my mouth refuses to speak.
But I'll summon my strength
and try to tell you anyways
how in my life all of a sudden
games ended and tragedy struck.
My brother was for me the whole world.
The earth, the sky,
and the whole known universe
have never been as vast
as his immense intelligence.
For me, the youngest one,
he always had consideration and care.
What I know now
my brother taught me.
And I truly looked at him
as if he were a God descended to earth.
So… walking and walking,

pi turnari a pigghiari
la via di lu mari
'un c'era autra strata d'u disertu.
A parti u cauru, a siti,
e mancu un pezz'i pani pi manciari,
c'eranu gran tirribili e sarbaggi
armali ca facevanu scantari.
E allura cu' potti dòrmiri dda notti?
Pi furtuna, cu li primi luci
di lu suli ca ntù celu avìa turnatu,
vittimu all'orizzonti
l'azzurru di lu mari.
'Unn'era miraggiu.
Era propriu a distesa marina.
Ma a strata pi gghiri 'ncontru all'acqua
avìa ntù menzu un castidduzzu anticu
ca pareva di gran tempu abbannunatu.
'Un c'era scrusciu e 'un si moveva
        nenti…
E nuatri camminàvamu,
camminàvamu,
camminàvamu …
A un certu puntu
na lingua di focu
partìu darreri u muru d'u casteddu.
Un corpu.
Un tron'i l'aria
spirtusò cu raggia
la pirfizioni di 'n silenziu stranu.
Stu bottu 'mprissionanti
era signali chiaru
di scoppiu di cannuni.
Silenziu.
U tempu di sbàttiri l'occhi
e a parti destra di me' frati
'un c'era cchiù.

per tornare a prendere
la via del mare
non c'era altra strada se non il deserto.
A parte il caldo e la sete,
e manco un pezzo di pane da
        mangiare,
c'erano grandi e terribili animali
selvaggi da far paura.
E allora chi poteva dormire la notte?
Per fortuna, con le prime luci
del sole che nel cielo era tornato,
vedemmo all'orizzonte
l'azzurro del mare.
Non era un miraggio.
Era proprio la distesa marina.
Ma la strada per andare incontro
        all'acqua
aveva nel mezzo un castelletto antico
che pareva da gran tempo
        abbandonato.
Non c'era rumore e non si muoveva
        niente…
E noialtri camminavamo,
camminavamo,
camminavamo…
A un certo punto
una lingua di fuoco
partì da dietro il muro del castello.
Un colpo.
Un tuono nell'aria
perforò con rabbia
la perfezione di un silenzio strano.
Sto botto impressionante
era il segnale chiaro
dello scoppio di un cannone.
Silenzio.
Il tempo di sbattere gli occhi
e la parte destra di mio fratello
non c'era più.

to go back to where we
set out to sea
there was no other way but the desert.
Heat and thirst aside,
there wasn't even a piece of bread to eat,
there were big and terrible,
terrifying savage animals.
Who could sleep at night?
Luckily, with the first rays
of the sun that had come back in the sky
we saw on the horizon
the blue of the sea.
It wasn't a mirage.
It really was the expanse of the sea.
But on the road to return to the water
there was an old small castle
that looked long abandoned.
There were no sounds and nothing stirred…
And we walked,
walked,
walked …
At some point
a tongue of flame
sprung from behind the wall of the castle.
A shot.
A thunder in the air
pierced with rage
the perfection of a strange silence.
This awesome explosion
was the clear signal
of a cannon fired.
Silence.
The time to blink
and the right side of my brother
was no longer there.

Si l'avìa purtata u focu	Se l'era portata via il fuoco
pizzuddi pizzuddi ntall'aria.	pezzo a pezzo nell'aria.
La parti sinistra	La parte sinistra
era curcata 'nterra.	era coricata in terra.
Era tutta 'n pirtuso e sanguinava.	Era tutta un buco e sanguinava.
Menzu frati oramai	Mezzo fratello ormai
era focu e ventu,	era fuoco e vento,
menzu frati arristava	mezzo fratello restava
terra e sangu.	terra e sangue.
Silenziu.	Silenzio.
Chi è sta cosa ca mi pigghia u pettu	Cos'è sta cosa che mi prende il petto
e strinci, strinci,	e stringe, stringe,
chi è — m'addumannava ntà ddu mentri	cos'è — mi chiedevo nel mentre
cull'occhi chiusi	con gli occhi chiusi
pi 'un vìdiri ddu scempiu scumminatu —	per non vedere lo scempio
	scombinato —
chi era?	cos'era?
Era duluri.	Era dolore.
Straziu.	Strazio.
Accuminciavu a ghiccari vuci.	Cominciai a dar voce.
Urlava.	Urlavo.
Santiava.	Bestemmiavo.
Chianceva.	Piangevo.
Ma 'unn'era tempu di duluri.	Ma non era tempo di dolore.
Era tempu di vinnitta e d'ira.	Era tempo di vendetta e ira.
"Grannissimi vigliacchi! Ora	"Grandissimi vigliacchi! Ora vi concio
v'agghiunciu!	io!
S'aviti ficatu niscìti!	Uscite da dove vi siete ficcati!
Niscìti subitu, surci ammucciati!	Uscite subito, sorci nascosti!
Niscìti trimanti cunigghi!"	Uscite tremanti conigli!"
Ma nuddu m'arrispunneva.	Ma nessuno mi rispondeva.
Nuddu mi dava saziu.	Nessuno mi dava retta.
E a me' vinnitta era senza birsagghiu.	E la mia vendetta era senza bersaglio.
Allura m'addinucchiavu	Allora mi inginocchiai
e ci dissi a me' frati	e dissi a mio fratello
comu s'ancora avissi statu vivu:	come se fosse stato ancora vivo:
"Susèmunni".	"Alziamoci".
'U pigghiavu…	Lo presi…

The fire had taken it away
piece by piece in the air.
The left side
lay on the ground.
It was all pierced and bleeding.
Half brother now
was fire and wind,
half brother remained
earth and blood.
Silence.
What is this thing that seizes my chest
and grips, grips,
what is it — I wondered then
with my eyes closed
not to see the havoc and confusion —
what was it?
It was pain.
Agony.
I started to scream.
I yelled.
I cursed.
I cried.
But there was no time for pain.
It was the time of revenge and wrath.
"Enormous cowards! I'll show you!
Come out from your hiding place!
Come out right now, hidden rats!
Come out, trembling chickens!"
But no one answered.
No one paid attention to me.
And my revenge lacked a target.
Then, I knelt
and I told my brother
as if he were still alive:
"Let's get up."
I picked him up…

'Un pisava nenti	Non pesava niente
dda menza cosa	una mezza cosa
senza sensu…	senza senso…
M'u misi d'accussì	Me lo misi così
darreri u coddu	dietro al collo
e accuminciavu a curriri	e cominciai a correre
direttu a lu casteddu	dritto al castello
sfidannu ddu 'nvisibili nimicu.	sfidando il nemico invisibile.
Finivu lu tragittu 'n trì secunni	Finii il tragitto in tre secondi
e quinni mi firmavu	e quindi mi fermai
davanzi a lu purtuni.	davanti al portone.
E arreri ai castiddani	E davanti ai castellani
iccannu vuci ci lanciavu a sfida.	a gran voce lanciai una sfida.
Doppu quarchi minutu	Dopo qualche minuto
'ntisi sunari un cornu	sentii suonare un corno
ca mi purtava annunziu	che mi annunciava
c'avissi nisciutu prestu 'n capitanu.	che sarebbe uscito presto un capitano.
E accussì successi.	E così avvenne.
Stu capitanu era guerrieru valurusu	Sto capitano era un guerriero valoroso
e si sintiu punciutu ntà l'unuri.	e si sentì punto nell'onore.
Unu di facci all'autru	Uno di fronte all'altro
accuminciammu allura	cominciammo allora
a darinni battagghia.	a dar battaglia.
Finu a quannu	Fino a quando,
satannu ntall'aria	saltando in aria
comu na tigri ircana	come una tigre ircana (persiana),
tantu acchianavu susu	tanto salii su
chi atterrannu di ddancapu	che atterrando di nuovo
ci assistavu 'n terribili finnenti	gli assestai un terribile fendente
ca ci spaccò la testa ntà du' pezzi	che gli spaccò la testa in due pezzi
e poi giù giù lu troncu ci tagghiavu	e poi giù giù gli tagliai il tronco
fino all'ossu sacru	fino all'osso sacro,
tantu ch'a fini	tanto che alla fine
cu 'n corpu di spata	con un colpo di spada
in dui l'avìa graputu.	l'avevo aperto in due.
E daccussì a me' frati vinnicavu.	E così vendicai mio fratello.

He weighted nothing,
a half thing
senseless...
I carried him thus
on my neck
and I began to run
straight to the castle
challenging the invisible enemy.
I ended my run in three seconds
and then I stopped
in front of the door.
Before the castle people
I yelled my challenge.
After a few minutes
I heard a horn blowing
announcing me
that soon a captain would come out.
And so it happened.
This captain was a valiant warrior
and he was stung to the quick.
Facing each other
we began
to battle.
Until,
leaping in the air
like a Persian tiger,
I jumped so high
that landing
I struck a terrible blow
that broke his head in two
and then all the way down I cut his body
to the sacrum,
so that in the end
with a swing of my sword
I had cut him in two.
So I avenged my brother.

Trasivu ntù casteddu vittoriosu.
Patruni da furtizza
subitu ordinavu
di muntarimi na tenda
propriu ntù puntu
unni me' frati avìa murutu.

'U lavavu,
'u cummigghiavu dintra nu linzolu,
e poi ci desi digna sipultura
senza virsari lacrima.
'Un vuleva chianciri davanzi a me' frati,
iddu 'un l'avissi suppurtatu.
Poi mi chiuivu
dintra dda tenda còmmoda e spaziusa
e quannu nuddu mi putìa taliari
acciminciò pi mmia
lu tempu di lu straziu.
E quattru jorna, quattru, stetti chiusu
a chianciri, a ululari,
stricànnumi 'nterra
manciannu a purviri
chi sempri,
quannu finisciunu i battagghi
havi sapuri di sangu abbruciatu.
Quannu finìu stu 'nfernu di duluri,
lassavu lu casteddu ô so' distinu
e cu na varca ca mi fici 'mpristari
pigghiavu u mari apertu
e accuminciavu arreri lu caminu.

Chistu è lu cuntu
ca mi tinìa ammucciatu dintr'u pettu.
Accogghi ntù to' cori
stu granni patimentu.

Entrai nel castello vittorioso.
Padrone della fortezza
subito ordinai
che mi montassero una tenda
proprio nel punto
in cui mio fratello era morto.

Lo lavai,
lo coprii dentro al lenzuolo,
e poi gli diedi degna sepoltura
senza versare una lacrima.
Non volevo piangere davanti a mio
        fratello,
lui non l'avrebbe sopportato.
Poi mi chiusi
dentro la tenda comoda e spaziosa
e quando nessuno mi poté vedere
cominciò per me
il tempo dello strazio.
E quattro giorni, quattro, stetti chiuso
a piangere, a ululare,
rivoltandomi in terra
mangiando la polvere
che sempre,
quando finiscono le battaglie
ha sapore di sangue bruciato.
Quando finì questo inferno di dolore,
lasciai il castello al suo destino
e con una barca che mi feci prestare
presi il mare aperto
e cominciai il cammino inverso.

Questo è il racconto
che mi tenevo nascosto nel petto.
Accogli nel tuo cuore
questo gran patimento.

I entered the castle victorious.
Master of the fort
I immediately ordered
that they pitch a tent
right where
my brother had died.

I washed him,
I covered him with a sheet
and then I gave him a proper burial
without shedding a tear.
I didn't want to cry in front of my brother,
he wouldn't have stood it.
Then I closed myself
into the comfortable and spacious tent
and when no one could see
the time of agony
began for me.
Four days, four, I remained inside
crying, wailing
rolling in the dirt
eating the dust
that always,
every time a battle ends,
tastes like burnt blood.
When this hell of pain was over
I left the castle to its destiny
and with a boat I borrowed
I took to the high seas
and began the trip home.

This is the tale
I kept hidden in my chest.
Welcome in thy heart
this great pain.

Ti lassu, amuri miu.
Mi chiamanu l'affari di la guerra.
Ti mannu du' rìali.
Un pugnali
— quannu tornu t'insignu a cafuddari
corpa e finnenti micidiali —
e un fazzulettu tuttu arricamatu
— quando tornu vogghiu ca m'asciuchi
stu chiantu ca 'un si voli prosciugari.

Ti lascio, amore mio.
Mi chiamano le faccende di guerra.
Ti mando dei regali.
Un pugnale
— quando torno ti insegno a infliggere
colpi e fendenti micidiali —
e un fazzoletto tutto ricamato
— quando torno voglio che mi asciughi
questo pianto che non si vuole arrestare.

Otello esce. Desdemona resta in scena con il pugnale in mano. Come invasata, simula le arti marziali di un combattimento immaginario. Dopo qualche istante esce anche lei, dirigendosi verso il fondo.

SOLDATO: Cu sti palori di guerra,
cu sti cunti di battagghia,
Otello 'a fici càdiri
pi sempri a li so' peri.
Cadìu Desdemona. Cadìu
sutta st'artigghiaria
di palori di morti.
Comu na vota dissi idda stissa:
"Arriniscisti a tràsiri
dintr'a la me' furtizza
e ora sì u patruni…".
Praticannu finu 'nfunnu l'ubbidienza
ca nun senti eccizioni,
addivintò Desdemona
chiddu c'Otello
si vosi 'nvintari
cu sta criatura.
E sempri la chiamò: "Guerriera Bedda".
'U 'ntisi chi me' aricchi,
'un cuntu fissarie: guerriera bedda.

SOLDATO: Con queste parole di guerra,
con queste parole di battaglia,
Otello la fece cadere
per sempre ai suoi piedi.
Cadde Desdemona. Cadde
sotto questa artiglieria
di parole di morte.
Come una volta disse lei stessa:
"Riuscisti a penetrare
dentro alla mia fortezza
e ora sei il padrone…".
Praticando fino in fondo l'obbedienza
che non sente eccezioni,
diventò Desdemona
quello che Otello
si volle inventare
con sta creatura.
E sempre la chiamò: "Bella Guerriera".
Lo sentii con le mie orecchie,
non racconto fesserie: bella guerriera.

Farewell, my love.
War business is calling me.
I send thee gifts.
A dagger
— when I'm back I'll teach thee to inflict
deadly blows and strikes —
and an embroidered handkerchief
— when I come back I want thee to dry
these tears that don't want to cease.

Exit Othello. Desdemona remains on stage, dagger in hand. As if possessed, she mimics martial arts in an imaginary duel. After a while she exits too, backstage.

SOLDIER: With these war words,
    with these battle words,
    Othello made her fall
    for ever at his feet.
    Desdemona fell. She fell
    under this artillery
    fire of words of death.
    As she herself said once:
    "Thou succeeded in penetrating
    my fortress
    and now thou are the master…"
    Practicing complete obedience
    With no exceptions,
    Desdemona became
    what Othello
    wanted to make
    of this woman.
    And he always called her: "my fair warrior."
    I heard it with my own ears,
    I'm not talking nonsense: my fair warrior.

La parti cchiù gintili
l'avìa purtata 'n doti
cu la so' ducazioni signurili
— pi cui sapìa cantari
comu 'n cardiddu,
sapìa sunari
comu l'ancilu d'u paraddisu,
e a manu avìa sapienti ntù ricamu —
ma iddu ci misi supra na curazza
pi strinciri dda parti fimminili
ca 'un si pò cuntrullari
cu palori, pricetti e cumanni,
dda parti scanusciuta e mistiriusa
ca l'omu 'un si pò pàciri
d'aviri a suppurtari.
Pi chistu iddu nni fici
na Diana cacciatrici
ca Veneri disprezza e onura Marti,
P'idda, oramai surdatu,
amuri o guerra o morti
eranu a stissa cosa:
vita racchiusa
ntù ferru 'i l'armatura,
contrastu, sacrificiu, rivirenza,
p'u martiriu putenti attrazioni.
Desdemona guerriera,
ti cunnannò a la morti l'ubbedienza.
A lu principiu
è azzurra e soavi
sta sorta 'i divozioni.
Ma poi addiventa
lugubri, murtali
e di culuri nivuru
comu na notti senza luna
quannu la tirannia d'amuri

La parte più gentile
l'aveva portata in dote
con la sua educazione signorile
— per cui sapeva cantare
come un cardellino,
sapeva suonare
come l'angelo del paradiso,
e aveva mano sapiente nel ricamo —
ma egli le mise addosso una corazza
per stringere le parti femminili
che non si possono controllare
con parole, precetti e comandi,
la parte sconosciuta e misteriosa
che l'uomo non si può dar pace
di dover sopportare.
Per questo egli ne fece
una Diana cacciatrice
che Venere disprezza e onora Marte,
Per lei, ormai soldato,
amore o guerra o morte
erano la stessa cosa:
vita rinchiusa
nel ferro dell'armatura,
contrasto, sacrificio, riverenza,
per il martirio potenti attrazioni.
Desdemona guerriera,
ti condannò a morte l'obbedienza.
Al principio
è azzurra e soave
questa sorta di devozione.
Ma poi diventa
lugubre, mortale
e di colore nero
come una notte senza luna
quando la tirannia dell'amore

The kindest side
she did bring as dowry
with her ladylike education
— which made her sing
like a cardinal,
play like
an angel of paradise,
embroider expertly —
but he made her wear an armour
to constrict the feminine parts
that can't be controlled
with words, instructions, and commands,
the mysterious and unknown side
that man can't come to terms
with handling.
That's why he turned her into
a hunting Diana
who despises Venus and honours Mars,
for her, now soldier,
love or war or death
were the same thing:
life enclosed
in the armour's iron,
adversity, sacrifice, reverence,
powerful attractions for martyrdom.
Warrior Desdemona,
obedience condemned you to death.
In the beginning
this sort of devotion
is serene and sweet.
But then it becomes
lugubrious, deadly
and black
like a night without the moon
when the tyranny of love

passannu lu so' scettru all'odiu e a lu rancuri pigghia la strata d'a pirsicuzioni.	passando il suo scettro all'odio e al rancore piglia la strada della persecuzione.

Entra Iago.

IAGO: Ma pi ddaveru,
 sti du' critini si jieru a nnamurari…
 e daccussì si penzanu filici…
 In ogni casu, ntà lu munnu
 cchiù forti di l'amuri è l'odiu,
 ca strinci lu respiru dintr'u pettu.
 Dici Desdemona ca 'u vosi pi maritu
 Picchì iddu ci cuntò li so' avvinturi
 e li so' viaggi chini di duluri.
 Otello 'nveci dici
 Chi sa vosi pigghiari pi mugghieri
 Picchì sta fimmina si cummuvìu di so'
  turmenti…
 'Nsomma: sulu pi chistu si juncero:
 pi na sula fissaria,
 pi na cosa 'nvintata, pi na cosa
  'mmaginata,
 dilliriu di l'amanti…
 Si 'nveci iu vulissi ora cuntari
 tutt'i ragiuni d'u risintimentu
 contra ddu barbaru sarbaggiu
 du nostru ginirali
 ci vulissiru jorna, simani,
 'nteri cicli di stagiuni.
 L'amuri? L'amuri esisti sulu
 ntà testa scunchiuruta
 d'a razza stravacanti
 di li pirduti amanti,
 sulu dda intra, dintr'a lu pinzeru.
 L'amuri è l'illusioni
 d'aviri nu vucconi d'infinitu
 pagatu cu du' liri.

IAGO: Ma per davvero
 sti due cretini si innamorarono…
 e così si pensano felici…
 In ogni caso, nel mondo
 più forte dell'amore è l'odio,
 che stringe il respiro nel petto.
 Dice Desdemona che lo volle per
  marito
 perché le raccontò le sue avventure
 e i suoi viaggi pieni di dolore.
 Otello invece dice
 che se la volle prendere per moglie
 perché sta donna si commosse dei
  suoi tormenti…
 Insomma: solo per questo si
  congiunsero:
 per una sola fesseria,
 per una cosa inventata, per una cosa
  immaginata,
 delirio di amanti…
 Se invece io volessi ora raccontare
 tutte le ragioni del risentimento
 contro quel barbaro selvaggio
 del nostro generale
 ci vorrebbero giorni, settimane,
 interi cicli di stagioni.
 L'amore? L'amore esiste solo
 nella testa sconclusionata
 della razza stravagante
 dei perduti amanti,
 solo là entra, nel pensiero.
 L'amore è l'illusione
 d'avere un boccone d'infinito
 pagato con due lire.

passing its sceptre
to hate and resentment
takes the road of persecution.

Enter Iago.

IAGO: Did these two cretins
fall in love for real…
and so they think themselves happy…
In any case, in the world,
stronger than love is hatred,
that constricts breathing in one's chest.
Desdemona says that she wanted him as a husband
because he told her of his adventures
and his travels filled with pain.
Othello instead says
that he wanted her as a bride
because she was moved by his sorrows…
In short: for this alone they mated:
for this hogwash,
for a made-up thing, imagined,
lovers' delirium…
If, instead, I wanted to tell
all the reasons for the resentment
against that savage barbarian,
our general,
it would take days, weeks,
whole cycles of seasons.
Love? Love exists only
in the erratic head
of the extravagant race
of lost lovers,
only there it enters, in thoughts.
Love is the illusion
of having a mouthful of infinity
for a few pennies.

È l'infinitu a purtata di manu
p'i cristiani ca sunnu mort'i fami.
L'odiu 'nveci è 'nfinitu pi ddaveru,
mai si sudisfa e mancu si sazìa.

È l'infinito a portata di mano
per gli uomini morti di fame.
L'odio invece è l'infinito per davvero,
mai si soddisfa e manco si sazia.

Otello raggiunge Iago che si finge assorto in un pensiero dopo aver visto un'ombra allontanarsi.

IAGO: Sta cosa a mmia 'un mi piaci…

IAGO: Questa cosa non mi piace…

OTELLO: Chi stai dicennu, Iago?

OTELLO: Che stai dicendo, Iago?

IAGO: Nenti… eccillenza… chi dicu…?
'Unn'u sacciu.

IAGO: Niente… Eccellenza… che
dico…? Non lo so.

OTELLO: Cu era ddu cristianu?
Mi parsi c'era Cassio
ca stava salutannu a me' mugghieri…

OTELLO: Chi era quell'uomo?
M'è sembrato che fosse Cassio
che stava salutando mia moglie…

IAGO: Cassio? Ma no, 'un pò essiri, signuri.
'Un pozzu cridiri ca s'arrassava
stricannu muru muru comu 'n latru
pigghiatu a lu 'mpruvisu d'u patruni
ca s'arricogghi anzi tempu a la casa.

IAGO: Cassio? Ma no, non può essere,
signore.
Non posso credere che si sarebbe
allontanato
strisciando rasente al muro come un
ladro
scoperto all'improvviso dal padrone
che ritorna prima del tempo a casa.

OTELLO: Iddu mi parsi a mmia.

OTELLO: A me pareva lui.

Entra Desdemona.

It is infinity within reach
for deadbeats.
Hatred, instead, is infinity for real,
it is never satisfied nor satiated.

Othello joins Iago who pretends to be deep in thought after seeing a shadow getting away.

IAGO: Ha? I like not that…

OTHELLO: What dost thou say, Iago?

IAGO: Nothing, my lord; or if — I know not what.

OTHELLO: Who was that man?
    Was not that Cassio
    Parted from my wife?

IAGO: Cassio, my lord? No, sure, it cannot be, sir.
    I cannot think it that he would steal away
    crawling by the wall like a thief
    suddenly discovered by the master
    returning home early.

OTHELLO: I do believe 'twas he.

Enter Desdemona.

DESDEMONA: E allora, mio signore? Stavo adesso
parlando con un uomo che ora soffre
e che vi supplica con tutto il cuore
di tornare a guardarlo con favore.

OTELLO: Cu'? Di cu' sta parrannu?

DESDEMONA: Di Cassio, il nostro buon luogotenente.
Se davvero possiedo qualche grazia
o potere capace d'influenzare
la vostra volontà e il vostro pensiero
allora sarà facile ottenere
un'immediata riconciliazione.
Vi prego, richiamatelo con voi.

OTELLO: Sinn'jiu ora ora?

DESDEMONA: Appena adesso, mio signore
è andato
in qualche luogo solo e disperato
a macerarsi nel suo turbamento.
Però non ha portato il suo dolore
tutto con sé, e io lo soffro in parte.
Per questo: richiamatelo con voi.

OTELLO: Ora 'unn'è cosa. N'autra vota, amuri.

DESDEMONA: Sarà tra poco, dolce amore mio?

OTELLO: Prestu prestu. Pi ttia, amuri duci.

DESDEMONA: Basta che stabiliate presto un tempo
e che non vada in là più di tre giorni.
Io vi assicuro che Cassio è pentito.
E inoltre la sua colpa, lo sappiamo,
— anche se in guerra è obbligato all'esempio
chi viene annoverato tra i migliori —
non è assolutamente da punire
se non con un rimprovero privato.
Allora, amore, quando può venire?
Ditemi, Otello. Davvero mi chiedo
dal fondo del mio cuore e ne sorrido

DESDEMONA: E allora, mio signore?
Stavo adesso
parlando con un uomo che ora soffre
e che vi supplica con tutto il cuore
di tornare a guardarlo con favore.

OTELLO: Chi? Di chi stai parlando?

DESDEMONA: Di Cassio, il nostro
buon luogotenente.
Se davvero possiedo qualche grazia
o potere capace d'influenzare
la vostra volontà e il vostro pensiero
allora sarà facile ottenere
un'immediata riconciliazione.
Vi prego, richiamatelo con voi.

OTELLO: Se n'è andato or ora?

DESDEMONA: Appena adesso, mio
signore è andato
in qualche luogo solo e disperato
a macerarsi nel suo turbamento.
Però non ha portato il suo dolore
tutto con sé, e anch'io soffro in parte.
Per questo: richiamatelo con voi.

OTELLO: Ora non è cosa. Un'altra volta, amore.

DESDEMONA: Sarà tra poco, dolce amore mio?

OTELLO: Presto presto. Per te, amore dolce.

DESDEMONA: Basta che stabiliate
presto un tempo
e che non vada in là più di tre giorni.
Io vi assicuro che Cassio è pentito.
E inoltre la sua colpa, lo sappiamo,
— anche se in guerra è obbligato all'esempio
chi viene annoverato tra i migliori —
non è assolutamente da punire
se non con un rimprovero privato.
Allora, amore, quando può venire?
Ditemi, Otello. Davvero mi chiedo
dal fondo del mio cuore e ne sorrido

DESDEMONA: How now, my lord? I have been
    talking with a suitor here who suffers
    and who begs you with all his heart
    to be back in your favour.

OTHELLO: Who is't you mean?

DESDEMONA: Why, our good lieutenant, Cassio.
    If I really have any grace
    or power to move
    your will and your thought
    then it will be easy to get
    a present reconciliation.
    I prithee call him back.

OTHELLO: Went he hence now?

DESDEMONA: Right now, my lord, he went
    somewhere alone and desperate
    to wallow in his upset.
    But he did not take all his grief
    with him, and I suffer with him.
    For this: call him back.

OTHELLO: Not now. Some other time, love.

DESDEMONA: Shall't be shortly, sweet my love?

OTHELLO: The sooner, sweet, for you.

DESDEMONA: I prithee name the time,
    but let it not exceed three days.
    I'faith Cassio's penitent.
    And yet his trespass, in our common reason
    — save that they say the wars must make example
    out of her best —
    is not at all a fault
    t'incur a private check.
    When shall he come, love?
    Tell me, Othello. I wonder in my soul
    and I smile

cosa mi chiedereste a vostra volta
che io vi negherei con piglio fermo
o improvvisando, come voi ora fate,
fragili scuse e distratti silenzi.
Ma come? Non è Michele Cassio
che sempre vi seguiva
nei primi tempi del corteggiamento
e che svariate volte
quando litigavamo vi difese?
Proprio per lui davvero mi obbligate
a tutto questo eccesso d'insistenza?
Ma sapete che ancora vi direi?

OTELLO: Famm'u fauri, bona, statti
cueta…
Dicci a Cassio ca si pò prisintari
nni mia quann'iddu voli, 'un pozzu certu
niàriti quarchi cosa, sangu miu.

DESDEMONA: Guardate: questo qui non
è un favore.
Se avessi veramente una richiesta
per mettere alla prova il vostro amore
allora sì dovrete stare in guardia
perché sarebbe certo un desiderio
molto difficile da accontentare.

OTELLO: 'Un c'è cosa ch'a ttia pozzu niàri.
Però ora tu m'ha' ffari un gran piaciri:
lassami stari ccà, solu cu mmia.

DESDEMONA: Nessun problema, addio
mio dolce amore.

OTELLO: Addìu cusuzza bedda. Ora
t'agghiunciu.

DESDEMONA: Sia quel che v'imporrà la
fantasia.
Qualunque cosa sia, per me è comando.

cosa mi chiedereste a vostra volta
che io vi negherei con piglio fermo
o improvvisando, come voi ora fate,
fragili scuse e distratti silenzi.
Ma come? Non è Michele Cassio
che sempre vi seguiva
nei primi tempi del corteggiamento
e che svariate volte
quando litigavamo vi difese?
Proprio per lui davvero mi obbligate
a tutto questo eccesso d'insistenza?
Ma sapete che ancora vi direi?

OTELLO: Fammi il favore, buona, stai
zitta…
Dì a Cassio che si può presentare
da me quando vuole, non posso certo
negarti qualcosa, sangue mio.

DESDEMONA: Guardate: questo qui
non è un favore.
Se avessi veramente una richiesta
per mettere alla prova il vostro amore
allora sì dovreste stare in guardia
perché sarebbe certo un desiderio
molto difficile da accontentare.

OTELLO: Non c'è cosa che ti posso
negare.
Però ora mi devi fare un gran piacere:
lasciami stare qua, solo con me stesso.

DESDEMONA: Nessun problema, addio
mio dolce amore.

OTELLO: Addio cosa bella. Ora ti
raggiungo.

DESDEMONA: Sia quel che v'imporrà la
fantasia.
Qualunque cosa sia, per me è
comando.

Esce Desdemona.

what would you ask me
that I should deny forcefully
or improvise, as you do now,
frail excuses and distracted silences.
What? Isn't it Michael Cassio
that came a-wooing with you
and so many a time
when we spoke dispraisingly, hath ta'en your part?
For him you force me
to this excessive insistence?
Do you know what else I could tell you?

OTHELLO: Prithee no more, keep silent...
Let Cassio come when he will —
I will deny thee nothing, my love.

DESDEMONA: Why, this is not a boon.
If I truly had a request
to test your love
then you should be alarmed
because it would certainly be a desire
difficult to fulfil.

OTHELLO: I will deny thee nothing.
Whereon, I do beseech thee, grant me this:
to leave me but a little to myself.

DESDEMONA: Shall I deny you? No! farewell, my sweet love.

OTHELLO: Farewell, beautiful thing. I'll come to thee straight.

DESDEMONA: Be as your fancies teach you.
Whate'er you be, I am obedient.

Exit Desdemona.

OTELLO: Mostru di maravigghia!
Puru si a perdiziuni
l'anima mia si pigghia
'u stissu sempri t'amu.
E quannu 'un t'amu cchiù
'un pozzu chi turnari
dda cosa cunfusa
d'abissu e turmentu
ddu Caos chinu d'angoscia
ca semu quannu mori lu disìu.

IAGO: Grannissimu signuri…

OTELLO: Dimmi Iago.

IAGO: Ntù tempu di la corti a la signura,
Cassio lu canuscìa lu vostru amuri?

OTELLO: Iddu tuttu sapìa dall'accuminciu.
D'unni ti veni e spercia sta dumanna?

IAGO: Nenti… Nenti… Cosa senza
'mpurtanza.
Cosa senza 'mpurtanza, bona sulu
p'arrisittari anticchia li pinzeri.

OTELLO: Tu sta' pinzannu quarchi cosa
amara.
Si m'ami, Iago, accumincia a parrari.

IAGO: Vossìa lu sapi bonu quantu l'amu.

OTELLO: E propriu picchì sacciu lu to'
beni,
e comu pisi sempri li palori
prima ca u ciatu acchiana e si fa vuci
ca tuttu lu to' 'mpacciu mi fa scantu.

IAGO: Riguardu a Cassio, lu pozzu giurari:
sugnu pirsuasu ca è cristianu onestu.

OTELLO: Puru iu sugnu pirsuasu.

IAGO: Avissi sempri l'omu
essiri nzoccu pari.
E chiddu ca 'unn'è nenti
A nenti assumigghiari.

OTELLO: Mostro di meraviglia!
Anche se la perdizione
si prende l'anima mia
ti amo sempre lo stesso.
E quando non t'amassi più
non potrei far altro se non ritornare
ad essere quella cosa confusa
d'abisso e di tormento
di Caos pieno d'angoscia
che siamo quando il desiderio è
morto.

IAGO: Grandissimo signore…

OTELLO: Dimmi Iago.

IAGO: Al tempo del corteggiamento della
signora,
Cassio era al corrente del vostro amore?

OTELLO: Sapeva tutto fin dall'inizio.
Da dove ti viene e sorge questa
domanda?

IAGO: Niente… Niente… Una cosa
senza importanza.
Una cosa senza importanza, buona solo
per rassettare un po' i pensieri.

OTELLO: Tu stai pensando qualche cosa
amara.
Se mi vuoi bene, Iago, comincia a
parlare.

IAGO: Voi sapete quanto mi state a cuore.

OTELLO: E proprio perché conosco il
tuo sentimento,
e come pesi sempre le parole
prima che il fiato salga e divenga voce
il tuo impaccio mi spaventa.

IAGO: Riguardo a Cassio, lo posso giurare:
sono convinto che sia un uomo onesto.

OTELLO: Anch'io ne sono convinto.

IAGO: Potesse sempre l'uomo
essere ciò che sembra.
E chi non è niente
a niente assomigliare.

OTHELLO: Excellent wretch!
　　Perdition catch my soul
　　but I do love thee.
　　And when I love thee not
　　I couldn't do anything but go back
　　to being that confused bundle
　　of abyss and torment
　　of Chaos full of angst
　　that we are when desire dies.

IAGO: My noble lord…

OTHELLO: What dost thou say, Iago?

IAGO: Did Michael Cassio, when you wooed my lady,
　　know of your love?

OTHELLO: He did, from first to last.
　　Why dost thou ask?

IAGO: No reason… Something of no consequence.
　　But for a satisfaction of my thought,
　　no further harm.

OTHELLO: Thou art thinking of a bitter thing.
　　If you love me, Iago, talk.

IAGO: My lord, you know I love you.

OTHELLO: For I know thou'rt full of love,　　　　　　　[omits **'and honesty'**]
　　and weigh'st thy words
　　before thou giv'st them breath
　　therefore these stops of thyne fright me the more.

IAGO: For Michael Cassio, I dare be sworn,
　　I think, that he is honest.

OTHELLO: I think so too.

IAGO: Men should be
　　what they seem —
　　or those that be not,
　　would they might seem none.

OTELLO: Sempri s'avissi a essiri
dda cosa chi unu pari.

IAGO: Si chistu è veru allura Cassio è onestu.

OTELLO: Sentu ca ntà sta frasi
ci manca quarchi cosa
di chiddu ca ntà testa ti firrìa.
Allura ti scungiuru:
parra cu mmia comu parri cu ttia.
E si u pinzeru è orribili,
'un ti scantari Iago,
orribili prisintami a palora.

IAGO: M'aviti a pirdunari, ginirali.
Certu lu vostru gradu mi custringi
cu franca divozioni all'ossirvanza
d'ogni cumannu ca vossìa disponi.
La me' pirsona 'nveci 'unn'è tinuta
a ffari cosa ca mancu li schiavi
sunnu 'ntimati da li so' signuri:
liberu è lu pinzeru
all'autri scanusciutu
e nuddu ci pò tràsiri
ca so' suvirchiaria.
Lu me' pinzeru 'un canusci patruni.

OTELLO: Tu contr'a mmia cungiuri
si penzi chi quarcunu
darrer'i spaddi sta facennu offisa
a mmia ca 'un sacciu nenti
e tu 'nveci sapennu nun m'avvisi.

IAGO: Voscenza, forsi su' pinzeri vili
e fausi e 'nfami. Ma chi ci haiu a ffari?
C'è casa unni trasennu
l'omu 'un si porta appressu lu so' fangu?
E avemu forsi pettu accussì puru

OTELLO: Sempre si deve essere
ciò che si pare.

IAGO: Se questo è vero allora Cassio è
onesto.

OTELLO: Sento che a questa frase
manca qualcosa
di ciò che ti frulla per la testa.
Allora ti scongiuro:
parla a me come parli a te stesso.
E se il pensiero è orribile,
non ti spaventare Iago,
orribile presenta la parola.

IAGO: Mi dovete perdonare, generale.
Certamente il vostro grado mi
costringe
con franca devozione all'obbedienza
ad ogni comando che voi date.
La mia persona invece non è tenuta
a far ciò che nemmeno agli schiavi
è ordinato dai loro padroni:
il pensiero è libero
sconosciuto agli altri
e nessuno ci può entrare
con la propria soverchieria.
Il mio pensiero non conosce padroni.

OTELLO: Tu congiuri contro di me
se pensi che qualcuno
alle mie spalle stia recando offesa
a me che non ne so niente
e tu invece, sapendolo, non mi avvisi.

IAGO: Signore, forse son pensieri vili
e falsi e infami. Ma che ci devo fare?
C'è una casa dove entrando
l'uomo non si porti dietro il suo
fango?
E abbiamo forse un petto così puro

OTELLO: Certain, men should be
    what they seem.

IAGO: Why, then I think Cassio's an honest man.

OTHELLO: I feel that this phrase   **Nay, yet there's more**
    is missing some   **in this**
    of what is mulling in your head.
    I prithee:
    speak to me as to thy thinkings.
    And if they are horrible   **As thou dost ruminate,**
    don't hesitate, Iago,   **and give thy worst of thoughts**
    and give me the horrible word.   **the worst of words.**

IAGO: Good my general, pardon me: **lord**
    I am bound by your rank
    faithfully to every act of duty
    to every command you impart.
    Personally, I am not bound
    to do what not even slaves   **to that all slaves are free to:**
    are ordered by their masters:
    thoughts are free
    unknown to others
    and no one can enter them
    by command.
    My thoughts know no master.

OTHELLO: Thou dost conspire against me   **thy friend, Iago,**
    if thou but think'st that someone   **him wronged**
    behind my back offends me
    without me knowing
    while thou, knowing, dost not warn me.   **and mak'st his ear a stranger to thy thoughts**

IAGO: My lord, perchance my thoughts are vile,
    and false and vicious. What of it?
    As where's that palace whereinto
    one's mud sometimes intrude not?   **foul things**
    Who has that breast so pure

ca l'ummira 'un ci càpi o lu suspettu?
L'ammettu, sugnu un tipu suspittusu.
È l'afflizioni di la me' natura
jiri a circari u mali e dunnegghiè
truvari lu piccatu unni s'alloca
chiddu chi all'autri pari onestu e puru.
Eppuru, c'haiu a ffari? Chistu sugnu.
Sugnu accussì e 'un mi pozzu canciari.
Macari viu cosi ca 'un ci su'...
Ci 'u dicu pi ddaveru, 'un s'appricassi
a tutti sti 'nvinzioni e fantasie
ca da me' testa nesciunu cunfuse.
'Un s'appricassi, si nni stassi cuetu.
Chiddu chi penzu lassamulu stari.
È bonu pi voscenza e quantu a mmia
megghiu stàrisi mutu e nun ciatari.

OTELLO: Chi senti diri? 'Un ti capisciu
    bonu.

IAGO: A cosa cchiù 'mpurtanti,
    masculu o fimmina 'un c'è diffirenza,
    è aviri cura di lu propriu nomu.
    Si quarcunu mi futti a vurza china
    'un m'ha' pigghiatu nenti di 'mpurtanti.
    Prima d'essiri mia era di nautru,
    ora addiventa so', cu si nni futti:
    i cosi sunnu fatti pi passari
    di manu 'n manu a tempu di ballettu...
    Ma si mi futti u nomu
    allora m'arruini:
    tu 'unn'addiventi ricco
    e a mmia 'un m'arresta nenti.

OTELLO: Vogghiu canusciri li to' pinzeri ...

IAGO: Fin'a quannu lu cori
    m'addimora ntù pettu
    sugnu patruni di li me' pinzeri
    e 'i tegnu sutta chiavi ntù me' scrignu.

---

che l'ombra non ci entri o il sospetto?
L'ammetto, sono un tipo sospettoso.
È l'afflizione della mia natura
andare a cercare il male e ovunque sia
trovare il peccato dove risiede
ciò che agli altri pare onesto e puro.
Eppure, che devo fare? È quello che sono.
Sono così e non mi posso cambiare.
Magari vedo cose che non ci sono...
Ve lo dico sul serio, non date peso
a tutte ste invenzioni e fantasie
che dalla mia testa nascono confuse.
Non date peso, state tranquillo.
Quello che penso lasciamolo stare.
È meglio per voi e quanto a me
meglio stare zitto e non fiatare.

OTELLO: Che sento dire? Non ti capisco
    bene.

IAGO: La cosa più importante,
    uomo o donna non c'è differenza,
    è avere cura del proprio nome.
    Se qualcuno mi ruba la borsa piena
    non mi ha preso nulla di importante.
    Prima di essere mia era di un altro,
    ora diventa sua; chi se ne frega:
    le cose sono fatte per passare
    di mano in mano a tempo di balletto...
    Ma se mi rubi il nome...
    allora mi rovini:
    tu non diventi ricco
    e a me non resta niente.

OTELLO: Voglio conoscerli i tuoi pensieri...

IAGO: Finché il cuore
    mi batte in petto
    sono padrone dei miei pensieri
    e li tengo sotto chiave nel mio scrigno.

where no uncleanly apprehensions enter?
As I confess I am the suspicious kind:
it is my nature's plague
to spy into abuses,
shape faults that others find honest and pure.
What can I do? This is who I am.
I am thus and I can't change.
Perchance I see what's not there…
Don't build yourself a trouble
out of this scattering and unsure
observance of my mind.
Take no notice, rest assured.
Let's leave my thoughts be.
'Tis for your good, as for me
better to keep silent and utter no breath.

OTHELLO: What dost thou mean?

IAGO: The most important thing,   **Good name in man — and woman — dear my lord,**
in man or woman, there's no difference,
is to safeguard one's name.   **is the immediate jewel of their souls**
Who steals my purse, steals trash:
'tis something nothing.
Before being mine it was someone else's,
now 'tis his; no harm:
things are made to move
from hand to hand as in a ballet…
but he that filches from me my good name…
ruins me:
he robs me of that which not enriches him,
and makes me poor indeed.

OTHELLO: By heaven, I'll know thy thoughts!

IAGO: Whilst my heart   **you cannot, if my heart were**
beats in my chest   **in your hand;**
I am master of my thoughts   **nor shall not,**
and I keep them locked in my box.   **whilst 'tis in my custody.**

OTELLO: Matri Santissima…!

IAGO: Signuri, stati arrassu
　　da chista Gilusia,
　　mostru cull'occhi virdi
　　ca s'addiverti pigghiannu pi fissa
　　a carni ca si mancia a muzzicuni.
　　Contentu è lu curnutu
　　chi sapi u so' distinu
　　e certu 'un soffri cchiù
　　picchì ora 'un'ama cchiù cu' l'ha'
　　　　'ngannatu.
　　Ma quant'abbìli fa
　　e agghiutti dispiaciri,
　　vuccuni di vilenu,
　　e u tempu 'un passa mai chinu d'affannu,
　　cu' affunna dintr'u mari di l'amuri
　　senza turnari a galla
　　e ntù scuru ddà sutta 'un vidi nenti,
　　si squagghia pi l'affettu ma 'un si fida,
　　dubbita eppuru è chinu di passiuni.

OTELLO: Grannissimu turmentu!

IAGO: Du celu, Signuruzzu, v'affacciati
　　e sempri nni scanzati
　　di chista gilusia
　　c'affliggi e fa 'mpossibili la vita.

OTELLO: Picchì? Rispunni Iago!
　　Picchì nn'havi a tuccari st'afflizioni?
　　Sta cosa 'unn'è pi mmia, t'u dicu chiaru.
　　A ttia forsi ti pari
　　Ca mi pozzu accullari
　　di vìviri accussì ntà stu turmentu?
　　Ma iu 'un ci penzu propriu…
　　Campàri cull'angoscia
　　da fimmina 'nfideli,
　　assicutannu a luna ca si cancia
　　pizzuddu pi pizzuddu ogni mumentu

OTELLO: Madre Santissima…!

IAGO: Signore, state lontano
　　da questa Gelosia,
　　mostro con gli occhi verdi
　　che si diverte a prendere per fessa
　　la carne di cui si nutre a morsi.
　　Contento è il cornuto
　　che conosce il suo destino
　　e certo non soffre più
　　perché ora non ama più chi l'ha
　　　　ingannato.
　　Ma quanta bile produce
　　e inghiotte dispiaceri,
　　bocconi di veleno,
　　e il tempo non passa mai pieno
　　　　d'affanno,
　　chi affonda nel mare dell'amore
　　senza tornare a galla
　　e nello scuro da sotto non vede niente,
　　si strugge per l'affetto ma non si fida,
　　dubita eppure è pieno di passione.

OTELLO: Grandissimo tormento!

IAGO: Dal cielo, Signore, affacciatevi
　　e sempre evitateci
　　questa gelosia
　　che affligge e rende impossibile la vita.

OTELLO: Perché? Rispondi Iago!
　　Perché non devo toccare questa
　　　　afflizione?
　　Questa cosa non fa per me,
　　te lo dico chiaramente.
　　A te forse pare
　　che mi possa accollare
　　di vivere così con sto tormento?
　　Ma io non ci penso proprio…
　　Vivere con l'angoscia
　　di una donna infedele,
　　rincorrendo la luna che cambia
　　pezzo a pezzo ogni momento

OTHELLO: Holy Mother of God…!   'Swounds!

IAGO: O beware, my lord
    of jealousy,
    it is the green-eyed monster
    which doth mock
    the meat it feeds on.
    That cuckold lives in bliss
    who, certain of his fate,
    loves not his wronger.
    But how much bile produces
    and swallows sorrows,
    morsels of poison,
    and time never passing full of angst,
    he who plunges in the sea of love
    without resurfacing
    and in its darkness from below sees nothing,
    is torn by affection but trusts not,
    doubts but is full of passion.

OTHELLO: Immense torment!   O misery!

IAGO: Lean over, Lord, from the heavens
    and always defend us
    from this jealousy
    that afflicts and makes life impossible.

OTHELLO: Why? Answer Iago!
    Why shouldn't I touch this affliction?
    This is not for me, I tell thee plainly.
    Think'st thou
    I would endure   I'd make a life of jealousy
    living with this torment?
    I think not…
    To live with the pangs
    of an unfaithful woman,
    following the changes of the moon
    piece by piece, in every moment

e iu darreri a idda
cu cori fattu servu
di chistu sintimentu livantinu?
T'u dicu arreri ca 'un ci penzu propriu.
Puru picchì accumincia a dubbitari
Sulu cu' ci havi u cori già dicisu.
E tu mi pò pigghiari pi capruni
si dugnu cuntu a vuci 'ncunsistenti
comu mi pari a to' ca mi fa stranu
vistu ca veni d'un cristianu onestu.
Eppuru pari vuci di curtigghiu,
vuci 'nvintata, assurda, stravacanti,
ca 'un vali nenti senza accetamentu.
L'occhi l'avìa Desdemona pi diri:
"Mi piaci propriu chistu pi maritu".
Prima d'u dubbiu, Iago,
ci voli a pirsuasioni.
Si mi pirsuadu poi m'ha' ddari i provi.
E doppu c'u pruvasti 'un c'è cchiù nenti:
si squagghianu ntall'aria
comu la nivi ô suli
amuri e gilusia
ca 'un ponnu stari 'nsemmula
dintra u me' stissu cori.

IAGO: Ginirali,
    pigghiàti stu discursu d'accussì
    pi comu a stu minutu v'apprisentu:
    ancora 'un parru cu certa sintenza,
    l'unica prova è lu me' 'ntindimentu.
    Taliàti bonu la vostra mugghieri,
    principalmenti quannu sta cu Cassio,
    cu l'occhi arrassu d'ogni pregiudiziu,
    fussi fiducia opùru gilusia.
    Iu sì ca sacciu bonu a custumanza
    di lu paisi di la vostra sposa

e io dietro a lei
col cuore reso schiavo
da questo sentimento imbroglione?
Ti ripeto che non ci penso proprio.
Anche perché comincia a dubitare
Solo chi ha il cuore già deciso.
E tu mi puoi prendere per caprone
se do retta a dicerie inconsistenti
come mi sembra la tua e mi sembra
    strano
visto che viene da un uomo onesto.
Eppure pare diceria di cortile,
diceria inventata, assurda, stravagante,
che non vale niente senza verificarla.
Gli occhi li aveva Desdemona per dire:
"Mi piace proprio questo per marito".
Prima del dubbio, Iago,
ci vuole la persuasione.
Se io mi persuado poi mi devi dare le
    prove.
E dopo che l'hai provato non c'è più
    niente:
si squagliano nell'aria
come la neve al sole
amore e gelosia
che non possono stare insieme
nello stesso cuore.

IAGO: Generale,
    prendete sto discorso così
    come ora ve lo presento:
    non parlo ancora con certezza,
    l'unica prova è quello che capisco.
    Guardate bene vostra moglie,
    principalmente quando sta con Cassio,
    con gli occhi privi di ogni pregiudizio,
    che sia fiducia o gelosia.
    Io sì che conosco bene gli usi
    del paese della vostra sposa

I after her,
my heart a slave
to this treacherous feeling?
I tell thee, not for me.
Also because to be once in doubt
is once to be resolved.
Exchange me for a goat
if I pay heed to such exsufflicate and blown surmises
matching thy inference, which seem odd
coming from an honest man.
Yet, it sounds like courtyard gossip,
invented, absurd, extravagant rumour,
worthless without proof.
Desdemona had eyes to say: for she had eyes and chose me
"I like this one for a husband."
Before doubt, Iago,   No, Iago, I'll see before I doubt.
persuasion is needed.
When I doubt, prove;
and, on the proof, there is no more but this:
love and jealousy,
which cannot live together
in the same heart,
dissolve in the air
like snow in the sun.

IAGO: General,
take this speech   receive it from me
as I am offering it now:
I speak not yet of proof,
the only proof is the one I understand.
Look to your wife,   observe her well with Cassio
mostly when she's with Cassio,
with eyes devoid of prejudice   wear your eyes thus,
not jealous nor secure.
I know well the customs   I know our country
of your bride's country   disposition well

e certu pozzu diri
ca i fimmini si grapinu lu cori
cu Signuruzzu cunfissannu 'nchiesa
tutta la pirvirsioni buttanesca
ca certu 'un ci va cuntanu ai mariti.
P'a fimmina sfrinata
'unn'è cosa virtuosa
circari di nun fari purcarìe
ma stari muta e 'un diri
a nuddu a so' lussuria.

OTELLO: Ma tu accussì mi dici?

IAGO: Pigghiò pi fissa u patri
quannu c'addivintò vostra mugghieri
e quannu si mustrava timurusa
du vostru aspettu d'omu colossali
dintra la carni ci crescìa la frevi
d'esseri di voscenza pussiduta.

OTELLO: È veru. Ci hai ragiuni.

IAGO: D'una ch'accussì nica e picciridda
già si mustrò 'ccillenti commedianti
nzoccu si pò aspittari ora vossìa?
No, mi dispiaci, 'u dicu pi ddaveru
ca di mia stissu iu mi disapprovu,
a pugni mi pigghiassi u me' tistuni…
Aviti a pirdunari sta 'nsullenza
ma soprattuttu ca vi vogghiu beni:
l'amuri ca vi portu
l'aviti a pirdunari.

OTELLO: A ttia Iago pi sempri
mi sentu 'ncatinatu.

IAGO: Mi pari ca stu fattu v'ha sturdutu.

OTELLO: Mancu na 'nticchia. 'Unn'ha
successu nenti.

IAGO: Parìti veru tuttu strancanciatu…

e posso dire con certezza
che le donne si aprono il cuore
col Signore confessando in chiesa
tutte le perversioni da puttane
che certamente non vanno a raccontare
ai mariti.
Per una donna sfrenata
non è cosa virtuosa
cercare di non fare porcherie
ma stare zitta e non confessare
a nessuno la sua lussuria.

OTELLO: Ma tu dici?

IAGO: Fece fesso il padre
quando diventò vostra moglie
e quando si mostrava timorosa
del vostro aspetto di uomo colossale
nella carne le cresceva la febbre
d'essere da voi posseduta.

OTELLO: È vero. Hai ragione.

IAGO: Da una che così piccola e giovane
già si mostrò eccellente attrice
cosa potete aspettarvi ora?
No, mi dispiace, lo dico per davvero
e non approvo me stesso,
mi piglierei a pugni sul testone…
Dovete perdonare questa insolenza
ma soprattutto perché vi voglio bene:
l'amore che vi porto
lo dovete perdonare.

OTELLO: A te Iago mi sento
per sempre incatenato.

IAGO: Mi pare che questa faccenda vi abbia
stordito.

OTELLO: Manco per niente. Non è successo
nulla.

IAGO: Sembrate del tutto trasformato…

and I can say with certainty
that women confessing in church
do let God see the whorish pranks
they dare not show their husbands.
For an unbridled woman
her best conscience
is not to leave't undone
but keep't unknown
and not confess her lust.

OTHELLO: Dost thou say so?

IAGO: She did deceive her father,
marrying you
and when she pretended to fear
your awesome looks
the fever to be possessed by you
mounted in her flesh.

OTHELLO: 'Tis true. Thou art right.

IAGO: What can you expect now
from one that so young
could give out such a performance?
No, I am sorry, in truth
and I am much to blame,
I would hit myself on the head…
I humbly do beseech you your pardon
for too much loving you:
you must forgive
the love I have for you

OTHELLO: I am bound to thee, Iago,
for ever.

IAGO: It seems to me you're moved.

OTHELLO: Not at all. Nothing happened.   **No, not much moved**

IAGO: You seem utterly transformed…

OTELLO: Picchì dici sti cosi?
    'Un sugnu stracanciatu.
    E 'u sai nzoccu alluntana
    d'a testa stu tirribili pinzeru?
    Lu cori onestu di la me' signura

IAGO: Sempri accussì lu sarba lu Signuri…

OTELLO: Eppuru… onestu Iago…
    Eppuru si a natura cancia strata
    e fatta differenti si snatura…

IAGO: U fattu è chistu: 'un fu vostra
      mugghieri
    accussì stravacanti 'i disprizzari
    dumanni 'i matrimoniu di picciotti
    ricchi, giuvini e beddi,
    di bona discinnenza e cumpaisani,
    mustrannu lu disìu contra natura?
    E chistu 'un fa pinzari
    a cori depravatu
    e carni purcariusa,
    pinzeri ca 'un canusciunu russuri
    'nchiappati di libìdini e lussuria?
    Ma u tempu ricunsigna lu giudiziu.
    E mittennu voscenza a paraguni
    cu li picciotti beddi e d'altu rangu
    vostra mugghieri certu havi rimorsu
    e pintimentu pi nu matrimoniu
    troppo affrittatu cu 'n cristianu anticu.

OTELLO: Vatinni, Iago, addiu, ora vatinni.
    E si veni a canusci quarchi cosa
    M'aspettu ca ntù 'n fiat m'u veni a dici.
    Lassami sulu, Iago, 'un ti siddiari.

IAGO (*uscendo*): Vi lassu sulu, illustri
    ginirali.

OTELLO: Picchì mi maritavu?
    Iago è criatura onesta e certamenti
    sapi cchiù cosi 'i chiddi ca mi dici.

OTELLO: Perché dici queste cose?
    Non sono trasformato.
    E lo sai cosa allontana
    dalla testa questo terribile pensiero?
    Il cuore onesto della mia signora.

IAGO: Sempre tale lo conservi il Signore…

OTELLO: Eppure… onesto Iago…
    eppure se la natura cambia strada
    e resa diversa si snatura…

IAGO: Il fatto è questo: non fu vostra moglie
    così stravagante da disprezzare
    domande di matrimonio di ragazzi
    ricchi, giovani e belli,
    di buona stirpe e compaesani,
    mostrando un desiderio contro natura?
    E questo non fa pensare
    a un cuore depravato
    e a carne da porca,
    pensieri che non conoscono il rossore
    sporchi di libidine e lussuria?
    Ma il tempo porta giudizio.
    E mettendovi a confronto
    coi giovani belli e d'alto rango
    vostra moglie di certo prova rimorso
    e pentimento per un matrimonio
    troppo affrettato con un uomo vecchio.

OTELLO: Vattene, Iago, addio, ora vattene.
    E se vieni a sapere qualche cosa
    mi aspetto che me lo venga a dire di
    corsa.
    Lasciami solo, Iago, non te la prendere.

IAGO (*uscendo*): Vi lascio solo, illustre
    generale.

OTELLO: Perché ho preso moglie?
    Iago è una creatura onesta e di certo
    sa più di quel che mi dice.

OTHELLO: Why sayest thou so?
    I am not transformed.
    And dost thou know what keeps at bay
    this terrible thought?
    My lady's honest heart.   **I do not think but Desdemona's honest.**

IAGO: May God keep it so …

OTHELLO: Yet… honest Iago…
    Yet how nature,
    Erring from itself changes…

IAGO: There's the point: wasn't your wife
    so extravagant to shun
    proposed matches of young   **As not to affect many proposed matches**
    rich and handsome,   **of her own clime, complexion, and degree**
    men of good breeding and from her land,
    showing a desire against nature?   **Whereto we see in all things nature tends**
    And doesn't this indicate
    a depraved heart
    lewd flesh,
    thoughts that know no blush
    tinted with lechery and lust?
    Time will tell.
    Comparing you
    with strapping young noblemen
    your wife surely regrets
    and repents too hasty a wedding
    with an old man.

OTHELLO: Leave, Iago, farewell, now leave.   **Farewell, farewell.**
    if thou comest to learn something   **if more thou dost perceive,**
    I expect thou to let me know at once.   **let me know more**
    Leave me, Iago, don't feel bad.   **Leave me, Iago.**

IAGO (*going*): I'll leave you alone, illustrious general   **My lord, I take my leave.**

OTHELLO: Why did I take a wife?   **Why did I marry?**
    Iago is an honest creature and for sure   **This honest creature doubtless sees**
    he sees more than he says.   **and knows more, much more than he unfolds.**

IAGO (*tornando*): Signuri me', iu priu lu
    vostru onuri,
  'un vi mittiti a scavari l'abissu
  dunni affunna d'a fimmina u disìu.
  Ma a voscenza ci dugnu stu cunsigghiu:
  puru si Cassio è dignu d'u so'gradu
  — e certu merita a locutinenza —
  'u facissi aspittari n'atra 'nticchia
  pi vìdiri cchiù chiaru
  lu so' comportamentu…
  E se vostra mugghieri
  'nsistisci cu primura
  pi fallu pirdunari,
  stu fattu quarchi cosa
  havi a significari…
  Arreri mi nni vaju.
  Voscenza binidica.

Iago esce.

OTELLO: Onestu com'a Iago nun c'è nuddu
  e nuddu megghiu d'iddu
  canusci u cori umanu
  cu tanta pricisioni.
  Forsi picchì iu sugnu furasteri
  e quannu parru 'un sacciu cunvirsari
  c'a lingua modda di li curtigiani,
  opuru picchì sciddicu cull'anni
  'nfunnu ô vadduni tristi d'a vicchiaia
  (puru si a mmia 'un mi pari accussì
      tantu…).
  Si nn'jiu. Sta traditura 'ngannatrici!
  Pi sempri l'haiu pirduta. Ora m'arresta
  di 'ncarricari l'odiu d'astutari
  lu 'ncendiu ca lu cori ora m'abbrucia.
  Sulu l'odiu è balsamu c'arrifrisca
  e cura li firiti di l'amuri.
  U matrimoniu è na granni illusioni.

IAGO (*tornando*): Signor mio onorato, io
    vi prego,
  non vi mettete a scavare l'abisso
  in cui affonda il desiderio di una donna.
  Vi do questo consiglio:
  anche se Cassio è degno del suo grado
  — e certo merita la luogotenenza —
  fatelo aspettare ancora un po'
  per veder più chiaramente
  il suo comportamento…
  E se vostra moglie
  insiste con la fretta
  per farlo perdonare,
  questo fatto deve
  voler dire qualcosa…
  Di nuovo me ne vado.
  Beneditemi.

OTELLO: Onesto come Iago non c'è
    nessuno
  e nessuno meglio di lui
  conosce il cuore umano
  con tanta precisione.
  Forse perché son straniero
  e quando parlo non so conversare
  con la lingua molle dei cortigiani,
  oppure perché scivolo con gli anni
  in fondo alle grandi valli tristi della
      vecchiaia
  (anche se a me non pare così tanto…).
  Se n'è andata. Sta traditrice ingannatrice!
  Per sempre l'ho perduta. Ora mi resta
  di far crescere l'odio per spegnere
  l'incendio che ora mi brucia il cuore.
  Solo l'odio è balsamo che rinfresca
  e cura le ferite d'amore.
  Il matrimonio è una grande illusione.

IAGO (*retuning*): My beloved lord, I prithee
    Do not dig in the abyss
    in which a woman's desire sinks.
    Let me give you this advice:
    even though Cassio is worthy of his rank
    — and for sure he deserves being lieutenant —
    let him wait a bit longer
    to see more clearly
    his behaviour…
    And if your wife
    insists that he be pardoned
    hurriedly,
    this must mean something…
    I once more take my leave.
    Bless me.

                My lord, I would I might entreat your
                honour, to scan this thing no farther

          although 'tis fit that Cassio have his place

          if you please to hold him off a while,
          you shall by that perceive him
          and his means
          Note if your lady
          strain his entertainment
          with any strong or vehement importunity;
          much will be seen in that
          I once more take my leave.

Exit Iago.

OTHELLO: No one is as honest as Iago
    and no one better than him
    knows the heart of men
    with such precision.
    Perchance for I'm a foreigner
    and when I speak I can't converse
    with the soft tongue of courtiers,
    or for I slip in years
    into the great valleys of old age
    (even though they don't seem so deep to me…).
    She's gone. That sneaky traitor!
    I have lost her for ever. All I have left
    is to feed my hatred to quell the fire
    that now burns my heart.
    Hatred alone is the balm that cools
    and cures love's wounds.
    Marriage is a great illusion.

          This fellow's of exceeding honesty
          and knows all qualities,
          with a learned spirit
          of human dealings.
          Haply, for I am black
          and have not those soft parts of
          conversation that chamberers have,
          or for I am declined
          into the vale of years
          yet that's not much
          I am abused
          and my relief
          must be to loathe her

          O curse of marriage,

Nni fa sèntiri nostri sti criature
accussì dilicati ntà facciata
ma chi nostri nun su' pi lu misteru
du corpu ca suverchia lu pinzeru.
A fimmina 'unn'u sapi mancu idda
chiddu c'adduma e avvampa la so' carni.
St'oceanu di libidini e lussuria
è na timpesta ca 'un si cueta mai,
na varca ca si perdi ntù cicluni.
E cu prova a cumprenniri
chi rutta veni a pigghia
sta sorta 'i 'mbarcazioni
ntù nivuru sprufunna
du mari unni s'affuca la ragiuni.
Meggiu nasciri rospu
e vìviri ntù fangu
di na paludi morta e putrafatta
c'aviri sulamenti un pizzuddicchiu
d'a stanza unn'addimora u sintimentu,
schifiata di lu toccu
'ngrasciatu di quarcunu
c'allorda, 'nchiappa e 'mpista lu canduri
e la dilicatizza di l'amuri.
È miu ddu locu e nuddu 'u pò
    ammurbari
trasennuci ammucciuni quannu nesciu
e chinu di scantu 'u lassu vacanti
mentri lu cori si finci sicuru
ma sutta sutta ntù silenziu trema.

Ci fa sentir nostre ste creature
così apparentemente delicate
ma che nostre non sono per il mistero
del corpo che sovrasta il pensiero.
Una donna non lo sa neanche lei
cosa accende e avvampa la sua carne.
Questo oceano di libidine e di lussuria
è una tempesta che non si quieta mai,
una barca che si perde nel ciclone.
E chi provi a comprendere
che rotta viene a prendere
sta sorta di imbarcazione
sprofonda nel nero
del mare in cui soffoca la ragione.
Meglio nascere rospo
e vivere nel fango
di una palude morta e putrefatta
che avere solamente un pezzettino
della stanza dove vive il sentimento,
disgustosa per il tocco
sudicio di qualcuno
che sporca, imbroglia e appesta il
    candore
e la delicatezza dell'amore.
È mio questo posto e nessuno lo può
    contaminare
entrandoci di nascosto quando esco
e pieno di paura lo lascio libero
mentre il cuore si finge sicuro
ma sotto sotto in silenzio trema.

Otello rimane in scena. È disteso per terra, spezzato in due dall'angoscia. Il soldato si rivolge al pubblico.

SOLDATO: Otello s'addumò
    Comu vagnatu d'ogghiu
    e subito avvampannu
    è cori ca sprufunna ntà lu 'nfernu.

SOLDATO: Otello si accese
    come bagnato d'odio
    e avvampando all'improvviso
    è il cuore che sprofonda nell'inferno.

It makes us feel ours these creatures
apparently so delicate
who are not, in fact, ours for the mystery
of the body that overtakes thought.
A woman doesn't even know
what lights up and burns her flesh.
This ocean of libido and lust
is a never quelled storm,
a skiff lost in a cyclone.
Whoever tries to understand
which route such a vessel
will take
plunges into the dark
sea in which reason suffocates.
Better to be born a toad
and live in mud
of a dead and putrefied swamp
than to have just a little piece
of the room where feelings live,
made disgusting by the greasy
touch of someone
who dirties, tricks, and pollutes the candour
and delicacy of love.
This place is mine and no one can contaminate it
entering unperceived when I go out
and, full of apprehension, leave it free
while the heart seems firm
but deep down silently quivers.

that we can call these delicate creatures ours
and not their appetites!

I'd rather be a toad
and live upon the vapour of a dungeon

than keep a corner in the thing I love
for other's uses.

Othello remains on stage. He's lying on the ground, broken by despair. The soldier addresses the audience.

SOLDIER: Othello lit up
as, soaked in hatred
and catching fire at once,
is the heart that plunges into hell.

Certu, lo focu di stu 'ncendiu
è Iago c'u pripara e l'alimenta.
Ma la sustanza cavura c'abbrucia,
u lignu ca si 'nfiamma,
è la menti d'Otello ca 'un sa fira
a suppurtari di la donna u gran misteru.
Iago è sinceru. 'Un dici fissarii:
a tuttu chiddu ca ci cunta a Otello
iddu stissu ci cridi pi ddaveru.
Pi Iago è cosa strana, innaturali,
chi Desdemona s'avìa curcatu
c'un vecchiu barbaru e straneru,
senza blasuni sparti.
Iago pinzava pi ddaveru chi Desdemona
né cchiù né menu d'autri fimmini
era sicuramenti na buttana.
Iago sapìa ca l'omu di principiu
è comu Otello, limpidu cristallu:
basta nu sputu e subitu si rumpi.
Pi chistu nunn'è è stranu
c'u nostru ginirali
ntà 'n attimu carìu dintr'u tranellu
ca ci cunzò l'alferi.
Otello c'era già dintra la riti.
U munnu è comu nuatri lu liggemu.
I palori di Iago
u nostru ginirali li liggìu
facennuli passari ntà lu 'mbutu
di na menti cu na certa 'nclinazioni.
Iago ci dissi: taliativi bonu
d'a gilusia, d'u mostru virdi
stativi luntanu.
E Otello fici so' stu gran cunsigghiu
Picchì 'un putìa truvari n'autra strata:
mai nenti gilusia
all'ùmmira d'u cori.

Certo, il fuoco di quest'incendio
è Iago che lo allestisce e alimenta.
Ma la sostanza calda che brucia,
il legno che si infiamma,
è la mente di Otello che non si fida
di sopportare il gran mistero della
    donna.
Iago è sincero. Non dice fesserie:
a tutto ciò che racconta a Otello
lui stesso ci crede per davvero.
Per Iago è cosa strana, innaturale,
che Desdemona si sia coricata
con un vecchio barbaro e straniero,
senza nobiltà per giunta.
Iago pensava per davvero che Desdemona
né più né meno delle altre donne
fosse sicuramente una puttana.
Iago sapeva che l'uomo di principî
è come Otello, un limpido cristallo:
basta uno sputo e subito si rompe.
Per questo non è strano
che il nostro generale
in un attimo cadde nel tranello
che gli preparò l'alfiere.
Otello era già nella rete.
Il mondo è come noi lo leggiamo.
Le parole di Iago
il nostro generale le lesse
facendole passare nell'imbuto
di una mente con una certa disposizione.
Iago gli disse: guardatevi bene
dalla gelosia, state lontano
dal mostro verde.
E Otello fece suo questo gran consiglio
perché non poteva trovare un'altra
    strada:
mai nessuna gelosia
all'ombra del cuore.

Sure, the fuel of this fire
is Iago, who sets it up and feeds it.
But the warm burning matter,
the wood catching fire
is the mind of Othello, who doesn't trust
himself to endure the great mystery of women.
Iago is honest. He is not lying:
he truly believes
everything he tells Othello.
For Iago it is strange, unnatural,
that Desdemona lay
with an old man, foreign and barbaric,
and not even noble.
Iago truly thought that Desdemona
no more, no less than other women
was surely a whore.
Iago knew that a principled man
is like Othello, clear as crystal:
a spit and it breaks.
That's why 'tis not strange
that our general
in a minute fell in the trap
the ensign prepared.
Othello was already in the net.
The world is how we read it.
Our general read
Iago's words
passing them through the funnel
of a predisposed mind.
Iago told him: beware
of jealousy, keep away
from the green-eyed monster.
And Othello took this suggestion to heart
because he could not find another way:
never any jealousy
in the heart's shade.

Si 'un ci pò stari amuri
allora ci havi a tràsiri disprezzu,
odiu ca cerca subitu vinnitta.
'Unn'è la gilusia la so' ossessioni.
U so' problema scava
'n funnu a li funnamenta
dunni l'amuri è pinzeru ideali
fattu di sita bianca e 'mmaculata.
Ma a fimmina è na cosa scanusciuta.
E quannu Iago 'u porta a ragiunari
e ci apprisenta chiara all'orizzonti
sta cosa ch'iddu avìa misu luntano
di l'occhi di la menti e di lu cori
eccu ch'a terra ferma
si grapi sutt'i peri,
s'agghiutti a iddu e puru
a lu so' perdutu amuri.

Se non ci può essere amore
allora deve entrarci il disprezzo,
l'odio che cerca subito vendetta.
Non è la gelosia la sua ossessione.
Il suo problema scava
in fondo alle fondamenta
in cui l'amore è pensiero ideale
fatto di seta bianca e immacolata.
Ma la donna è una cosa sconosciuta.
E quando Iago lo porta a ragionare
e gli presenta chiara all'orizzonte
questa cosa che lui aveva messo lontano
dagli occhi dalla mente e dal cuore
ecco che la terra ferma
si apre sotto i piedi,
se lo inghiotte insieme
al suo perduto amore.

In alto una linea di luce taglia l'oscurità come una lama sottile. Una Desdemona contemporanea — una delle tante di tutti i tempi — è distesa, in bilico sul vuoto. In abiti moderni è vestita a festa.

DESDEMONA: Un giorno in più…
  non me l'hai dato.
  Neanche un minuto
  per farmi recitare una preghiera…
  Ed ora spegni
  questa fiammella spersa
  ormai tra cielo e terra…

  E dunque rubo il tempo
  che adesso stai impiegando
  per togliermi la vita a mani nude.

  Lo so, me ne sto andando…

DESDEMONA: Un giorno in più…
  non me l'hai dato.
  Neanche un minuto
  per farmi recitare una preghiera…
  Ed ora spegni
  questa fiammella spersa
  ormai tra cielo e terra…

  E dunque rubo il tempo
  che adesso stai impiegando
  per togliermi la vita a mani nude.

  Lo so, me ne sto andando…

If there can't be love
then there must be contempt,
hatred that immediately seeks revenge.
Jealousy is not his obsession.
His problem digs deep
into the foundations
where love is ideal thought
made of white and spotless silk.
But a woman is an unknown thing.
And when Iago makes him think
and offers him, clear on the horizon,
this thing that he had placed far
away from the eyes, the mind, and the heart
then firm ground
opens up from beneath his feet,
and swallows him along
with his lost love.

Up above a spotlight cuts the darkness as a thin blade. A contemporary Desdemona — one of the many women of all times — is reclined, perched on the brink of nothingness. She is dressed up, in modern clothes.

DESDEMONA: One more day…
    thou didst not give it to me.
    Not even a minute
    to let me say a prayer…
    and now thou put out
    the light of this flame
    now lost between heaven and earth…

    So now I steal the time
    thou art using
    to take my life with your bare hands.

    I know, I am done…

Non te ne accorgi
ma mentre mi uccidi
anche tu stai morendo a poco a poco.

Ormai ti cerco solo
al di là di te
dove tu stesso più non sei,
al di là della vita ormai.
E proverò a trovare
di nuovo la tua voce dentro il buio.

Quando da me non uscirà più alcun
      respiro
e tu sfiorandomi
non potrai non pensare all'inverno,
ecco che allora sarà chiaro
che il mio amore ha natura di pietra
di roccia costante, di sasso,
di marmo che resiste al tuo scalpello.
L'amore che inflessibile mi uccide…

E ti amo ancora.
Anche se sei oramai
luce invisibile sperduta nel gelo dei
      tuoi occhi
ormai di ghiaccio.

Entriamo quindi in questa stanza buia.

Adesso mi sfiora
quest'ultimo imbocco di vento.
Lo catturo.
Lo lascio scivolare dal naso
giù giù fino alla bocca…
E col sapore trattenuto
di questo piccolo tesoro d'aria,

Non te ne accorgi
ma mentre mi uccidi
anche tu stai morendo a poco a poco.

Ormai ti cerco solo
al di là di te
dove tu stesso più non sei,
al di là della vita ormai.
E proverò a trovare
di nuovo la tua voce dentro il buio.

Quando da me non uscirà più alcun
      respiro
e tu sfiorandomi
non potrai non pensare all'inverno,
ecco che allora sarà chiaro
che il mio amore ha natura di pietra
di roccia costante, di sasso,
di marmo che resiste al tuo scalpello.
L'amore che inflessibile mi uccide…

E ti amo ancora.
Anche se sei oramai
luce invisibile sperduta
nel gelo dei tuoi occhi
ormai di ghiaccio.

Entriamo quindi in questa stanza buia.

Adesso mi sfiora
quest'ultimo imbocco di vento.
Lo catturo.
Lo lascio scivolare dal naso
giù giù fino alla bocca…
E col sapore trattenuto
di questo piccolo tesoro d'aria,

Thou dost not see it
But as thou kill'st me
Thou diest with me little by little.

By now I only seek thee
beyond thyself
where thou art no longer,
beyond life, now.
And I will try to find again
thy voice in the darkness.

When no breath will come from me
and thou, touching me,
wilt not be able to avoid thinking of winter,
then it will be clear
that my love shares the nature of stone,
solid rock, pebble,
marble resisting your chisel.
Love that, unyielding, kills me…

And I still love thee.
Even though now thou art
an invisible light lost
in the coldness of your eyes
now icy.

Let's then enter this dark room.

Now this last gust of wind
brushes over me.
I seize it.
I let it slide down the nose
down into my mouth…
And with the kept flavour
of this little treasure of air,

prima di restituirlo al mondo
adesso tremo.

Adesso muoio.

Baciami le labbra
anche per me,
sto per andare.

E un silenzio nuovo, inatteso,
mai più mi sveglierà al mattino.

prima di restituirlo al mondo
adesso tremo.

Adesso muoio.

Baciami le labbra
anche per me,
sto per andare.

E un silenzio nuovo, inatteso,
mai più mi sveglierà al mattino.

Iago raggiunge di nuovo il generale che nel frattempo era rimasto a terra a ruminare il suo dolore.

OTELLO: Fausa! Fausa cu mmia!
  Nzoccu significava a so' lussuria
  Pi mmia can nun vìdìa e nun sapìa?
  Essennu nenti, iu nenti suffrìa
  Mancannu lu pinzeru, 'un c'era dannu.
  Si a ttia t'arrubbano e tu 'un tinn'adduni
  è comu si 'un t'avissiru arrubbatu.

IAGO: Di sintiri sti cosi mi dispiaci

OTELLO: Addìu jorna sireni, addìu pi
    sempri.
  Addìu tempu sbriùsu di la menti.
  Addìu forti guirreri 'mpinnacchiati
  cummattimenti liggindari addìu.
  Addìu, addìu a li vuci di cavaddi,
  addìu trummi firrigne, addìu tammuri
  c'aizzanu lu spirdu di battagghia,
  friscalettu che spirtusa l'aricchi
  addìu, riali stinnardu, orgogliu addìu
  parata di surdati e ogni signali
  c'accrisci unuri e vantu di la guerra
  addìu a li machini pi lu stirminiu

OTELLO: Falsa! Falsa con me!
  Cosa significava la sua lussuria
  per me che non vedevo e non sapevo?
  Essendo niente, io non soffrivo per
    niente.
  Mancando il pensiero, non c'era danno.
  Se ti derubano e non te ne accorgi
  è come se non ti avessero derubato.

IAGO: Mi dispiace sentire queste cose.

OTELLO: Addio giorni sereni, addio per
    sempre.
  Addio tempo spensierato della mente.
  Addio forti guerrieri impennacchiati,
  combattimenti leggendari addio.
  Addio, addio alle voci dei cavalli,
  addio trombe di ferro, addio tamburi
  che aizzano lo spirito della battaglia,
  fischietto che perfora le orecchie
  addio, reale stendardo, orgoglio addio
  parata di soldati e ogni segnale
  che accresce l'onore e il vanto della
    guerra
  addio alle macchine per lo sterminio

before returning it to the world
I now tremble.

Now I die.

Kiss my lips
for me too,
I'm about to leave.

And no new, unexpected silence,
will ever wake me again in the morning.

Iago re-joins Othello who, in the meantime, had remained on the floor nursing his pain

OTHELLO: False! False to me!
    What did her lust mean   **What sense had I in her stolen hours of lust?**
    to me who didn't see and didn't know?   **I saw't not, thought it not**
    being nothing, I suffered nothing.
    Without the thought, there was no damage.   **— it harm'd not me**
    He that is robbed, not wanting what is stolen,
    Let him not know't, and he's not robbed at all.

IAGO: I am sorry to hear this.

OTHELLO: Farewell happy days, farewell for ever.
    Farewell carefree time of the mind.   **Farwell the tranquil mind**
    Farewell strong plumed knights,   **Farewell the plumèd troops,**
    legendary fights, farewell.   **and the big wars that makes ambition virtue**
    O, farewell! Farewell thee neighing steed
    farewell iron trumpets, farewell   **shrill trump**
    spirit-stirring drum,
    t'ear-piercing fife,
    farewell, the royal banner, pride farewell   **and all quality**
    soldier parade and every sign
    that augments the honour and glory of war   **pride, pomp, and circumstance of**
    farewell you mortal engines   **glorious war;**

chi sonanu 'n tirribili ribbùmmu
c'acchiana fin'u monti unni sta Giovi.
A tuttu chistu munnu scintillanti
e chinu d'avvintura dicu: addìu!
'Un c'è cchiù nenti, ormai tuttu finìu.
U cumpitu d'Otello s'a cunchiusu.

IAGO: Pussibili ca semu junti a chistu?

OTELLO: T'ha' stari mutu pezz'i dilinquenti!
E parra sulu si pò dimustrari
ca pi ddaveru lu me grann'amuri
è comu l'autri fimmini buttana.
Cull'occhi mi l'ha' rènniri prisenti
cu provi ca 'un si ponnu dubitari
ca vasinnò, ti giuru, ha' stari accura
di chiddu ca i me' manu ponnu fari.
Megghiu si tu avissi nasciutu cani
chiuttostu ch'a me' raggia cuntrastari.

IAGO: A chistu semu junti pi ddaveru?

OTELLO: Fammill'abbiriri sta cosa atruci.
O pirlomenu dunami na prova
ca 'unn'havi aneddi o ganci unni
appizzari
un sulu dubbiu, vasinnò t'ammazzu.

IAGO: Signuri me', iu ci vulissi diri…

OTELLO: Si stai 'nfangannu a idda e a
mmia turtùri,
'un perdiri cchiù tempu pi prijari!

IAGO: Cori di Gèsu e tutti Santi 'ncelu
taliàti di sta parti e difinniti
sta povera criatura svinturata!
Ma siti omu? E l'anima l'aviti?
V'arresta ancora 'ntesta anticchia 'i
sennu?
Lassatimi e u Signuri v'accumpagna!
Ma fuvu foddi? Cu' m'u fici fari?
Iu fuvu onestu e chistu è lu ringraziu?
Oh munnu, munnu, cchiù nun ti
canusciu!

che suonano un terribile rimbombo
che sale fino al monte dove sta Giove.
A tutto questo mondo scintillante e
pieno d'avventura dico: addio!
Non c'è più niente, ormai tutto è finito.
Il compito di Otello s'è concluso.

IAGO: Possibile che siamo giunti a questo?

OTELLO: Devi stare zitto pezzo di
delinquente!
E parla solo se puoi dimostrare
che per davvero il mio grande amore
è come le altre donne una puttana.
Con gli occhi me lo devi far presente
con prove che non si possono dubitare
che se no, ti giuro, devi stare attento
a ciò che le mie mani possono fare.
Meglio se fossi nato cane
piuttosto che contrastare la mia rabbia.

IAGO: Siamo giunti a questo per davvero?

OTELLO: Fammela vedere sta cosa atroce.
O perlomeno dammi una prova
che non ci siano anelli o
ganci a cui appendere
un solo dubbio, se no ti ammazzo.

IAGO: Signore mio, io vi vorrei dire…

OTELLO: Se stai infangando lei e
torturando me,
non perdere più tempo a pregare!

IAGO: Cuore di Gesù e tutti i santi del cielo
guardate da sta parte e difendete
questa povera creatura sventurata!
Ma siete uomo? E l'anima l'avete?
Vi resta ancora in testa un po' di senno?
Lasciatemi e Dio vi assista!
Ma sono stato pazzo? Chi me lo fece
fare?
Son stato onesto e questo è il
ringraziamento?
Oh, mondo, mondo, non ti riconosco
più!

playing a terrible thunder
that mounts all the way up to Jupiter's mount.
To all this shiny world
full of adventure I say: farewell!
There's nothing left, 'tis all over now.
Othello's occupation's gone.

IAGO: Can it be that we've come to this?

Is't possible, my lord?

OTHELLO: You must keep silent, you villain!
Speak only if you can prove
that for real my great love
is like all other women a whore.

Be sure thou prove my love a whore!

You must give me the ocular proof,
proof that cannot be doubted
otherwise, I swear, you must beware
of what my hands can do.
Thou hadst been better have been born a dog
than answer my waked wrath!

IAGO: Is't come to this, truly?

OTHELLO: Make me to see't, this atrocious thing.
Or, at least, so prove it
that the probation bear no hinge nor loop
to hang a doubt on — or woe upon thy life!

IAGO: My noble lord, I would say…

OTHELLO: If thou dost slander her an torture me,
never pray more!

IAGO: Jesus' heart and all the saints in heaven
look this way and defend
this poor unfortunate creature!
Are you a man? Have you a soul?

or sense

Have you still some sense in your head?
Let go of me and God help you!
Have I been mad? Why did I ever…?

O wretched fool
That lov'st to make thy honesty a vice!

I was honest and this is what I get?
O world, world, I don't recognize you!

Munnu crudeli, munnu 'mprissionanti,
vidi nzoccu succedi e pigghia appunti
è chistu lu distinu
pi l'omu onestu e francu.
Certu mi fici bonu sta lizioni:
si chista è a consiguenza di l'amuri
megghiu starisi sulu e senz'amici.

OTELLO: 'Un ti nni jiri, Iago, ti scungiuru.
Ma chi ci pozzu fari s'iddu criu
'nsemmula me' mugghieri
onesta e sdisonesta
e tu 'nsemmula francu e farabutto?
Chi nzoccu dici è veru e puru 'ngannu?
Pi chistu t'addumannu di pruvari
Lu quatru c'addipinci chi palori
cu fatti ca 'un si ponnu cuntistari.
E pinzari chi l'amuri da me' vita
candido avìa lu nomu comu a facci
di Diana cacciatrici 'mmaculata.
'Nveci accomòra è 'nchiappato e scurusu
comu la facci di me' china di bili,
cchiù nivura di notti senza luna.
Certu a la morti 'un manca la manera
pi cogghiri di 'nterra na criatura
e falla accumudari all'autru munnu…
Ma prima avissi a essiri sicuru.

IAGO: Ma comu si pò fari, ginirali?
Vossìa forsi vulissi
c'a vucca spalancata
taliari la mugghieri
mentri un picciotto 'a pigghia e la
pussedi
e comu nu cavaddu s'accavadda?

OTELLO: Malidizioni e morti!

Mondo crudele, mondo impressionante,
ho visto quel che succede e prendo nota:
è questo il destino
per l'uomo onesto e franco.
Certo mi ha fatto bene questa lezione:
se questa è la conseguenza dell'amore
meglio stare solo e senza amici.

OTELLO: Non te ne andare, Iago, ti
scongiuro.
Ma che ci posso fare se credo
allo stesso tempo mia moglie
onesta e disonesta
e tu franco e farabutto?
Che ciò che dici è vero ma
anche un inganno?
Per questo ti domando di provare
il quadro che dipingi con le parole
con fatti che non si possano contestare.
E pensare che l'amore della mia vita
candido aveva il nome come la faccia
di Diana cacciatrice immacolata.
Invece adesso è sporco e scuro
come la faccia mia piena di bile,
più nera di una notte senza luna.
Certo alla morte non manca il modo
di raccogliere da terra una creatura
e farla accomodare all'altro mondo…
Ma prima devo essere sicuro.

IAGO: Ma come si può fare, generale?
Voi forse vorreste
con la bocca spalancata
guardare vostra moglie
mentre un giovane la prende e la possiede
e come un cavallo se l'ingroppa?

OTELLO: Maledizione e morte!

O monstrous world, amazing world,
I saw how it works and took notice:
this is the destiny
of a frank and honest man.
Surely this lesson was welcome:
if this is the consequence of love
better to be alone and friendless.

To be direct and honest is not safe.
I thank you for this profit,
and from hence I'll love no friend,
sith love breeds such offence.

OTHELLO: Nay, stay, Iago, prithee.
What can I do if I think
At the same time my wife be
honest and dishonest
and thou just and a villain?
That what you say is true but also a trick?
For this I ask you to prove
the picture you paint with words
with facts that no one can dispute.
To think that the love of my life
had a name as clean as the face
of Diana, immaculate huntress.
now, instead, it is as begrimed and black
as mine own face full of bile,
darker than a night without the moon.
Surely death knows how
to pick a person from the earth
and let her into the other world…
But first I have to be sure.

I think my wife be honest, and think she is not
I think that thou art just, and think thou art not

her name, that was as fresh
as Dian's visage,

IAGO: How can that be, general?
Would you,
your mouth agape,
want to watch your wife
as a young man takes and tups her
and as a horse mounts her?

Would you the supervisor grossly gape on?
Behold her tupped?

OTHELLO: Death and damnation!

IAGO: Si 'un sunnu propriu fissa
  Starann'accura a 'un fàrisi truvari.
  Chi sunnu, serpi? Scimie, lupi, crape,
  armali c'hannu sempri ddu pruritu?
  Mi pari assai difficili
  'ncoccialli mentri Cassio
  ntù vostru lettu joca
  la parti d'u muntuni e s'addiverti.
  Unn'è, chista, cirtizza
  ca nuddu vi pò dari.
  Allura pò bastari a cundannari
  a 'mputaziuni e tracci cunsistenti
  ca portanu davanzi a lu purtuni
  dunni la virità ci havi a so' casa.

OTELLO: A prova dunami ca è traditura,
  prova viventi, prova manifesta.

IAGO: Stu 'ncarricu 'un mi piaci eppuru
    dicu,
  spintu dill'onestà e d'a cumprinsiuni
  p'a vostra cunnizioni dilicata,
  dicu ca sugnu prontu a gghiri avanti.
  Chista ci l'hè cuntari picchì è cosa
  Chi a mmia, quannu chi fu, fici
    'mprissioni.
  N'arreri quarchi jornu succirìu
  ca stavamu curcati ciancu a ciancu
  cu Cassio dintr'a tenda militari.
  Botta di sali avìa un duluri 'i denti
  ca 'un mi faceva dòrmiri pi nenti
  tuttu accupatu dintra st'afflizioni.
  Comu sapiti ci sunnu cristiani
  cull'arma e u sintimentu sempri pronti
  a nèsciri d'a vucca cu lu ciatu.
  E cuntanu durmennu i loro affari
  grapenu all'autri a porta chi cunnuci
  dintra la virità ca si fa 'nsonnu.

IAGO: Se non sono proprio fessi
  staranno attenti a non farsi trovare.
  Cosa sono, serpenti? Scimmie, lupi,
    capre,
  animali che hanno sempre un prurito?
  Mi pare molto difficile
  sorprenderli mentre Cassio
  nel vostro letto gioca
  la parte di un montone e si diverte.
  Questa è una certezza
  che nessuno vi può dare.
  Allora possono bastare a condannare
  l'imputazione e le tracce consistenti
  che portano davanti al portone
  dove la verità sta di casa.

OTELLO: Dammi la prova che è traditrice,
  prova vivente, prova manifesta.

IAGO: Quest'incarico non mi piace eppure
    dico,
  spinto dall'onestà e dalla comprensione
  per la vostra condizione delicata,
  dico che sono pronto ad andare avanti.
  Questa ve la devo raccontare
  perché è una cosa
  che a me, quando accadde, fece
    impressione.
  Qualche giorno fa successe
  che eravamo coricati fianco a fianco
  con Cassio nella tenda militare.
  Maledizione, avevo un mal di denti
  che non mi faceva dormire per niente
  tutto avvolto in quest'afflizione.
  Come sapete ci sono uomini
  con anima e sentimenti sempre pronti
  a uscire dalla bocca col respiro.
  E raccontano dormendo gli affari loro
  aprendo agli altri la porta che conduce
  alla verità che si fa nel sogno.

IAGO: If they are not dumb
    They will be careful not to get caught.
    What are they, snakes? Monkeys, wolves, goats,
    animals that always have an itch?
    I think it very difficult
    to catch them as Cassio
    plays in your bed
    the part of a ram and has his fun.
    This is a certainty
    that no one can give you.
    The accusation and the consistent clues
    that lead to the door
    where truth resides
    may suffice, then, to condemn.

> It were a tedious difficulty, I think
> to bring them to that prospect.
> Were they as prime as goats, as hot as monkeys,
> as salt as wolves in pride

OTHELLO: Give me a reason she's disloyal,
    living proof, obvious proof.

IAGO: I do not like the office; yet I say,
    pricked by foolish honesty and understanding
    for your delicate condition,
    I say I am ready to go on.
    I have to tell you this one because
    when it happened it struck me.
    A few days ago it happened
    that we were lying side by side
    with Cassio in the military tent.
    Damn, I had such a toothache
    that didn't let me sleep at all
    overwhelmed by this affliction.
    As you know, there are men
    with soul and feelings always ready
    to leave their mouths with a breath.
    And, sleeping, they tell their affairs
    opening the door to others
    to the truth that lives in sleep.

> I lay with Cassio lately;
> and, being troubled with a raging tooth,
> I could not sleep.

> There are a kind of men
> so loose of soul that in their sleep will mutter
> their affairs.

Ci 'ntisi diri a Cassio: "Amuri duci,
Desdemona ti priu am'a stari accura,
tinemul'ammucciata sta passioni
cu l'arti ca ci voli e l'attinzioni
pi 'un darici a Otello cognizioni
di quantu stu piaciri n'arricrìa".
M'abbrazza, a manu strinci e mi cafudda
Ntà vucca na vasata accussì forti
Quasi scippannu i labbra a muzzicuni.
Doppu m'annagghia a coscia cu na jamma
mi strinci e mentri simula l'amplessu
mi vasa arreri e dici: "Malasorti
fu chidda ca ti desi ô ginirali".

OTELLO: Giuru ch'a scannu! A tagghiu pezzi pezzi!

IAGO: Voscenza si carmassi. Stassi cuetu.
Certu era sulu 'nsonnu.
P'aviri la cirtizza ancora è prestu.
Cchiuttostu mi dicissi, ginirali,
ci vitti mai pi casu un fazzulettu
a vostra mugghieri
strinciutu ntì manu
cu certi fraguluni ricamati?

OTELLO: Unu accussì ci l'avìa arrialatu:
fu propriu chiddu u primu pinzerinu
ca ci mannavu qann'eramu ziti.

IAGO: Sta cosa 'unn'a sapìa e 'nveci sacciu,
picchì cull'occhi mia l'haiu viduta,
ca Cassio s'asciucava a vucca e a varva
cu fazzulettu di la vostra sposa.

OTELLO: Si fussi propriu chiddu...

Intesi dire a Cassio: "Amore dolce,
Desdemona ti prego
dobbiamo stare attenti,
teniamola nascosta questa passione
con l'arte che ci vuole e l'attenzione
per non dare a Otello la percezione
di quanto questo piacere allieti".
Mi abbraccia, mi stringe la mano e mi preme
in bocca un bacio così forte
che quasi mi porta via le labbra a morsi.
Poi mi prende la coscia e con una gamba
mi stringe e mentre simula l'amplesso
mi bacia di nuovo e dice: "Mala sorte
fu quella che ti diede al generale".

OTELLO: Giuro che la scanno! La taglio a pezzettini!

IAGO: Calmatevi. State tranquillo.
Di sicuro era solo un sogno.
Per avere la certezza è ancora presto.
Piuttosto ditemi, generale,
avete mai visto a vostra moglie
stretto tra le mani
un fazzoletto
con delle fragole ricamate?

OTELLO: Uno così glielo avevo regalato io:
fu proprio quello il primo pensierino
che le inviai quando eravamo fidanzati.

IAGO: Questa cosa non la sapevo ma so,
perché l'ho visto coi miei occhi,
che Cassio si asciugava la bocca e la barba
col fazzoletto della vostra sposa.

OTELLO: Se fosse proprio quello...

I heard Cassio say: "Sweet love,
Desdemona, I prithee let us be wary,
let us hide this passion
with the art and care needed
not to give Othello the perception
of how this pleasure is enjoyable."
He embraced me, held my hand and smacked
a kiss on my mouth so hard
that he almost bit my mouth off.
Then he seized my thigh and with a leg
he held me and, as he mimed intercourse,
he kissed me again and said: "Bad luck
that gave you to the general."

'Sweet Desdemona

our loves

**And then, sir, would he gripe and wring my hand
cry 'o, sweet creature!' and kiss me hard,
as if he plucked up kisses by the roots
that grew upon my lips, then laid his leg
over my thigh, and sighed, and kissed, and then
cried 'Cursed fate that gave thee to the Moor!'**

OTHELLO: I swear I'll slaughter her! I'll cut her in pieces!

IAGO: Calm down. Don't fret.
It was surely just a dream.
It is too soon to be certain.
Rather tell me, general,
have you not sometimes seen
a handkerchief
spotted with strawberries
in your wife's hand?

OTHELLO: I gave her such a one:
'twas my first gift
that I sent her when we were courting.

IAGO: I know not that but I know,
because I saw it with mine own eyes,
that Cassio wiped his mouth and beard
with your wife's handkerchief.

OTHELLO: If it be that…

IAGO: …s'agghiunci a l'autri provi,
  ca certu 'un sunnu picca,
  e portanu a sintenza di cunnanna.

OTELLO: Iago talìami bonu,
  talìami mentri ciusciu
  (*soffia in aria*)
  talìami mentri ciusciu
  l'amuri e 'u ricunsignu ô paraddisu.
  Sinn'acchianassi e spirissi luntanu,
  ntù celu d'unni 'n jornu avìa caduto.
  Eccu! 'Un c'è cchiù! 'Ntall'aria s'ha'
    pirdutu…
  Vinnitta nivura comu lu 'nfernu
  nesci da to' tirribili caverna,
  pi fari giustizia
  sta manu accumpagna!
  E tu, pirdutu Amuri,
  lassannu a signuria,
  ci ha' cunsignari all'Odiu scettru e tronu
  chi stava ncardinatu dintra u cori.

IAGO: Stativi bonu!

OTELLO: Sangu! Sangu! Sangu!

IAGO: Stativi bonu! 'N pocu di pacenza:
  u vostru 'ntindimentu pò canciari.

OTELLO: Canciari, Iago? Mai!
  Darreri nun si torna!
  (*Otello si inginocchia*)
  Ora Iago m'inchinu.
  E stannu addinucchiatu
  a me' palora 'mpignu
  cu sacru giuramentu di vinnitta.

IAGO: 'Un vi susiti ancora.
  Stativi addinucchiatu.
  (*Iago si inginocchia*)

IAGO: …si aggiungerebbe alle altre prove,
  che certo non sono poche,
  e portano una sentenza di condanna.

OTELLO: Iago guardami bene,
  guardami mentre soffio
  (*soffia in aria*)
  guardami mentre soffio via
  l'amore e lo riconsegno al paradiso.
  Che se ne salga e sparisca lontano,
  nel cielo da cui un giorno era caduto.
  Ecco! Non c'è più! Si è perso nell'aria…
  Vendetta nera come l'inferno
  esci dalla tua terribile caverna,
  per fare giustizia
  accompagna questa mano!
  E tu, perduto Amore,
  lasciando il tuo potere,
  devi consegnare all'Odio scettro e trono
  che erano incardinati nel cuore.

IAGO: State calmo!

OTELLO: Sangue! Sangue! Sangue!

IAGO: State calmo! Un po' di pazienza:
  il vostro giudizio può cambiare.

OTELLO: Cambiare, Iago? Mai!
  Non si torna indietro!
  (*Otello si inginocchia*)
  Ora Iago mi chino.
  E stando inginocchiato
  La mia parola impegno
  A un sacro giuramento di vendetta.

IAGO: Non vi alzate ancora.
  State in ginocchio.
  (*Iago si inginocchia*)

IAGO: …it would add on to the other proofs
    that surely are not few,
    and bring a damning sentence.

OTHELLO: Look here, Iago,
    look at me while I blow
    (*he blows in the air*)
    look at me while I blow
    my love back up to heaven.
    May it go up and disappear far
    in the sky from whence it fell.
    There! It's gone! Lost in the air…
    Arise, black Vengeance from thy hollow hell
    to bring justice
    lead this hand!
    Relinquishing your power
    yield up, lost Love,
    thy crown and hearted throne
    to tyrannous Hate.

IAGO: Calm down!

OTHELLO: O, blood, blood, blood!

IAGO: Calm down! Patience, I say:
    your mind perhaps may change.

OTHELLO: Change, Iago? Never!
    There's no going back!
    (*Othello kneels*)
    now Iago I kneel.
    And by kneeling I here engage my words
    In a sacred vow of revenge.

IAGO: Do not rise yet.
    Keep kneeling
    (*Iago kneels*)

Chiamu a tistimoniari
li stiddi di lu celu
e tutti l'elementi
chi dunanu sustanza all'universu:
Iago 'mpigna la forza d'u so' 'ngignu
e metti manu e cori a lu sirviziu
d'Otello ca 'un si mirita st'offisa.
Mi 'mpignu all'ossirvanza
d'ogni cumannamentu
ca porta a cumpimentu la vinnitta
puru s'avissi a spargiri lu sangu.
(si rimettono in piedi)

OTELLO: Di chistu grann'amuri ti ringraziu.
    Entru tri jorna vogghiu ca mi dici
    chi Cassio si nn'ha' gghiutu a l'autru
      munnu.

IAGO: Facissi cuntu ca l'amicu Cassio
    fussi già stinnicchiatu sutta terra.
    Desdemona lassatila campari…

OTELLO: Signuri, malidici sta buttana!
    Sia sempri maliditta! Maliditta!
    Camina ora cu mmia, fraternu amicu.
    Vogghiu truvari lu giustu strumentu
    pi darici la morti a stu demoniu.
    E tu, accussì fideli, addivintasti
    lu me' locotinenti, onestu Iago.

IAGO: Vostru pi sempri, amatu ginirali.

OTELLO (*alzandosi in piedi*): 'Un pozzu
    stari fermu.
    Susèmunni e marciamu.
    Sentu ca caminari mi fa bonu.
    Marciamu, caminamu, caminamu,
    e macari curremu
    accussì mi svarìu…

Otello e Iago marciano insieme.

Chiamo a testimoniare
le stelle del cielo
e tutti gli elementi
che danno sostanza all'universo:
Iago impegna la forza del suo ingegno
e mette mano e cuore al servizio
di Otello che non si merita quest'offesa.
Mi impegno all'osservanza
di ogni ordine
che porti a compimento la vendetta
anche se dovessi spargere del sangue.
(si rimettono in piedi)

OTELLO: Di questo gran amore ti ringrazio.
    Entro tre giorni voglio che mi dica
    che Cassio se n'è andato all'altro mondo.

IAGO: Fate conto che l'amico Cassio
    sia già steso sotto terra.
    Desdemona lasciatela campare…

OTELLO: Signore, maledici sta puttana!
    Sia sempre maledetta! Maledetta!
    Cammina ora con me, amico fraterno.
    Voglio trovare il giusto strumento
    per dare la morte a sto demonio.
    E tu, così fedele, sei diventato
    mio luogotenente, onesto Iago.

IAGO: Vostro per sempre, amato generale.

OTELLO (*alzandosi in piedi*): Non posso
    stare fermo.
    Alziamoci e marciamo.
    Sento che camminare mi fa bene.
    Marciamo, camminiamo, camminiamo,
    e magari corriamo
    così mi distraggo…

I call as witnesses
the stars above
and all the elements
that sustain the universe:
Iago here devotes the strength of his wit
And puts hand and heart to the service
Of Othello, who does not deserve this offence.
I vow to comply with
every order
that brings to fruition his revenge
even if I need to shed blood.
(*they rise*)

Witness, you ever-burning lights above,
you elements that clip us round about

Witness that here Iago doth give up
the execution of his wit, hands, heart,
to the wronged Othello's service.
Let him command
and to obey shall be in me remorse,
what bloody business ever.

OTHELLO: I thank thee for this great love.
Within these three days let me hear thee say
that Cassio's not alive.

IAGO: Count upon friend Cassio
Being already under the earth.
Let Desdemona live…

OTHELLO: God, damn this lewd minx!
May she be damned for always! Damn her!
Walk with me, brotherly friend.
I want to find the right means
to put this demon to death.
And thou, so faithful, are now
my lieutenant, honest Iago.

IAGO: I am your own for ever, beloved general.

OTHELLO (*raising*): I can't stand still.
Let's stand and walk.
Methinks walking does me good.
Let's march, walk, walk,
perchance run
so I'll distract myself…

Othello and Iago march together.

OTELLO: Nenti! Nenti! Si pur unni
    spicciamu
    resta u pinzeru fissu e nun si movi,
    resta u pinzeru ccà ntù ciriveddu
    e scava comu 'n tarlu la so' tana.

IAGO: Nzoccu pinzati? Vasi?

OTELLO: Ca certu si vasaru…

IAGO: Abbrazzi e vasi luntani dill'occhi
    dintra quarchi ricoviru sigretu…

OTELLO: E vasi e tuccatine,
    carizzi, pumiciati…
    sti cosi certu 'un sunnu autorizzati…

IAGO: E starisi alla nuda cull'amicu
    'nsemmula stinnicchiati 'ncapu ô lettu…

OTELLO: Nuda ntù letto? E chistu nunn'è
    mali?
    Comu si fa a nun dàrisi pinzeru
    di chista cosa lorda e ripugnanti.

IAGO: Lassannu stare chistu, si ci dugnu
    a me' mugghieri 'ndonu un fazzulettu…

Iago interrompe la sua frase. Silenzio.

OTELLO: 'Un ti firmari! Parra! Chi vo' diri?
    Era megghiu si m'avissi scurdatu
    d'avirici arrialatu u fazzulettu.
    E 'nveci stu pinzeru 'un m'abbannuna:
    è chiovu fissu chiantatu ntù cori,
    'nfusca la menti e nun fa ragiunari.
    E dunca l'avi Cassio u fazzulettu?

IAGO: Ma chista è cos'i nenti a paraguni
    di quantu mi cuntò Michele Cassio.

OTELLO: Picchì, Michele Cassio dissi cosa?

IAGO: Disse nun sacciu cosa c'avìa fattu…

OTELLO: Niente! Niente! Se anche ci
    spicciamo
    resta il pensiero fisso e non si muove,
    resta il pensiero qui nel cervello
    e scava come un tarlo la sua tana.

IAGO: A cosa pensate? Ai baci?

OTELLO: Che certo si baciarono…

IAGO: Abbracci e baci lontani dagli occhi
    in qualche anfratto segreto…

OTELLO: E baci e toccatine,
    carezze, pomiciate…
    queste cose certo non sono autorizzate

IAGO: E starsene nuda con l'amico
    insieme stesi nel letto…

OTELLO: Nuda nel letto? E questo non
    è male?
    Come si fa a non darsi pensiero
    di questa cosa sporca e ripugnante?

IAGO: A parte questo, se dessi
    in dono a mia moglie un fazzoletto…

OTELLO: Non ti fermare! Parla! Che vuoi
    dire?
    Era meglio che mi fossi scordato
    di averle regalato il fazzoletto.
    E invece sto pensiero non mi lascia:
    è un chiodo fisso piantato nel cuore,
    oscura la mente e non fa ragionare.
    E quindi Cassio ha il fazzoletto?

IAGO: Ma questo è niente confronto
    a quello che mi raccontò Michele Cassio.

OTELLO: Perché, Michele Cassio cosa disse?

IAGO: Disse non so cosa avesse fatto…

OTHELLO: Nothing! Nothing! Even if we hurry along
    the thought is fixed and unmovable,
    the thought stays here in my brain
    and burrows like a woodworm.

IAGO: What are you thinking? About kisses?

OTHELLO: For sure they kissed…

IAGO: Embraces and kisses far from prying eyes
    in some secret hideout…

to kiss in private?

OTHELLO: And kisses and touching,
    caresses, petting…
    these for sure are unauthorized things…

an unauthorized kiss!

IAGO: And being naked with her friend
    together in bed…

OTHELLO: Naked in bed? And not mean harm?
    How can one not think about
    such a dirty and repulsive thing?

IAGO: That aside, but if I gave
    my wife a handkerchief as a gift…

Iago interrupts his phrase. Silence.

OTHELLO: Don't stop! Speak! What dost thou mean?
    I would most gladly have forgot
    I gave her the handkerchief.
    Instead this thought doesn't leave me:
    it's a thorn solidly stuck in my heart,
    it obfuscated the mind and prevents from thinking.
    So Cassio hath the handkerchief?

IAGO: That is nothing compared to
    what Michael Cassio told me.

OTHELLO: Why, what hath Michael Cassio said?

IAGO: He said — I know not what he did…

OTELLO: Fattu? Chi sta dicennu? Nzoccu fici?

IAGO: Si curcò… si infilò…

OTELLO: Dintr'a cu' s'infilò?

IAGO: Dintr'a vostra signura.

OTELLO: Ma propriu dintr'a idda?

IAGO: Dintr'a idda, supr'a idda, unn'egghiè…

OTELLO: Dintr'a idda, supr'a idda, unn'egghiè.
Buttana, buttanissima d'u 'nfernu!
U fazzulettu, a cunfissiuni
u fa…zzuletto, la cu…nfissiuni, u fa…zzuletto…
Diavulu chi cunfessi, ora t'abbruciu.
Opuru fari tuttu alla riversa:
prima abbruciari e doppu cunfissari.
Ahi ahi, staiu murennu, staiu trimannu…
Si 'un ci fussi quarchi cosa, oscura e senza nomu, cosa ca 'un si sapi diri, è certu c'a natura 'un si lassassi ntà nenti traviari — staiu trimannu. Sta cosa chi nni fa addannari — talìa comu tremu — sta cosa ca ntà fimmina 'un pò stari senza farimi strammiari — tremu comu n'aceddu vagnato — senza c'a testa accumincia a firriari e 'un si pò cchiù firmari. 'Un sunnu li palori ca mi fannu strantuliari — tremu e sugnu chinu di sururi. Bedda matri! Naschi, arricchi e labbra! Pussibili? 'Un ci crìu. Naschi, arricchi e labbra! Pi ddaveru? — a testa mi firrìa, 'un ci sugnu cchiù. Cunfissari? U fazzulettu! Lu dimoniu! — a vucca l'haiu ntà panza e pigghia u cori a muzzicuni… stu dimoniu…! 'un sugnu cchiù dda cosa chi parrava — u fazzulettu! — unni staiu jiennu?… unni staiu currennu?… c'è sulu u fazzulettu! U fazzulettu!

OTELLO: Fatto? Che stai dicendo? Che fece?

IAGO: Si coricò… si infilò…

OTELLO: Dentro a cosa s'infilò?

IAGO: Nella vostra signora.

OTELLO: Ma proprio dentro a lei?

IAGO: Dentro a lei, su di lei, ovunque…

OTELLO: Dentro a lei, su di lei, ovunque.
Puttana, puttanissima dell'inferno!
Il fazzoletto, la confessione,
il fa…zzoletto, la co…nfessione, il fa…zzoletto…
Diavolo che confessi, ora ti brucio.
Oppure fare tutto al contrario:
prima ti brucio e poi confessi.
Ahi ahi, sto morendo, sto tremando…
Se non ci fosse qualche cosa, oscura e senza nome, cosa che non si sa dire, è certo che la natura non si lascerebbe traviare da nulla — sto tremando. Sta cosa che ci fa dannare — guarda come tremo — sta cosa che nella donna non può stare senza farmi impazzire — tremo come un uccello bagnato — senza che la testa cominci a girare e non si possa più fermare. Non sono le parole che mi fanno andare in convulsioni — tremo e sono tutto sudato. Madre mia! Narici, orecchie e labbra! Possibile? Non ci credo. Narici, orecchie e labbra! Per davvero? — la testa mi gira, non ci sono più. Confessare? Il fazzoletto! Il demonio! — la bocca ce l'ho nella pancia e prende il cuore a morsi… sto demonio…! Non so più di cosa si parlava — il fazzoletto! — Dove sto andando?… dove sto correndo?… c'è solo il fazzoletto! Il fazzoletto!

Otello sviene. Iago lentamente lo raggiunge, constatando da vicino il suo crollo.

OTHELLO: Did? What art thou saying? What hath he done?

IAGO: Lie… got in…

OTHELLO: Got into what?

IAGO: Into your lady.

OTHELLO: Into her, art thou sure?

IAGO: In her, on her, everywhere…

OTHELLO: In her, on her, everywhere.
    Whore, great whore of hell!
    Handkerchief, confession
    hand…kerchief, co…nfession, hand…kerchief…
    Devil who confesses, now I'll burn you.
    Or do the opposite:
    first I burn you, then you confess.
    Ahi ahi, I'm dying, I'm trembling…
    If there weren't something, obscure and nameless, something that can't be named, it is certain that nature would not be swayed by anything — I'm trembling. This thing that drives us crazy — look how I'm trembling — this thing that can't stay in a woman without making me crazy — I'm trembling like a wet bird — without having one's head spin without ever stopping. It's not words that make me convulse — I tremble and I'm all sweaty. Mother! Noses, ears, and lips! Is't possible? I don't believe it. Noses, ears, and lips! For real? — my head is spinning, I'm no longer here. Confess? Handkerchief? O, devil! — my mouth is in my stomach and it's biting off my heart… this demon…! I no longer know what I was saying — the handkerchief! — where am I going?... where am I running? There is just the handkerchief! The handkerchief!

Othello faints. Iago slowly joins him, checking his fall from up close.

SOLDATO: "Quannu finisci amuri
    ntù Caos arreri torna lu pinzeru"
    a un certo puntu dissi u ginirali.
    Chi schiantu… chi caduta…
    Nta stu mumentu Otello s'ha' pirduto…
    'Un c'è… sinn'jiu… spirìu…
    A casa abbannunò lu so' pinzeru.
    'Un c'è cchiù sennu, 'un c'è cchiù
        'ntindimentu.
    È cosa iccata 'nterra e senza vuci.
    E ora? Comu si torna arreri
    ntù munnu unni ci su' l'autri cristiani?
    O si susi malinconicu e s'addanna
    manciannusi lu cori,
    circannu di livarisi di mmenzu,
    opuru acchiana arreri u ginirali
    'ncapu all'eroicu pedistallu
    facennusi aiutari
    pi nèsciri 'i sta sorta 'i cunfusioni
    dall'odiu chi cerca subito vinnitta.
    E chistu è lu stratuni
    chi pigghia u gran surdatu.
    Ntall'omu c'è na parti scanusciuta
    ca domina e suverchia menti e cori.
    Nuatri semu propriu lu misteru
    di comu arrispunnemu a stu cumannu,
    a sta palora d'ordini sigreta,
    puru si nun sapemu d'unni arriva.
    E si quarcosa 'ntacca sta palora
    allura tutta quanta la pirsona
    di corpu si cunfunni
    e perdi orientamentu e dirizioni.
    Cull'amuri chi finisci,
    tuttu Otello di corpu spirisci…

SOLDATO: "Quando finisce l'amore
    il pensiero torna indietro nel Caos"
    disse a un certo punto il generale.
    Che schianto… che caduta…
    In questo momento Otello si è perso…
    Non c'è… se n'è andato… sparito…
    Ha lasciato a casa il pensiero.
    Non c'è più senno, non c'è più
        comprensione.
    È una cosa gettata a terra e senza voce.
    E ora? Come si torna indietro
    nel mondo dove ci sono gli altri uomini?
    O si alza malinconico e si danna
    mangiandosi il cuore,
    cercando di levarsi di mezzo,
    oppure sale di nuovo il generale
    in cima al piedistallo d'eroe
    facendosi aiutare
    per uscire da questa specie di confusione
    dall'odio che cerca subito vendetta.
    E questa è la strada
    che prende il gran soldato.
    Nell'uomo c'è una parte sconosciuta
    che domina e sovrasta mente e cuore.
    Noi siamo proprio il mistero
    di come rispondiamo a questo ordine,
    a questa parola d'ordine segreta,
    anche se non sappiamo da dove arriva.
    E se qualcosa intacca questa parola
    allora tutta la persona
    di colpo si confonde
    e perde orientamento e direzione.
    Con l'amore che finisce,
    tutto Otello di colpo sparisce…

SOLDIER: "When love ends
    thought goes back into Chaos"
    said the general at some point.
    What a crash... what a fall...
    In this moment Othello is lost...
    He is not there... he's gone... disappeared...
    He left thought at home.
    There's no more sense, no more understanding.
    He is a thing strewn on the ground and voiceless.
    And now? How does one go back
    to the world of men?
    Either he gets up, melancholic, and he damns himself
    eating his heart out,
    trying to step aside,
    or the general climbs again
    on top of the hero's pedestal
    seeking help
    to get out of this sort of confusion
    of hatred that looks for immediate revenge.
    This is the way
    that the great soldier takes.
    In man there's an unknown side
    that dominates and towers over mind and heart.
    We are the mystery
    of how we respond to this order,
    to this secret password,
    even if we don't know from whence it comes.
    And if something tarnishes this word
    then the whole person
    suddenly gets confused
    and loses bearings and direction.
    With love ending
    all of Othello suddenly disappears...

Mentri saluta pi sempri a so' mugghieri
Otello a Otello stissu dici addìu.
U nostru ginirali scoppa 'nterra
picchì ntall'ossessioni e ntall'angoscia
svanisci tutta quanta la pirsona.
Curri dannatu, curri cu primura,
Otello ora pi chiudiri stu tagghiu
e 'un fari sanguinari a ferita.

Mentre saluta per sempre sua moglie
Otello a Otello stesso dice addio.
Il nostro generale cade a terra
perché nell'ossessione e nell'angoscia
svanisce tutta la persona.
Corre dannato, corre di fretta,
Otello ora per chiudere sto taglio
e non far sanguinare la ferita.

Mentre il soldato torna in proscenio, Iago scuote Otello fino a rianimarlo.

IAGO: V'aviti a cumpurtari comu 'n omu.
 'Ntu munnu nun si cuntanu i curnuti.
 Sti puvireddi tornanu ntù lettu
 e abbrazzanu i mugghieri mascariati
 du fangu di l'amuri clandistinu
 e restanu accussì tutt'inchiappati
 senza sapillu di dda purcarìa.
 Chiddu ca 'un si pò propriu suppurtari
 è spàrtiri lu lettu
 c'a fimmina buttana
 cridennula pi sbagghiu casta e pura.
 Nonsi. 'Unn'è cosa mia.
 Pi mmia megghiu canusciri e sapiri.

OTELLO: Sugnu ammiratu da to' granni
 scenza.

IAGO: S'ammucciassi n'anticchia agghiriddà.
 M'haiu a 'ncuntrari cu Michele Cassio.
 Circati di spiari di 'n agnuni,
 senza ch'iddu vi vidi,
 lu visu, l'esprissioni,
 si parra nzoccu dici,
 si ridi, si mi cunta quarchi cosa
 supra l'inquacchiu cu la vostra spusa.

IAGO: Vi dovete comportare da uomo.
 Nel mondo non si contano i cornuti.
 Sti poveretti tornano a letto
 e abbracciano le mogli mascherate
 col fango dell'amore clandestino
 e restano così tutti macchiati
 senza saperlo da quella porcheria.
 Quello che non si può proprio
  sopportare
 è condividere il letto
 con una donna puttana
 credendola per sbaglio casta e pura.
 No. Non è cosa mia.
 Per me meglio conoscere e sapere.

OTELLO: Sono ammirato da tanta saggezza.

IAGO: Nascondetevi un po' da quella parte.
 Mi devo incontrare con Michele Cassio.
 Cercate di spiare da un angolo,
 senza ch'egli vi veda,
 il viso, l'espressione,
 se parla ciò che dice,
 se ride, se mi racconta qualcosa
 delle schifezze con la vostra sposa.

As he for ever says good-bye to his wife
Othello to Othello himself says good-bye.
Our general falls on the ground
because in obsession and angst
the whole person disappears.
He runs, damned, he runs with haste,
Othello now to close this cut
and not let the wound bleed.

While the soldier gets back to the proscenium, Iago shakes Othello until he revives.

IAGO: You need to be a man.
    Too many cuckolds in the world to count.
    These poor wretches go back to bed
    and embrace their wives, masked
    in the mud of a clandestine love
    and get stained, unknowingly, by that filth.
    What is unbearable
    is to share a bed
    with a whore
    believing her, mistakenly, chaste and pure.
    No. it's not my thing.
    For me it's better to know.

        Good sir, be a man:
        there's millions now alive
        that nightly lie in those unproper beds,
        which they dare swear peculiar.

        O, 'tis the spite of hell, the fiend's arch-mock,
        to lip a wanton in a secure couch
        and to suppose her chaste.

OTHELLO: O, thou art wise; 'tis certain.

IAGO: Stand you a while apart;
    I have to meet Michael Cassio.
    Try to spy from a corner,
    without being seen by him,
    the face, the expression,
    if he speaks, what he says,
    if he laughs, if he tells me something
    of the filth with your wife.

        Do but encave yourself

        and mark the fleers, the gibes,
        and notable scorns
        that dwell in every region of his face.

Iu cu dumanni annagghiu l'argumentu
di comi, dovi, quannu si pirderu
dintr'a l'abissu scuru d'u piccatu.
Stativ'accura a lèggiri ogni gestu,
ogni mossa, ogni signu, ogni musioni.
Sti formi accussì chiari
diventanu cuncettu
pi rènniri cchiù forti
ntù cori a pirsuasioni
ca 'unn'è cosa 'nvintata u tradimentu.
Ma suprattuttu ci voli pacenza!
Si siti omu aviti a stari carmu.
O siti sulu un carricu di bili?
Circati d'ubbligarivi un cuntegnu.

OTELLO: Sentimi bonu, Iago, all'apparenza
carmu mi portu e chino di pacenza.
Ma chiddu c'ora ammuccia stu tiatru
è lu me' cori assitato di sangu.

IAGO: Chistu mi pari bonu. Ora jitivinni.
Iu vaju 'ncontru a ddu fangu di Cassio.

Io con le domande affronto l'argomento
di come, dove, quando si persero
nell'abisso scuro del peccato.
State attento a leggere ogni gesto,
ogni mossa, ogni segno, ogni movimento.
Ste forme così chiare
diventano concetto
per rendere più forte
nel cuore la persuasione
che non è una cosa inventata il
tradimento.
Ma soprattutto ci vuole pazienza!
Se siete uomo dovete stare calmo.
O siete solo carico di bile?
Cercate di darvi un contegno.

OTELLO: Sentimi bene, Iago, all'apparenza
sembro calmo e pieno di pazienza.
Ma quello che nasconde sta commedia
è il mio cuore assetato di sangue.

IAGO: Questo va bene. Ora andate.
Io vado incontro al fango di Cassio.

Otello si mette un po' in disparte. Sulla parete di fondo verranno proiettate delle ombre. Sono figure imprecise, opache. Macchie che si contraggono e dilatano emettendo suoni lontani e distorti. Saranno comprensibili solo le osservazioni e i commenti di Otello.

OTELLO: Sentilo comu ridi.
Puru si nun l'ammetti
Cu' ridi dici u veru.
Mentri ca ridi, iu ti conzu a festa.
E bravo ch'ora cunti lu piccatu
di comu m'allurdasti li linzola.
Ntà stu mentri lu to' nasu lo vju bonu.

OTELLO: Sentilo come ride.
Anche se non l'ammette
chi ride dice il vero.
Mentre ridi, io ti concio a festa.
E bravo che ora racconti il peccato
di come mi sporcasti le lenzuola.
In questo momento il tuo naso lo vedo
bene.

I will question him about
how, where, when they lost themselves
in the obscure abyss of sin.
Make sure you read every gesture,
every move, every sign, every motion.
These ways so clear
become an idea
that strengthens
in the heart the persuasion
that betrayal is not invented.
But most of all, patience!
If you're a man you have to keep calm.   *Or shall I say you're all in all in spleen*
Or are you just full of bile?   *And nothing of a man.*
Try to keep cool.

OTHELLO: Listen carefully, Iago, outwardly
I seem calm and full of patience.   *I will be found most cunning in my patience*
But what this comedy hides   *but — dost thou hear? — most bloody.*
is my bloodthirsty heart.

IAGO: This is fine. Now go.   *That's not amiss*
I will go face Cassio's mud.

Othello hides. On the back wall will be projected shadows. They are blurry figures, opaque. Spots that contract and expand emitting far and distorted sounds. Only Othello's observations and comments will be understandable.

OTHELLO: Look how he laughs already.
Even if he denies it
who laughs tells the truth.
While you laugh, I'll tear you to pieces.
Now you're telling the sin
of how you got my sheets dirty.
I can see your nose well now.

Manca sulu lu cani c'a su mancia
Doppu ca di la facci t'u scippavu.
Chi staiu virennu? Chiddu è u fazzulettu
Ca ci rialavu tannu a me' mugghieri.
E ora Cassio tantu lu disprezza
che già lu desi a nn'autra pi riàlu?

Manca solo il cane che se lo mangia
dopo che te l'ho staccato dalla faccia.
Cosa vedo? Quello è il fazzoletto
che regalai un tempo a mia moglie.
E ora Cassio tanto lo disprezza
che già lo ha dato a un'altra in regalo?

Le strane e contorte figure si dileguano. Poco dopo torna in scena Iago.

OTELLO: M'addivintò lu cori
    cchiù duru di na petra.
    'U pigghiu a cazzuttuni
    e si scunocchia a manu.
    U munnu nun ci havi
    Criatura cchiù duci.
    Putissi stari ô lato
    di quarchi 'mpiraturi
    pi fallu suttastari ô so cumannu.
    Stanotti già la vita l'abbannuna…
    Ntall'universu 'un c'è biddizza uguali.
    A cùsiri s'a fira
    c'avugghia dilicata,
    eccelli poi ntall'arti du ricamu.
    'Ncantevuli lu sonu
    ca nesci d'u so' liutu
    e canta cu na vuci 'i rusignolu
    ca l'orsu cchiù sirvaggiu l'ammanzisci.
    E comu ci camina l'intellettu …
    chi supira in artizza Muncibeddu.
    A fantasia poi l'havi scunfinata
    e aperta comu chidda d'un poeta.

OTELLO: Il cuore mi è diventato
    più duro di una pietra.
    Se lo prendo a cazzotti
    si distrugge la mano.
    Il mondo non ha
    creatura più dolce.
    Potrebbe stare a lato
    di qualche imperatore
    per farlo sottostare ai suoi ordini.
    Stanotte già la vita l'abbandona…
    Nell'universo non c'è bellezza uguale.
    A cucire è andata
    con l'ago delicato,
    eccelle poi nell'arte del ricamo.
    Incantevole il suono
    che esce dal suo liuto
    e canta con una voce da usignolo
    che l'orso più selvaggio si
    ammansisce.
    E come le funziona l'intelletto…
    che supera in altezza l'Etna.
    La fantasia poi ha sconfinata
    e aperta come quella di un poeta.

The only thing missing is a dog to eat it   **O, I see that nose of yours**
after I rip it from your face.   **but not that dog I shall throw it to.**
What do I see? That is the handkerchief   **By heaven, that should be my handkerchief.**
That I once gave to my wife.
And now Cassio scorns it so
That he has already given it to another as a gift?

The odd and distorted figures depart. Shortly after Iago gets back.

OTHELLO: My heart has become   **My heart is turned to stone**
   harder than stone.   **I strike it, and it hurts my hand.**
   If I punch it
   my hands gets broken.
   The world hath not
   a sweeter creature.
   She could be
   by an emperor's side
   and order him around.
   Tonight life is already leaving her…
   The universe contains no beauty equal to hers.
   She went to sew
   with a delicate needle,   **so delicate with her needle**
   she excels in embroidery.
   Enchanting is the sound   **an admirable musician**
   coming from her lute
   and she sings like a nightingale
   that could charm the wildest bear.   **she will sing the savageness out of a bear**
   And how her brain works…
   it surpasses Mount Etna's height.
   Her fantasy's unbridled   **so high and plenteous wit and invention!**
   and open as a poet's.

Alle loro spalle, in una remota lontananza come di sogno, la luce a poco a poco rivela la presenza di Desdemona con un bastone in mano. Si sta esercitando simulando i colpi da portare all'avversario in un eventuale combattimento. Questa visione continua fino alla conclusione del dialogo tra Otello e Iago. Alla fine la luce aumenterà, descrivendo un unico spazio per la scena successiva tra Otello e Desdemona.

OTELLO: E poi st'addivintannu un gran
  surdatu
  ca porta fin'in funnu lu cumannu
  si puri si jocassi la so' vita.

IAGO: Propriu pi sti dilizie
  cchiù miritèvuli di punizioni:
  cchiù 'nfami è cu' disperdi i so' virtuti.

OTELLO: Chistu è sicuru, Iago. Chi piccatu!
  Chi piccatu, Iago.
  Chistu è 'n gran piccatu!

IAGO: 'Un vi capisciu propriu, ginirali.
  Si a so' malignità tantu vi piaci
  lassati ca vi porta ancora offisa.

OTELLO: Appen'annagghiu 'a tagghiu pezzi
  pezzi!
  Iago, ti prju di darimi u vilenu.
  Stanotti. Stanotti. E quando ca 'ncontru
  è megghiu ca 'un ci parru vasinnò…
  poi va finisci chi la so' biddizza
  e di lu corpu la so' pirfizioni
  a menti mi cunfùnninu e lu dubbiu
  ci fa li scarpi a la risoluzioni.
  Stanotti 'u fazzu, quant'è ver'Iddiu.

IAGO: Sta cosa 'un si risolvi cu vilenu.
  L'aviti a suffucari ntù so' lettu,
  ntù lettu di l'amuri profanatu.

OTELLO: E poi sta diventando un gran
  soldato
  che porta fino in fondo un ordine
  se pure ne andasse della sua vita.

IAGO: Proprio per queste delizie
  è più meritevole di punizione:
  più infame è chi disperde le sue virtù.

OTELLO: Questo è sicuro, Iago. Che
  peccato!
  Che peccato, Iago.
  Questo è un gran peccato!

IAGO: Non vi capisco proprio, generale.
  Se la sua malignità vi piace tanto
  Lasciate che vi porti ancora offesa.

OTELLO: Appena l'acchiappo la taglio a
  pezzi!
  Iago, ti prego di darmi il veleno.
  Stanotte. Stanotte. E quando l'incontro
  è meglio che non le parli se no…
  poi va a finire che la sua bellezza
  e la perfezione del suo corpo
  mi confondano la mente e il dubbio
  faccia le scarpe alla risoluzione.
  Stanotte lo faccio, quant'è vero Iddio.

IAGO: Questa cosa non si risolve col veleno.
  Dovete soffocarla nel suo letto,
  nel letto dell'amore profanato.

Behind their backs, far as in a dream, light slowly reveals Desdemona with a stick in hand. She is exercising, simulating the strokes she would inflict on an opponent in combat. This vision continues until the end of Othello and Iago's dialogue. At the end, light will increase in intensity to give way to the following scene between Othello and Desdemona.

OTHELLO: Moreover, she is becoming a great soldier
    who will follow through an order
    should her life depend on it.

IAGO: For these qualities alone   **She's the worse for all this.**
    she's even more deserving of punishment:
    even fouler to dissipate her virtues.

OTHELLO: That's certain, Iago. Yet the pity of it!
    The pity of it, Iago.
    This is a great pity!

IAGO: I don't understand you, general.
    If you're so fond over her iniquity
    give her patent to offend.

OTHELLO: As soon as I get her I'll chop her into messes!
    Iago, get me some poison.
    This night. This night. When I see her
    it's better if I don't speak to her…   **I'll not expostulate with her**
    lest her beauty   **lest her body and beauty**
    and the perfection of her body
    confound my mind and doubt   **unprovide my mind again**
    unsettle resolution.
    This night, Iago, as God is my witness.

IAGO: Do not do it with poison.
    Strangle her in her bed,
    even the bed she hath contaminated.

OTELLO: Mi piaci lu to' sensu di giustizia.
   E quannu parri, Iago, 'un sbagghi mai.

IAGO: E quantu a Cassio: è Iago u beccamortu
   Ca prestu lu spidisci ô campusantu.
   A menzannotti v'u fazzu sapiri.

OTELLO: A vita mia accumincia a menzannotti.

OTELLO: Mi piace il tuo senso di giustizia.
   E quando parli, Iago, non sbagli mai.

IAGO: E quanto a Cassio: è Iago il becchino
   che presto lo spedirà al camposanto.
   A mezzanotte vi faccio sapere.

OTELLO: La mia vita comincia a mezzanotte.

Desdemona, che ha ultimato il suo esercizio marziale, si accorge della presenza di Otello e gli va incontro festante.

DESDEMONA: Che ve ne pare del vostro soldato?

OTELLO: Dunami la to' manu, amuri miu.

DESDEMONA: Che ve ne pare del vostro soldato?

OTELLO: Dammi la mano, amore mio.

Desdemona si avvicina e s'inginocchia davanti a Otello, come si trovasse di fronte a un padre confessore. Dopo qualche attimo di esitazione porge la mano a suo marito.

OTELLO: Umida daccussì 'un m'aspittava...
   Tutta vagnata sta manu, lu corpu
   ti suda 'nfunnu e sutta sutta avvampa...
   Poi 'n supirfici cu st'acqua si vagna
   la peddi di st'umuri e sti vapuri.
   Pi chistu tutt'i carni sunnu moddi...

DESDEMONA: La morbidezza delle mani
      è frutto
   della mia giovinezza e del destino
   che non mi ha riservato alcun dolore.

OTELLO: Umida così non me l'aspettavo...
   Tutta bagnata sta mano, il corpo
   ti suda in fondo e sotto sotto avvampa...
   Poi in superficie con quest'acqua si bagna
   la pelle di questi umori e questi vapori.
   Per questo tutta la carne è molle...

DESDEMONA: La morbidezza delle mani
      è frutto
   della mia giovinezza e del destino
   che non mi ha riservato alcun dolore.

OTHELLO: I like thy brand of justice. **Good, good, the justice of it pleases, very good.**
　　When thou speakest, Iago, thou art never wrong.

IAGO: And for Cassio: Iago is the undertaker **let me be his undertaker:**
　　who will soon send him to the cemetery.
　　I'll let you know by midnight. **you shall hear more by midnight.**

OTHELLO: My life begins at midnight.

Desdemona, who has finished her last martial exercise, notices Othello's presence and runs to him, jubilant.

DESDEMONA: What do you think of your soldier?

OTHELLO: Give me your hand, my love.

Desdemona approaches and kneels in front of Othello, as if in front of a priest. After a moment's hesitation she gives him her hand.

OTHELLO: I did not expect it to be so moist…
　　This hand is moist, your body
　　sweats deeply and underneath burns…
　　Then on the surface this water wets
　　the skin with these humours and vapours.
　　That's why the whole flesh is soft…

DESDEMONA: The softness of my hands is the product
　　of my youth and of destiny **it yet hath felt no age, nor known no sorrow.**
　　that has given me no sorrows.

OTELLO: Ricchizza e abbunnanza voli diri
 e cori ginirusu, chista manu
 accussì cauda, chi quasi si squagghia,
 accussì cauda, chi quarìa lu cori
 di tutti chiddi c'a ponnu tuccari.
 Essennu accussì cauda la to' manu
 Ci havi bisognu di mudirazioni
 pi fari scìnniri a timpiratura,
 ci voli u gelu di la prigiunia
 passata ô friscu dintra na galera,
 djunu poi ci voli e pinitenza,
 nu pocu d'esercizi spirituali,
 rosari a teccapigghia e divozioni,
 'nsomma rinunzia, misura e prudenza
 e suprattuttu mortificazioni
 picchì ccà dintra sentu un diavulettu,
 'u sentu ca si movi. E comu suda…!
 'U sentu ca si voli arribbillari…!
 Bona sta manu, onesta pi ddaveru
 Picchì sudannu svela lu so' 'nfernu.

DESDEMONA: Direi che è onesta invece
 solamente
 perché vi ha dichiarato la passione
 che a voi mi lega offrendovi il mio cuore.

OTELLO: Na vota ntà li stemmi e li blasuni
 era lu cori c'offriva la manu.
 E 'nveci ntà sti tempi dipravati
 ci sunnu sulu mani senza cori.

OTELLO: Ricchezza e abbondanza vuol dire
 e cuore generoso, questa mano
 così calda, che quasi si squaglia,
 così calda, che riscalda il cuore
 di tutti quelli che la possono toccare.
 Essendo così calda la tua mano
 c'è bisogno di moderazione
 per far scendere la temperatura,
 ci vuole il gelo della prigionia
 passata al fresco in una galera,
 digiuno poi ci vuole e penitenza,
 un po' di esercizio spirituale,
 rosari a ripetizione e devozioni,
 insomma rinunce, misura e prudenza
 e soprattutto mortificazione
 perché qui dentro sento un diavoletto,
 lo sento che si muove. E come suda…!
 Lo sento che si vuole ribellare…!
 Buona questa mano, onesta per davvero
 perché sudando svela il suo inferno.

DESDEMONA: Direi che è onesta invece
 solamente
 perché vi ha dichiarato la passione
 che a voi mi lega offrendovi il mio cuore.

OTELLO: Una volta tra stemmi e blasoni
 era il cuore che offriva la mano.
 E invece in questi tempi depravati
 ci sono solo mani senza cuore.

Desdemona si alza e accenna una corsa verso il fondo.

OTHELLO: It means richness and abundance
    and a generous heart, this hand
    so warm that it almost melts,
    so warm that it warms the heart
    of all those who may touch it.
    Your hand being so warm,
    moderation is needed;
    to lower the temperature,
    what is needed is the chill of captivity   **This hand of yours requires**
    spent in the coldness of a prison,   **a sequester from liberty**
    fasting and penitence,   **— fasting and prayer,**
    some spiritual exercises,   **much castigation, exercise devout**
    repeated rosaries and devotion,
    sacrifices, measure and prudence
    but mostly mortification
    because I sense a little demon in here,   **for there's a young and sweating devil here**
    I feel him move. And how he sweats…!   **that commonly rebels.**
    I feel he wants to rebel…!
    'Tis a good hand, a frank one
    because by sweating it reveals its hell.

DESDEMONA: I would say it's frank only   **You may indeed say so;**
    because it has declared the passion   **for 'twas that hand that gave away my heart.**
    that binds me to you, by offering my heart.

OTHELLO: It used to be that, among coats of arms   **The heart of old gave hands,**
    and escutcheons, the heart offered the hand.   **But our new heraldry is hands, not hearts.**
    Now, in these depraved times,
    there are only heartless hands.

Desdemona stands up and starts running upstage.

OTELLO: Unni sta' jiennu? Veni ccà, ti prju.

DESDEMONA: Che cosa vuole ancora il
mio signore?

OTELLO: Famm'abbidiri bonu
dintr'all'occhi.
Senza calari a testa!
Nta facci m'ha' taliari!

DESDEMONA: Di nuovo mi inginocchio
a supplicarvi:
cosa volete dire? Io non comprendo
il senso di parole
che suonano stonate
se dette in preda a furia sconosciuta.

OTELLO: Na cosa ora m'ha' ddiri:
cu' sì tu pi ddaveru?
"Che cosa sei tu?" pi essiri cchiù chiaru
ntà to' parrata a dumanna traducu.
"Che cosa sei?"! Nzoccu sì tu? Rispunni!

DESDEMONA: Vostra moglie, signore.
La vostra sincera e devota moglie.

OTELLO: Si t'a firi: giura! Accussì t'addanni.
Ma quannu mori e scìddichi ntù 'nfernu,
li diavuli virennuti ammantata
d'una luci celesti e ancelicata
t'addannirannu arreri p'u spaventu.
Giurami, si t'a firi, ca sì onesta!

DESDEMONA: Il cielo che ci guarda lo
sa bene.

OTELLO: U celu vidi a ttia e pinz'a lu
'nfernu!
Picchì sì fausa comu lu dimoniu.

DESDEMONA: Falsa con chi? Verso di
chi, signore?
Falsa in che modo? Non mi so spiegare…

OTELLO (*piangendo*): Desdemona, amunì!
A vo' finiri?
Vatinni! Ora ti supplicu: vatinni!

OTELLO: Dove stai andando? Vieni qui,
ti prego.

DESDEMONA: Che cosa vuole ancora il
mio signore?

OTELLO: Fammi vedere bene gli occhi.
Senza abbassare la testa!
In faccia mi devi guardare!

DESDEMONA: Di nuovo mi inginocchio
a supplicarvi:
cosa volete dire? Io non comprendo
il senso di parole
che suonano stonate
se dette in preda a furia sconosciuta.

OTELLO: Ora mi devi dire una cosa:
chi sei tu per davvero?
"Che cosa sei tu?" per essere più chiaro
ti traduco la domanda nella tua lingua.
"Che cosa sei?"! Cosa sei tu? Rispondi!

DESDEMONA: Vostra moglie, signore.
La vostra sincera e devota moglie.

OTELLO: Se ci riesci: giura! Così ti danni.
Ma quando muori e scendi all'inferno
i diavoli vedendoti ammantata
d'una luce celeste e angelicata
ti danneranno di nuovo per lo spavento.
Giuramelo, se ci riesci, che sei onesta!

DESDEMONA: Il cielo che ci guarda lo
sa bene.

OTELLO: Il cielo vede te e pensa all'inferno!
Perché sei falsa come il demonio.

DESDEMONA: Falsa con chi? Verso di
chi, signore?
Falsa in che modo? Non mi so spiegare…

OTELLO (*piangendo*): Desdemona,
andiamo! La vuoi finire?
Vattene! Ora ti supplico: vattene!

OTHELLO: Where art thou going? Come hither, I prithee.

DESDEMONA: What is my lord's pleasure?

OTHELLO: Let me see thine eyes.
    Don't lower thy head!
    Look in my face!

DESDEMONA: Upon my knee, I beg you
    what doth your speech import? I don't understand
    the meaning of words   **I understand a fury in your words**
    that sound off-key   **but not the words.**
    if uttered with unknown fury.

OTHELLO: Now thou hast to tell me something:
    who art thou, in truth?   **What art thou?**
    "Who art thou?" to be clearer
    I will translate the question in your parlance.
    "Who are you?" What are you? Answer!

DESDEMONA: Your wife, my lord,
    your true and loyal wife.

OTHELLO: Come swear it! Damn thyself.
    But when you descend to hell   **Lest, being like one of heaven,**
    devils, seeing thee wrapped   **the devils themselves**
    in a celestial and angelical light,   **should fear to seize thee.**
    will double damn thee out of fright.   **Therefore be double-damned**
    Swear, if thou dare, thou art honest!

DESDEMONA: Heaven doth truly know it.

OTHELLO: Heaven sees thee and thinks of hell!   **Heaven truly knows that thou art false as hell.**
    Because thou art false as the demon.

DESDEMONA: False with whom? To whom, my lord?
    How am I false? I can't understand…
OTHELLO (*crying*): Desdemon, come! Would thou stop this?
    Away! I prithee: away!

DESDEMONA: Che giorno incomprensibile
    e straziante…
  Non piangete…! Non piangete…!

OTELLO: Si puru a lu celu
  ci avissi piaciutu
  mittirimi alla prova cu duluri,
  opuru c'ogni sorta d'afflizioni,
  farimi chioviri a vijogna 'ntesta
  nsemmul'a tutt'un carricu 'i svinture
  e si m'avissi calatu ntù mari
  d'orribili miserie fin'ô punto
  d'agghiùttiri stu mali e d'affucari,
  opuru si m'avissi 'mprigionatu
  e cunnannatu a morti ogni spiranza,
  avessi mantinutu nquarchi agnuni,
  nquarchi minimo loco
  di l'arma smisurata,
  un pizzuddicchiu nicu di pacenza.
  Solu 'n pizzuddu m'avissi bastatu.
  E 'nveci arriducirimi a birsagghiu
  d'u tempu chi m'addita a so' zimbello,
  esempiu di taliari cu disprezzu
  ntà st'epuca di diginerazioni…
  E puru chistu avissi suppurtatu.
  Ma esseri scippatu di lu beni
  ch'aveva diliziatu lu me' cori,
  di chidda sula cosa
  che fa vàliri a pena
  di vìviri o murìri,
  la fonti dunni l'esistenza scurri
  se 'un voli arriducirisi a disertu,
  chistu daveru 'un si pò suppurtari…

DESDEMONA: Che giorno incomprensibile
    e straziante…
  Non piangete…! Non piangete…!

OTELLO: Se pure al cielo
  fosse piaciuto
  mettermi alla prova coi dolori,
  oppure con ogni sorta d'afflizione,
  farmi piovere la vergogna in testa
  insieme a tutto un carico di sventure
  e se mi avesse calato nel mare
  di orribili miserie fino al punto
  d'inghiottire sto male e di affogare,
  oppure se mi avesse imprigionato
  e condannato a morte ogni speranza,
  avrei mantenuto in qualche angolo,
  in qualche piccolissimo luogo
  dell'anima smisurata,
  un pezzettino piccolo di pazienza.
  Solo un pezzetto mi sarebbe bastato.
  E invece mi ha ridotto a bersaglio
  del tempo che mi addita come zimbello
  esempio da guardare con disprezzo
  in quest'epoca di degenerazione…
  E pure questo avrei sopportato.
  Ma essere derubato del bene
  che aveva deliziato il mio cuore,
  di quella sola cosa
  che fa valer la pena
  di vivere o morire,
  la fonte dove l'esistenza scorre
  se non vuole condurre al deserto,
  questo davvero non si può sopportare…

DESDEMONA: What a puzzling and heart-wrenching day…

Don't weep…! Don't weep…!   **Alas, the heavy day, why do you weep?**

OTHELLO: Had it pleased heaven
to try me with afflictions,
had they rained all kind of sores
and shames on my bare head,
along with a plethora of misfortunes
and had they dropped me in a sea
of horrible miseries until
I swallowed this pain and drowned,
or given to captivity me
and my utmost hopes,
I would have kept in some corner   **I should have found in some place of my soul**
in some tiny place of my infinite soul   **a drop of patience**
a teeny piece of patience
just a drop would have sufficed.
Instead, I have been reduced to a target   **but alas, to make me**
of time that points its finger at me with derision   **the fixèd figure for the scorn of time,**
an example to be looked at with scorn   **to point its slow and moving finger at!**
in these degenerate times…
Yet could I bear that too.
But to be robbed of the love
that had delighted my heart,
of that single thing
that makes it worth it
to live or to die,
the source from whence existence flows
to avoid running into the desert,
this is truly unbearable…

DESDEMONA: La mia lealtà…
come vi sfugge?

OTELLO: Chianciu, haiu l'occhi vunci,
ma certu 'un sugnu orbu
e vju la to' lialtà, nun ti scantari.
Sì onesta comu li muscuni virdi,
pilusi, ca ci pinnulìa d'a vucca
lu ciumi granni di bava 'mpastata
di pisciu co la mmerda
liccata mmenz'â strata.
O ciuri beddu e dilicatu, ciuri
ca 'mbriachi i sensi cu lu to' prufumu,
avissi statu megghiu pi lu munnu
si tu ccà mmenzu mai avissi nasciutu

DESDEMONA: Io non mi rendo conto
del torto che ho commesso.

OTELLO: A testa mi sbattissi forti ô muru.
E pi ddaveru nun mi dugnu paci:
chi cummittisti? — 'un ci pozzu pinzari —
chi cummittisti, sparti m'addumanni?
Si iu vulissi cuntari i to' piccati,
la vucca, i labbra e tutti li masciddi
m'addivintasseru tizzuni ardenti.
P'u fetu u celu s'attuppassi u nasu
a luna pi 'un taliari si vutassi
a n'autra banna e u ventu gran ruffianu
chi quannu passa è tutt'un vasa vasa,
pi 'un sèntiri sta sorta 'i purcarie
ntù ventri di la terra s'ammucciassi.
"Chi cummittivu?" Buttana e sfruntata!

DESDEMONA: Il cielo vede che mi fate
torto.

OTELLO: Picchì? Vo' diri can nun sì
buttana?

DESDEMONA: La mia lealtà…
come vi sfugge?

OTELLO: Piango, ho gli occhi sporchi,
ma certo non sono cieco
e vedo la tua lealtà, non t'impaurire.
Sei onesta come i mosconi verdi,
pelosi, a cui pende dalla bocca
un gran fiume di bava impastata
di piscio e merda
leccata in mezzo alla strada.
O fiore bello e delicato, fiore
che ubriachi i sensi col tuo profumo,
sarebbe stato meglio per il mondo
se tu qui in mezzo non fossi mai nata.

DESDEMONA: Io non mi rendo conto
del torto che ho commesso.

OTELLO: Mi sbatterei la testa forte contro
il muro.
E per davvero non mi do pace:
che hai fatto? — non ci posso pensare —
che hai fatto, per giunta mi domandi?
Se io volessi raccontare i tuoi peccati,
la bocca, le labbra e tutte le mascelle
mi diventerebbero tizzoni ardenti.
Per la puzza il cielo si tapperebbe il naso,
la luna per non guardare si volterebbe
da un'altra parte e il vento gran ruffiano
che quando passa è tutto un bacia bacia,
per non sentire questa sorta di porcherie
si nasconderebbe nel ventre della terra.
"Che ho fatto?" Puttana e sfrontata!

DESDEMONA: Il cielo vede che mi fate
torto.

OTELLO: Perché? Vuoi dire che non sei
puttana?

DESDEMONA: My honesty…
How can you miss it?

OTHELLO: I cry, my eyes are dirty,
but I'm not blind
and I see thy honesty, fear not.
Thou art as honest as green flies,
hairy, sticky slime
of piss and shit
licked in the streets
hanging from their mouths.
O, beautiful and delicate flower,   **O thou black weed, who art so lovely fair,**
inebriating the senses with your perfume   **and smell'st so sweet that the sense aches at thee**
would thou hadst ne'er been born!

DESDEMONA: Alas, what ignorant sin
have I committed?

OTHELLO: I should slam my head against a wall.
I can't get over it:
what committed? — I can't think of it —
'committed,' thou askest me?
Would I want to speak thy sins,   **I should make very forges of my cheeks**
my mouth, lips, and jaws   **that would to cinders burn up modesty**
would turn into burning coals.   **Did I but speak thy deeds. What committed?**
Heaven would stop its nose for the stench,   **heaven stops the nose at it,**
the moon would turn away not to watch   **and the moon winks;**
and the wind, great tease   **the bawdy wind that kisses all it meets**
who's all kisses when he passes by,   **is hushed within the hollow mine of earth**
not to hear this filth would hide in the earth's bosom.   **and will not hear't.**
'What committed?' Impudent strumpet!

DESDEMONA: By heaven you do me wrong.

OTHELLO: Why? Are you not a strumpet?

DESDEMONA: No!
Se il fatto di volere preservare
questo mio scrigno da ogni tocco impuro
significa non essere sgualdrina
allora, mi dispiace, non lo sono.

OTELLO: Ncà certu 'un sì sgualdrina, sì
buttana.

DESDEMONA: Non credo proprio.
Sull'anima mia.

OTELLO: Domando scusa, 'u sacciu, mi
sbagghiavu.
T'avìa scanciatu pi na gran buttana.

DESDEMONA: Che il cielo ci perdoni!

DESDEMONA: No!
Ma se il fatto di volere preservare
questo mio scrigno da ogni tocco impuro
significa non essere sgualdrina
allora, mi dispiace, non lo sono.

OTELLO: Ma certo, non sei sgualdrina,
sei puttana.

DESDEMONA: Non credo proprio.
Sull'anima mia.

OTELLO: Domando scusa, lo so, mi sono
sbagliato.
Ti avevo confusa con una gran puttana.

DESDEMONA: Che il cielo ci perdoni!

Otello esce. Desdemona, stremata, si stende per terra e si addormenta. Dopo qualche secondo il soldato le si avvicina come a portarle un ultimo saluto.

SOLDATO: "Ci sunnu cosi chi passanu.
Comu la vita.
Ci sunnu cosi c'arrestanu. Comu
l'amuri."
Chistu pari ca ti sta' 'nsunnannu.
Dormi. Com'è ca dormi?
Ora t'agghiunci lu to' sposu
p'ammazzariti, già 'u sai,
'u capisti bonu, eppuru dormi?
Picchì si pigghiata
Ntù 'nsonnu d'amuri.
Amuri ca 'un si ferma 'nnanzi a nenti,
amuri ca darreri nun ci torna.

SOLDATO: "Ci sono cose che passano.
Come la vita.
Ci sono cose che cessano. Come
l'amore."
Ti sembra di star sognando questo.
Dormi. Come puoi dormire?
Ora ti raggiungerà il tuo sposo
per ammazzarti, già lo sai,
lo hai capito bene, eppure dormi?
Perché sei presa
in un sonno d'amore.
Amore che non si ferma davanti a niente,
amore che indietro non torna.

DESDEMONA: No!
    If wanting to preserve   **if to preserve this vessel for my lord**
    this vessel from any impure touch   **from any other foul unlawful touch**
    means not to be a strumpet   **be not to be a strumpet, I am none.**
    then, I'm sorry, I am none.

OTHELLO: Of course, thou art not a strumpet, thou art a whore.

DESDEMONA: I don't think so. Upon my soul.   **No, as I shall be saved.**

OTHELLO: I beg thy pardon, I know, I was wrong.
    I took thee for a filthy whore.

DESDEMONA: O heaven forgive us!

Exit Othello. Desdemona, exhausted, lies down and falls asleep. After a few seconds the soldier gets close to her, as if to give her a last good-bye.

SOLDIER: "There are things that pass. Like life.
    There are things that end. Like love."
    You think you are dreaming this.
    Sleep. How can you sleep?
    Your groom will join you now
    to kill you, you know it,
    you understood, yet you sleep?
    Because you're caught
    in a love dream.
    Love that stops at nothing,
    love that can't backtrack.

Ora ch'u tempu strinci
e Otello t'u pirdisti,
Amuri è lu to' novu ginirali.
Sula camini, 'ncontru a la ruina.
Sula, 'ncontru a sta terra di nissunu.
Cu ti vidi passari vidi luci
'nflissibili, ustinata.
Putevi ammucciariti, scappari,
putevi addumannari aiutu a to' cucinu…
e 'nvece nenti. 'Un ti fermi. Camini.
Putevi cafuddarici
'n gran corpu di pugnali
ora ca ti 'nsignasti
a mulinari spati.
E 'nveci a n'atra 'nticchia
quannu ti veni a chiama u ginirali
darreri a iddu tu camini e 'un canci
    strata.
E cchiù iddu addiventa notti, abissu
    scuru,
chiossai pari divinu u to' splinnuri,
luci ca mancu a morti pò astutari.
A vita 'un ti 'ntiressa. È forsi vita
u tempu senza u tempu d'u disìu?
Pi ttia sarbari a vita 'unn'havi sensu.
Sulu ti premi sarbari l'amuri.

Ora che il tempo stringe
e hai perso Otello,
l'Amore è il tuo nuovo generale.
Cammini sola, incontro alla rovina.
Sola, incontro a questa terra di nessuno.
Chi ti ha vista passare ha visto la luce
inflessibile, ostinata.
Potevi nasconderti, scappare,
potevi domandare aiuto a tuo cugino…
e invece niente. Non ti fermi. Cammini.
Potevi sferrare
un gran colpo di pugnale
ora che ti ha insegnato
a tirar di spada.
E invece tra un altro po'
quando ti verrà a chiamare il generale
gli camminerai dietro e non cambierai
    strada.
E più lui diventa notte, abisso scuro,
più ancora sembra divino il tuo
    splendore,
luce che nemmeno la morte può
    spegnere.
La vita non ti interessa. È forse vita
il tempo senza il tempo del desiderio?
Per te conservare la vita non ha senso.
Solo ti preme conservare l'amore.

Il soldato si allontana. Desdemona sta ancora dormendo.

Un elegante Iago moderno, galeotto novecentesco e spinto all'introspezione, seduto su una sedia, aspetta che un pittore finisca il suo ritratto. È l'ora d'aria e il direttore della prigione gli ha consentito d'indossare per l'occasione l'abito scuro, con tanto di cravatta.

Now that time is running out
and you have lost Othello,
Love is your new general.
Alone you walk, towards disaster.
Alone, towards this no man's land.
Those who saw you pass saw the light
inflexible, obstinate.
You could have hidden, ran,
you could have asked your cousin…
But nothing. You don't stop. You walk.
You could have inflicted
an awesome dagger wound
now that he taught you
how to fence.
Instead, in a little while,
when the general calls
you will walk behind him an stay the course.
The more he becomes night, dark abyss,
the more divine your splendour seems,
light that not even death can extinguish.
Life does not interest you. Is it life,
time without the time of desire?
Preserving your life is meaningless to you.
Only preserving love makes sense.

The soldier leaves. Desdemona is still asleep.

An elegant modern Iago, introspective twentieth-century prisoner, sitting on a chair waits for a painter to finish his portrait. It's his yard time and the prison director has allowed him to wear a dark suit and tie for the occasion.

IAGO: Quantu tempu t'abbisogna ancora?
’Un m'a firu a stari fermu… t'arrimini?
Quantu ci metti a finìri stu ritrattu?
Ora ti cuntu quarchi cosa
ca forsi ti pò aiutari ntù travagghiu,
pi rènniri st'abbozzu cchiù pricisu.
Accuminciamu di lu nomu… Iago:
forsi veni di Santiago, u santu prutitturi
di la Spagna…
Età? Vintott'anni… l'età di lu giudiziu…
Riligioni? Dicunu ca sugnu satanista…
Inveci 'unn'è veru. 'Un sugnu nenti,
com'u Signuruzzu.
Sì, nenti…
Picchì, nzoccu è dda cosa ca chiamamu
Dio?
Nenti è… nenti:
è sulu fumu
c'acchiana 'n celu
mentri c'u munnu abbrucia.
Travagghiu? Era surdatu, ora sugnu
carciratu
p'istigazioni e participazioni
a plurimu omicidiu,
’ngannu, plagiu, altu tradimentu.
Mi piaci la licanza.
’Nfatti ci haiu a diri grazie
ô diritturi d'u carciri
ca mi detti sta cravatta
pi farimi stu bellu ritrattu.
Mi piaci l'oziu, l'oziu solitariu.
’Nveci a la genti
’un ci piaci stari sula.
’Un sapi stari 'mmersa
dintra la propria dispirazioni.
E cridi di scurdarisi sta cruci
jiennu firriannu a circari l'amuri.
Ca poi l'amuri è sempri
Comu tèniri 'n manu
nu specchiu diformanti:

IAGO: Di quanto tempo hai bisogno ancora?
Non ce la faccio a stare fermo… ti
sbrighi?
Quanto ci metti a finire sto ritratto?
Ora ti racconto una cosa
che forse ti può aiutare nel lavoro,
per rendere sto quadro più preciso.
Cominciamo dal nome… Iago:
forse viene da Santiago, il santo
protettore della Spagna…
Età? Ventotto anni… l'età del giudizio…
Religione? Dicono che sia satanista…
Invece non è vero. Non sono niente,
come il Signore.
Sì, niente…
Perché cos'è quello che chiamiamo Dio?
Non è niente… niente:
è solo fumo
che sale in cielo
mentre il mondo brucia.
Lavoro? Ero soldato, ora sono carcerato
per istigazione e partecipazione
a plurimo omicidio,
inganno, plagio, alto tradimento.
Mi piace l'eleganza.
Infatti devo ringraziare
il direttore del carcere
che mi ha dato questa cravatta
per farmi questo bel ritratto.
Mi piace l'ozio, l'ozio solitario.
Invece alla gente
non piace stare sola.
Non sa stare immersa
nella propria disperazione.
E crede di scordarsi sta croce
andando in giro a cercare l'amore.
Che poi l'amore è sempre
come tenere in mano
uno specchio deformante:

IAGO: How much time do you still need?
I can't stand still… would you hurry?
How long does it take to finish this portrait?
Let me tell you something
that may help you as you work,
to make this portrait more precise.
Let's begin with the name… Iago:
perhaps it comes from Santiago, the saint patron of Spain…
Age? Twenty-eight years old… the age of reason…
Religion? They say I'm a Satanist…
That's not true. I'm nothing, like the Lord.
Yes, nothing…
What is what we call God?
It's nothing… nothing:
it is just smoke
that ascends in the sky
as the world burns.
Work? I was a soldier, now I'm a prisoner
for instigation and participation
in multiple homicides,
fraud, plagiarism, high treason.
I like elegance.
I need to thank
the director of the prison
who lent me this tie
to have this nice portrait made.
I like leisure, solitary leisure.
People, though,
don't like to be alone.
They don't know how to wallow
in their own desperation.
And they think they can forget this cross
by going around looking for love.
In the end love is always
like holding a fun-house mirror:

supra videmu a facci di l'amata
ma sutta s'ammuccia lu nostru dilliriu,
sutta s'ammuccia la nostra miseria
ca s'apprisenta cu mintiti spogghi.
E puru a rilazioni d'ordini sessuali 'un
    m'intiressa…
'Un mi 'ntiressa tràsiri dintra a n'atra
    cosa.
E di mia stissu nèsciri 'un mi piaci.
Sugnu sempri ccà, pressu di mia,
o comùncui ntall'immidiati vicinanzi.
Certu, u fattu ca l'amuri 'un mi 'ntiressa
forsi è duvutu… almenu… si propriu
    haiu a pinzari
a na cosa 'mpurtanti da me' vita…
forsi quannu capivu p'a prima vota
ca i fimmini su' tutti buttani.
Eh, eh!
"Tranni li matri e li soru"… unu pò diri.
No, no, propriu li matri.
A cuminciari dalli matri su' buttani…
T'u dicu pi spirienza pirsunali.
Tannu avìa quartordici anni
e a me' matri ci vulìa cchiù beni da me'
    vita.
Pi mmia truvari na mugghieri,
quannu c'avissi statu,
avissi duvutu significari
truvari na fimmina comu a me' matri.
Mi parìa u ritrattu
dill'onestà, d'a gintilizza…
Passavamu 'nsaccu 'i tempu 'nsemmula
a parrari, schirzari, farinni carizzi…
E mi piaceva assai talialla
mentri ca discorreva cu me' patri
mentri ca si vasavanu p'a strata
cu tinirizza, dicennusi palori
ca parevano arrubbati
a li poeti antichi.

sopra vediamo la faccia dell'amata
ma sotto si nasconde il nostro delirio,
sotto si nasconde la nostra miseria
che si presenta sotto mentite spoglie.
E pure le relazioni sessuali non mi
    interessano…
Non mi interessa entrare in un'altra cosa.
E uscire da me stesso non mi piace.
Sono sempre qui, vicino a me,
o comunque nelle immediate vicinanze.
Certo, il fatto che l'amore non mi
    interessi
forse è dovuto… almeno… se proprio
    ci devo pensare
a una cosa importante della mia vita…
forse quando capii per la prima volta
che tutte le donne sono puttane.
Eh, eh!
"Tranne le madri e le sorelle"… si
    potrebbe dire.
No, no, proprio le madri.
A cominciare dalle madri sono puttane…
Te lo dico per esperienza personale.
Quando avevo quattordici anni
a mia madre volevo bene più della mia
    vita.
Per me trovare una moglie,
quando fosse venuto il tempo,
avrebbe voluto dire
trovare una donna come mia madre.
Mi sembrava il ritratto
dell'onestà, della gentilezza…
Passavamo un sacco di tempo insieme
a parlare, scherzare, farci carezze…
E mi piaceva tanto guardarla
mentre parlava con mio padre
mentre si baciavano per la strada
con tenerezza, dicendosi parole
che sembravano rubate
agli antichi poeti.

on it we see the beloved's face
but underneath hides our delirium,
underneath hides our misery
hiding behind a smokescreen.
Sexual relations don't interest me either...
I'm not interested in entering another thing.
Nor do I like to get outside of myself.
I'm always here, close to me,
or in the immediate surroundings.
Sure, the fact that love doesn't interest me
perhaps depends... well... if I really think hard,
on something important in my life...
perhaps when I first realized
that all women are whores.
Eh, eh!
"Except for mothers and sisters"... one may object.
No, no, mothers first.
They're whores, mothers before others...
I'm talking from personal experience.
When I was fourteen
and I loved my mother more than life itself.
For me finding a wife,
when the time would come,
would have meant
finding a woman like my mother.
She seemed to me like the portrait
of honesty, of kindness...
We used to spend a lot of time together
talking, joking, holding each other...
And I liked so much to look at her
while she talked with my father
while they kissed in the street
tenderly, exchanging words
that seemed stolen
from ancient poets.

Un jornu
c'avìa nisciutu prima di la scola
picchì n'avìa mancatu un prufissuri,
turnavu â casa prima d'u tempu.
Ci vulìa fari na surprisa
e mi 'nfilavu dintra
trasennu d'a finestra d'u curtigghiu.
M'avvicinavu â stanz'i lettu
dunni ogni notti
secunnu mia l'amuri rinascìa
tra me' matri e me patri
curcati ciancu a ciancu.
E 'nveci
già camminannu p'u currituri
sinteva strane vuci
comu d'armali c'a vucca appujata ntì
    cuscini…
'Unn'avìa mai sintutu a me' matri
cantari cu sta vuci di piacìri…
e u masculu 'un parrava forti
comu a me' patri
ma araciu araciu pi 'un fàrisi sèntiri
mentri facìa piccatu cu me' matri.
Accuminciavu a sudari,
u corpu mi trimava…
d'un latu vulìa scappari…
ma poi mi vinni forti a tintazioni
d'jiri a taliari.
E accussì fici… e vitti…
Vitti dda cosa
Ca l'omu 'un pò sapiri…
A vitti 'ncapu u lettu di me' matri…
Poi mi vutavu e senza diri nenti
niscivu arreri d'a finestra
comu si u latru avissi statu iu.

Un giorno,
che ero uscito prima da scuola
perché era mancato un professore,
tornai a casa prima del tempo.
Volevo farle una sorpresa
e mi infilai dentro
entrando da una finestra del cortile.
Mi avvicinai alla stanza da letto
dove ogni notte
secondo me l'amore rinasceva
tra mia madre e mio padre
coricati fianco a fianco.
E invece
già camminando per il corridoio
sentivo strane voci
come di animali con la bocca appoggiata
    al cuscino…
Non avevo mai sentito mia madre
cantare con sta voce di piacere…
e il maschio non parlava forte
come mio padre
ma piano piano per non farsi sentire
mentre faceva peccato con mia madre.
Cominciai a sudare,
il corpo mi tremava…
da un lato volevo scappare…
ma poi mi venne forte la tentazione
di andare a vedere.
E così feci… e vidi…
Vidi una cosa
che non si può sapere…
La vidi sul letto di mia madre…
Poi mi voltai e senza dir niente
uscii nuovamente dalla finestra
come se il ladro fossi stato io.

One day
that I had left school earlier
because a professor was absent,
I returned home sooner than usual.
I wanted to surprise her
and I got in
from a window in the courtyard.
I got close to the bedroom
where I thought
that every night love was reborn
between my mother and my father
lying next to each other.
Instead,
in the hallway
I heard odd voices
as of animals with their mouths on the pillow…
I had never heard my mother
sing with this pleasure voice…
and the man did not speak as loudly
as my father
but softly, not to be heard
while he sinned with my mother.
I started to tremble,
my body shook…
on the one hand I wanted to run away…
but then I was tempted
to go see.
And so I did… and I saw…
I saw something
that cannot be described…
I saw it on my mother's bed…
Then I turned around without a word
I got out of the same window
as if I were the thief.

E 'nveci dintr'a casa
c'era quarcuno ca s'avìa arrubbatu
a me' matri e a me' 'nnucenza
di picciutteddu 'nnamuratu di l'amuri.
Ddocu finìu lu jocu.
E u lettu 'un m'u spartivu mai
mancu cu me' mugghieri,
ca mi vosi pigghiari
sulu pi spicciari
li sirvizzi di la casa.
Na fimmina ci voli…
Ma sulu pi spicciari li sirvizzi…
U lettu no. U lettu nun si sparti…
U lettu servi sulu pi durmìri
Opuru pi studiari…
U lettu è megghiu di na biblioteca,
c'è tutta la duttrina di lu munnu…
'Un c'è bisognu di libbra
e mancu di lenti o cannucchiali
o viaggi o spirimenti…
basta curcarisi ntù letto…
e accuminciari a chianciri,
a chianciri cull'occhi ca s'abbrucianu
pu sali ca nesci u stissu quannu l'acqua
d'i lacrimi s'ha' prosciugatu.
Tuttu ntù munnu è chiantu,
tuttu è lamentu.
Tuttu ntù munnu è patimentu.
U restu è sulu 'ngannu,
tiatru, jocu di travisamentu.

E invece in casa
c'era qualcuno che si era rubato
mia madre e la mia innocenza
di ragazzino innamorato dell'amore.
Là finì il gioco.
E non condivisi mai un letto
neanche con mia moglie,
che mi volli prendere
solo per sbrigare
le faccende di casa.
Una donna ci vuole…
Ma solo per sbrigare le faccende…
Il letto no. Il letto non si condivide…
Il letto serve solo per dormire
oppure per studiare…
Il letto è meglio di una biblioteca,
c'è tutto il sapere del mondo…
Non c'è bisogno di libri
e nemmeno di lenti o cannocchiali
o viaggi o esperimenti…
basta coricarsi nel letto…
e cominciare a piangere,
a piangere con gli occhi che bruciano
per il sale che ne esce quando l'acqua
delle lacrime si è asciugata.
Tutto il mondo è pianto,
tutto è lamento.
Tutto nel mondo è sofferenza.
Il resto è solo inganno,
teatro, gioco di travisamento.

Buio.

Instead, at home
there was someone who had stolen
my mother and the innocence
of a boy in love with love.
The game ended there.
And I never shared a bed
not even with my wife,
whom I married
only to clean
the house.
You need a woman…
But only to clean the house…
Not for the bed. The bed can't be shared…
The bed is just to sleep
or to study.
A bed is better than a library,
all the knowledge in the world is there…
One needs no books
nor lenses or binoculars
nor trips or experiments…
just lie on the bed…
and begin to cry,
to cry with eyes that sting
for the salt that comes out when the water
of tears has dried.
All the world is tears,
all is wailing.
The rest is just deception,
theatre, perverse games.

Darkness.

Otello si avvicina a Desdemona vincendo il buio della stanza col piccolo lume di una candela.

OTELLO: A causa è chista. A causa è chista:
    'u sacciu.
  È chista la ragiuni, casti stiddi,
  ca 'un pozzu numinari picchì sona
  d'in facci a la purizza comu offisa
  A causa c'è. Ma certu 'un vogghiu diri
  c'ora accumincia u sangu a spargimentu.
  Nenti sangu, né tagghi, né firite:
  'un vogghiu guastari
  'nchiappari lu biancu
  di la so' peddi chiara comu nivi
  e liscia comu tomba d'alabastru.
  Ma c'havi a mòriri, chistu è sicuru.
  Spettanu uffiziu e 'ncarricu ô maritu.
  E scancillanu a idda
  d'u munnu si scancilla
  la 'nclinazioni so' p'u tradimentu
  ca pò tuccari ad autri doppu 'i mia.
  Ora facemu scuru.
  Prima astutam'a luci
  e poi astutamu st'autra bedda luci…
  S'astutu a vampicedda 'i sta cannìla
  'a pozzu, si mi pentu, riaddumari.
  Ma si ora ciusciu forti e astutu a ttia,
  ca sì l'esempiu d'ogni pirfizioni,
  a luci d'a to' vita 'un pò turnari
  mancu s'arrubbu a torcia di Prometeo.
  A luci to' s'astutu 'un si riadduma…
  E se ti coggiu, rosa, comu crisci
  doppu ca d'u jardinu ti scippavu?
  Lu ciuri pigghiatu
  sdisciura d'un ciatu.
  Vogghiu ciarari bonu lu prufumu
  ca nesci di la vucca di sta rosa
  stannu azziccatu cu nasu a lu stelu.
  (la bacia)

OTELLO: La causa è questa.
  La causa è questa: lo so.
  È questa la ragione, caste stelle,
  che non posso nominare perché suona
  come un'offesa in faccia alla purezza.
  La causa c'è. Ma certo non voglio dire
  che ora comincia lo spargimento di
    sangue.
  Niente sangue, né tagli, né ferite:
  non voglio rovinare
  sporcare il bianco
  della sua pelle chiara come neve
  e liscia come tomba di alabastro.
  Ma deve morire, questo è sicuro.
  Spettano al marito il dovere e l'incarico.
  E cancellando lei
  dal mondo si cancella
  la sua propensità al tradimento
  che potrebbe toccare ad altri dopo di me.
  Ora facciamo scuro.
  Prima spegniamo la luce
  E poi spegniamo quest'altra bella luce…
  Se spengo la fiammella di questa candela
  la posso, se mi pento, riaccendere.
  Ma se io ora soffio forte e spengo te,
  che sei l'esempio di ogni perfezione,
  la luce della tua vita non può tornare
  nemmeno se rubo la torcia di Prometeo.
  Se spengo la luce tua non si riaccende…
  E se ti colgo, rosa, come cresci
  dopo che ti ho rubato dal giardino?
  Il fiore colto
  appassisce in un attimo.
  Voglio annusare bene il profumo
  che esce dalla bocca di questa rosa
  stando attaccato col naso allo stelo.
  (la bacia)

Othello gets near Desdemona fighting the darkness in the house with the small flame of a candle.

OTHELLO: It is the cause, it is the cause: I know.
   It is the cause, you chaste stars,
   that I can't name because it sounds   **let me not name it to you**
   like an offense to purity.
   It is the cause. Yet I'll not shed her blood.
   No blood, nor cuts, nor wounds:
   I don't want to scar,   **nor scar that whiter skin of hers than snow**
   mar the white   **and smooth as monumental alabaster.**
   of her skin clear as snow
   and smooth as an alabaster tomb.
   Yet she must die, that's for sure.
   It is the husband's duty and chore.
   Erasing her,
   her propensity to betrayal
   is erased as well
   else she'll betray more men after me.
   Let's create darkness now.
   Put out the light,
   and then put out this other nice light…
   If I quench the flame of this candle
   I can, should I repent, its former light restore.
   But once blowing hard I put out thine,
   paragon of every perfection,
   thy light I cannot relume
   not even if I steal Prometheus' torch.
   If I extinguish thy light it does not relume…
   And if I pluck thee, rose, how dost thou grow   **When I have plucked thy rose**
   once I stole thee from the garden?   **I cannot give it vital growth again.**
   A picked flower   **It needs must wither**
   wilts in a moment.
   I want to smell the perfume
   that comes from the mouth of this rose
   my nose glued to the stem.
   (*he kisses her*)

Alitu ca mi porti mparadisu,
si a testa accussì tantu ora mi 'mbriachi
a spata va finisci ca mi cari
e 'un pozzu fari bonu u giustizieri.
Amuri, nautru vasu… nautru vasu…
ntù munnu 'un c'è figura
ca ti pò supirari in armunia.
E vistu ca ntà morti
lu corpu trova la so' pirfizioni
prima t'ammazzu e doppu t'amu ancora.
Nautru vaso. Ti giuro che chistu è
    l'urtimu
ti giuro nautru sulu, nautru sulu…
Ma comu pò na cosa accussì duci
ntù stissu mentri essiri fatali?
Basta di sugghiuzzari e sulu chiantu
pò nesciri di l'occhi
cu lacrimi crudeli.
Cilesti è lu duluri
Ca strinci a carni dunni trova amuri.
Eccu ca grapi l'occhi: s'arruspigghia.

DESDEMONA: Otello… mio signore…

OTELLO: Desdemona… chi fa'?
    T'addummiscisti?
Veni ntà stanza 'i lettu
e priparamu ntà bianchi linzola
lu postu diputatu ô sacrificiu.
Veni, acchianamu susu, caminamu.
Purtamu prestu st'attu a cumpimentu.

DESDEMONA (*completando la sua
    vestizione*):
Eccomi, mio signore. Fate strada.
Senz'incertezze il fedele soldato
vi seguirà sul campo di battaglia.

Alito che mi porti in paradiso
se la testa così tanto ora mi ubriachi
va a finire che la spada mi cade
e non posso far bene il giustiziere.
Amore, un altro bacio… un altro
    bacio…
nel mondo non c'è immagine
che ti possa superare in armonia.
E visto che nella morte
il corpo trova la sua perfezione
prima ti ammazzo e poi ti amo ancora.
Un altro bacio. Ti giuro che questo è
    l'ultimo
ti giuro un altro solo, un altro solo…
Ma come può una cosa così dolce
allo stesso tempo essere fatale?
Basta singhiozzare e solo il pianto
può uscire dagli occhi
con le lacrime crudeli.
Celeste è il dolore
che stringe la carne dove trova amore.
Ecco che apre gli occhi, si sveglia.

DESDEMONA: Otello… mio signore…

OTELLO: Desdemona… che fai? Ti sei
    addormentata?
Vieni in camera da letto
e prepariamo tra le bianche lenzuola
il posto votato al sacrificio.
Vieni, saliamo su, camminiamo.
Portiamo a compimento quest'atto
    presto.

DESDEMONA (*completando la sua
    vestizione*):
Eccomi, mio signore. Fate strada.
Senz'incertezze il fedele soldato
vi seguirà sul campo di battaglia.

Otello e Desdemona s'arrampicano sulla vetta di una camera da letto che sembra sospesa in cima a un monte.

Breath that leads to paradise **O balmy breath, that doth almost persuade**
if thou inebriatest me this way **justice to break her sword**
my sword will fall
and I won't be a good executioner.
My love, one more kiss… one more…
in the world there is no image
that can surpass thee in harmony.
And since in death
the body finds its perfection **Be thus when thou art dead, and I will kill thee**
first I'll kill thee and then love thee after. **and love thee after**
One more kiss. I swear 'tis the last one
I swear, one more… one more…
So sweet was ne'er so fatal.
Enough sobbing and only crying
can come out of eyes **I must weep**
with cruel tears.
This sorrow's heavenly
It strikes the flesh where it doth love.
She's opening her eyes. She wakes.

DESDEMONA: Othello… my lord…

OTHELLO: How now, Desdemona…? Didst thou sleep?
Come to the bedroom
and let's prepare, among white sheets,
the place for the sacrifice.
Come, let's go up, let's walk.
Let's get this over soon.

DESDEMONA (*getting dressed*):
Here I am, my lord. Lead the way.
The faithful soldier will follow you
on the battlefield with no hesitation.

Othello and Desdemona climb to the top of a bedroom that seems perched on a mountain.

OTELLO: Stasera li dicisti i to' preghieri?

DESDEMONA: Sì, mio signore.

OTELLO: E già facisti bonu.
Eppuru, si ntà testa ti suvveni
Quarchi dilittu ca 'unn'hai cunfissatu,
sullecita na presta assoluzioni.

DESDEMONA: Ahimè, cos'intendete, mio
signore?

OTELLO: Strata facennu, mentri caminamu,
battit'u pettu e grapiti lu cori
pi cunfissari ô celo li piccati
ch'ancora 'un ci dicisti a lu parrinu.
Ca certu nun ti vogghiu assassinari
prima c'u spirdu to' s'ha' puliziatu.
Puru si a ttia ti mannu all'autru munnu
l'arma 'un m'attocca, 'unn'a pozzu
ammazzari.

DESDEMONA: Parlate di ammazzare?

OTELLO: Certamenti.

DESDEMONA: Che il cielo abbia pietà…

OTELLO: E così sia!
Amen, cu tutt'u cori.

DESDEMONA: Se ancora vi ispirate al
vostro cuore
posso sperare che mi grazierete…

OTELLO: Chi dici? 'Un ti capisciu…

DESDEMONA: Perché impaurirmi proprio
non saprei
visto che in me non trovo
neppure l'ombra lieve di un peccato.

OTELLO: Ti dissi: arricanusci i to' piccati.

DESDEMONA: L'amore che vi porto è il
mio peccato.

OTELLO: Ha' mòriri pi chistu.

OTELLO: Stasera le hai dette le preghiere?

DESDEMONA: Sì, mio signore.

OTELLO: E hai fatto bene.
Eppure, se ti viene in mente
qualche delitto che non hai confessato,
richiedi una veloce assoluzione.

DESDEMONA: Ahimè, cos'intendete, mio
signore?

OTELLO: Strada facendo, mentre
camminiamo,
battiti il petto e apriti il cuore
per confessare al cielo i peccati
che ancora non hai detto al prete.
Che certo non ti voglio assassinare
prima che il tuo spirito si sia pulito.
Anche se ti mando all'altro mondo
l'anima non mi tocca, non ti posso
ammazzare.

DESDEMONA: Parlate di ammazzare?

OTELLO: Certamente.

DESDEMONA: Che il cielo abbia pietà…

OTELLO: E così sia!
Amen, con tutto il cuore.

DESDEMONA: Se ancora vi ispirate al
vostro cuore
posso sperare che mi grazierete…

OTELLO: Che dici? Non ti capisco…

DESDEMONA: Perché impaurirmi proprio
non saprei
visto che in me non trovo
neppure l'ombra lieve di un peccato.

OTELLO: Ti ho detto: ammetti i tuoi
peccati.

DESDEMONA: L'amore che vi porto è il
mio peccato.

OTELLO: Devi morire per questo.

OTHELLO: Have you prayed tonight?

DESDEMONA: Ay, my lord.

OTHELLO: You did well.
 If you bethink yourself of any crime
 unreconciled as yet to heaven and grace
 solicit for it straight.

DESDEMONA: Alas, my lord, what may you mean by that?

OTHELLO: Along the way, as we walk,
 beat your chest and open your heart
 to confess to heaven the sins
 that you have not confessed to the priest yet.
 I would not kill
 thy unpreparèd spirit.
 Even if I send thee to the other world
 thy soul does not belong to me, I can't kill thee.

DESDEMONA: Talk you of killing?

OTHELLO: Ay, I do.

DESDEMONA: Then heaven have mercy on me…

OTHELLO: So let it be!
 Amen, with all my heart.

DESDEMONA: If you talk about your heart   **If you say so, I hope you will not kill me.**
 I may still hope you'll spare me.

OTHELLO: What sayest thou? I don't understand thee…

DESDEMONA: Why I should fear I know not
 since guiltiness I know not, not at all.

OTHELLO: I told thee: think on thy sins.

DESDEMONA: They are loves I bear to you.

OTHELLO: Ay, and for that thou diest.

DESDEMONA: È innaturale
la morte che assassina per amore.
Ahimè, perché ora vi mordete il labbro?
Sembra che una passione sanguinaria
il corpo vi attraversi. Sono segni
che non lasciano dubbi. Eppure spero
che non riguardi me la vostra furia.

OTELLO: Zìttati du' minuti
e dimmi n'autra cosa.

DESDEMONA: Risponderò a ogni cosa
che chiedete.

OTELLO: U fazzulettu chi t'avìa rialatu,
inveci di sarballu
ci 'u cunsignasti a Cassio!
'U sa' quantu l'amava e ci tinìa…

DESDEMONA: Giuro sulla mia vita e sul
destino
che attende la mia anima immortale
che questo non è vero. E se volete
chiamate Cassio e a lui stesso chiedete.

OTELLO: Ti staiu cunzannu u lettu di la
morti:
vidi di stari accura a lu spirgiuru.

DESDEMONA: Sto per morire?

OTELLO: Certu. Esattamenti.
E puru s'insistisci a spirgiurari
ormai pi ttia nun cancia la sintenza:
è cosa certa ca t'haiu ammazzari.

DESDEMONA: E allora che il Signore
abbia pietà di me.

OTELLO: E iu rispunnu: "Amen"!

DESDEMONA: Chiedo pietà anche a voi.
Mai nella vita
vi ho fatto torto e non ho amato Cassio
se non di quell'affetto consentito
dagli usi di una semplice amicizia.
Il fazzoletto poi non gliel'ho dato.

DESDEMONA: È innaturale
la morte che assassina per amore.
Ahimè, perché ora vi mordete il labbro?
Sembra che una passione sanguinaria
il corpo vi attraversi. Sono segni
che non lasciano dubbi. Eppure spero
che non riguardi me la vostra furia.

OTELLO: Stai zitta due minuti
e dimmi un'altra cosa.

DESDEMONA: Risponderò a ogni cosa
che chiedete.

OTELLO: Il fazzoletto che ti avevo regalato,
invece di conservarlo
lo desti a Cassio!
Lo sai quanto lo amassi e ci tenessi…

DESDEMONA: Giuro sulla mia vita e sul
destino
che attende la mia anima immortale
che questo non è vero. E se volete
chiamate Cassio e a lui stesso chiedete.

OTELLO: Ti sto preparando il letto della
morte:
vedi di stare attenta allo spergiuro.

DESDEMONA: Sto per morire?

OTELLO: Certo. Esattamente.
E anche se insisti a spergiurare
ormai per te non cambia la sentenza:
è cosa certa che ti devo ammazzare.

DESDEMONA: E allora che il Signore
abbia pietà di me.

OTELLO: E io rispondo: "Amen"!

DESDEMONA: Chiedo pietà anche a voi.
Mai nella vita
vi ho fatto torto e non ho amato Cassio
se non di quell'affetto consentito
dagli usi di una semplice amicizia.
Il fazzoletto poi non gliel'ho dato.

DESDEMONA: That death's unnatural
    that kills for loving.
    Alas, why gnaw you so your nether lip?
    Some bloody passion
    shakes your very frame. They are
    unmistakable signs. But yet I hope
    that your fury does not point on me.

OTHELLO: Peace, be silent for two minutes
    and tell me something else

DESDEMONA: I will answer anything you ask.

OTHELLO: That handkerchief which I gave thee,
    instead of keeping it
    thou gav'st to Cassio!
    Thou knowest how I loved and cherished it…

DESDEMONA: By my life and the destiny
    that awaits my immortal soul
    I swear 'tis not true. Send for Cassio
    and ask him.

OTHELLO: I'm preparing thee thy death-bed:
    take heed of perjury.

DESDEMONA: I'm about to die?

OTHELLO: Yes, presently.
    Even if thou insist in thy perjury
    the sentence is the same:
    it is certain that I have to kill thee.

DESDEMONA: Then Lord
    have mercy on me.

OTHELLO: I say, Amen!

DESDEMONA: And have you mercy too. I never did
    offend you in my life; never loved Cassio
    if not with that affection allowed
    by the customs of a simple friendship.
    I never gave him the handkerchief.

OTELLO: M'ha' ffari bistimiari? U fazzulettu
ci 'u vitti ntì so' manu, traditura!
U cori tu accussì m'u fa' di petra
e chiddu ca pi mmia era 'n sacrificiu
— e a parti ca facìa era u sacerdoti —
ora addiventa sulu scannatina,
ammazzatina senza cirimonia.
T'u dicu arreri: 'u vitti u fazzulettu!

DESDEMONA: Allora certamente l'ha trovato.
Mandatelo a chiamare e che confessi
in che maniera se n'è impossessato.

OTELLO: Cunfissò?

DESDEMONA: Che cosa?

OTELLO: Chi c'era cosa.

DESDEMONA: Qualcosa di non lecito tra noi?

OTELLO: E puru m'addumanni?

DESDEMONA: Non lo può dire.

OTELLO: Nenti oramai pò diri.
A vucca ci attuppò l'onesto Iago.

DESDEMONA: Cosa intendete? Allora forse è morto?

OTELLO: Si Cassio avissi avuto tanti vite
quantu capiddi ca ci aveva 'ntesta
tutti d'un corpu l'avissi affruntati
e tutti massacrati pi vinnitta.

DESDEMONA: Povero Cassio, alle spalle tradito.
E povera Desdemona perduta.

OTELLO: Ma comu nun t'affrunti
di chianciri pi Cassio 'nfaci a mmia!

DESDEMONA: Mandatemi in esilio, se volete.
Ma vi scongiuro: no, non mi uccidete.

OTELLO: Grandissima buttana.

OTELLO: Mi vuoi far bestemmiare? Il fazzoletto
gliel'ho visto tra le mani, traditrice!
Il cuore tu così me lo rendi di pietra
e quello che per me era un sacrificio
— e la parte che avevo era quella del sacerdote —
adesso diventa solo un'esecuzione,
un'ammazzata senza cerimonia.
Te lo dico di nuovo: il fazzoletto l'ho visto!

DESDEMONA: Allora certamente l'ha trovato.
Mandatelo a chiamare e che confessi
in che maniera se n'è impossessato.

OTELLO: Ha confessato?

DESDEMONA: Che cosa?

OTELLO: Che c'era cosa.

DESDEMONA: Qualcosa di non lecito tra noi?

OTELLO: Me lo domandi pure?

DESDEMONA: Non lo può dire.

OTELLO: Non può dire più niente oramai.
La bocca gli ha chiuso l'onesto Iago.

DESDEMONA: Cosa intendete? Allora forse è morto?

OTELLO: Se Cassio avesse avuto tante vite
quanti capelli aveva in testa
tutti insieme li avrei affrontati
e tutti massacrati per vendetta.

DESDEMONA: Povero Cassio, alle spalle tradito.
E povera Desdemona perduta.

OTELLO: Ma come non ti vergogni
di piangere per Cassio di fronte a me!

DESDEMONA: Mandatemi in esilio, se volete.
Ma vi scongiuro: no, non mi uccidete.

OTELLO: Grandissima puttana.

OTHELLO: Dost thou want me to curse? I saw
 my handkerchief in's hand, traitor!
 Thou dost stone my heart
 and makes me call what I intend to do
 — and I pictured myself the high priest —
 a murder, which I thought a sacrifice,
 a killing with no ceremony.
 I repeat: I saw the handkerchief!

DESDEMONA: He found it then.
 Send for him and let him confess
 how he came in possession of it.

OTHELLO: He hath confessed?

DESDEMONA: What, my lord?

OTHELLO: That he hath used thee.

DESDEMONA: How? Unlawfully?

OTHELLO: Thou askst?

DESDEMONA: He will not say so.

OTHELLO: He can no longer say anything.
 Honest Iago hath ta'en order.   **No, his mouth is stopped**

DESDEMONA: What do you mean? What, is he dead?

OTHELLO: Had Cassio had as many lives
 as hair on his head   **Had all his hairs been lives, my great revenge**
 all together I would have faced them   **had stomach for them all.**
 and all together massacred for revenge.

DESDEMONA: Alas, Cassio is betrayed.
 and Desdemona undone.

OTHELLO: Art thou not ashamed   **Weep'st thou for him to my face?**
 to weep for him to my face!

DESDEMONA: Banish me, if you wish.
 But I prithee: kill me not.

OTHELLO: Down strumpet.

DESDEMONA: Ammazzatemi domani,
vi prego.
Un'altra notte fatemi gustare
la gioia sconfinata della vita.

OTELLO: 'Un si nni parra propriu.

DESDEMONA: Ancora una mezz'ora.

OTELLO: Sta cosa s'havi a ffari.

DESDEMONA: Il tempo di finire una
preghiera.

OTELLO: Si fici tardu. Ormai si fici tardu.

DESDEMONA: Signore, vi scongiuro, mio
signore…

OTELLO: Picchì sta mania di ristari 'n vita?
'Unn'u capisti ca nun sì cchiù nenti?

DESDEMONA: Se davvero per voi non
sono niente
lasciatemi cadere lentamente
nel cuore dell'abisso, nel suo fondo,
e non con una mano svelta e sbrigativa.

OTELLO: 'U sa'? C'è nenti e nenti.
Pi mmia stu nenti, u to' assoluto nenti,
hav'a stari ammucciatu sutta terra.
Iu vogghiu caminari ntà stu munnu
senza lu scantu di 'ncuntrari arreri
stu nenti ca mi fici 'nnamurari.

DESDEMONA: E allora fate quello che
dovete
guardandomi negli occhi con amore.
La morte in questo modo…
è dolce sopportare…

DESDEMONA: Ammazzatemi domani,
vi prego.
Un'altra notte fatemi gustare
la gioia sconfinata della vita.

OTELLO: Non se ne parla proprio.

DESDEMONA: Ancora una mezz'ora.

OTELLO: Questa cosa s'ha da fare.

DESDEMONA: Il tempo di finire una
preghiera.

OTELLO: Si è fatto tardi. Ormai si è fatto
tardi.

DESDEMONA: Signore, vi scongiuro, mio
signore…

OTELLO: Perché sta mania di restare in vita?
Non lo capisci che non sei più niente?

DESDEMONA: Se davvero per voi non
sono niente
lasciatemi cadere lentamente
nel cuore dell'abisso, nel suo fondo,
e non con una mano svelta e sbrigativa.

OTELLO: Lo sai? C'è niente e niente
Per me sto niente, il tuo niente assoluto,
deve stare nascosto sotto terra.
Io voglio camminare in questo mondo
senza la paura di incontrare di nuovo
questo niente che mi fece innamorare.

DESDEMONA: E allora fate quello che
dovete
guardandomi negli occhi con amore
La morte in questo modo…
è dolce sopportare…

Desdemona consegna a Otello il pugnale ricevuto durante il corteggiamento.

DESDEMONA: Kill me tomorrow, I beseech you.
　　Let me enjoy another night
　　the boundless joy of life.

OTHELLO: Not a chance.

DESDEMONA: But half an hour?

OTHELLO: This has to be done.

DESDEMONA: The time to say a prayer.

OTHELLO: It is too late. It is too late now.

DESDEMONA: Lord, I beseech you, my lord…

OTHELLO: Why this obsession with staying alive?
　　Don't you understand you're nothing now?

DESDEMONA: If for you I'm really nothing
　　let me fall slowly
　　in the heart of the abyss, at its bottom,
　　not with quick and hurried hand.

OTHELLO: You know? There are different kinds of nothing.
　　For me this nothing, your absolute nothing,
　　you have to remain hidden underground
　　I want to walk this earth
　　without fear to run into
　　this nothing that made me fall in love.

DESDEMONA: Then do what you must
　　looking at me with eyes of love.
　　Death this way…
　　is sweet to endure…

Desdemona gives Othello the dagger received during their courtship.

Let me live tonight

DESDEMONA: Volevo diventare
per te come la spada
o come il tuo pugnale
con cui sferrare quel colpo segreto
che nell'ora del pericolo estremo
assicura la vita.
Un'arma nelle tue mani.
Un'arma scintillante e fedele.
Come la lama che presto mi uccide…

OTELLO: Nessuna lama, solo mani, amore.
Adesso ti addormento
senza sangue, né tagli, né ferite.
Con le mie mani ti addormento, amore.

DESDEMONA: Ricordi il tempo delle
passeggiate
Ci fermavamo quasi ad ogni passo
ad ascoltare come fa la notte
quando si calma il vento.
E sentivamo che lì dentro,
nel mondo all'improvviso silenzioso,
solo noi eravamo vivi,
solo noi guardavamo la luna.

Otello si avvicina alla sua sposa e le stringe il collo fino a soffocarla.

OTELLO: Adesso dormi! Dormi! Dormi!
Dormi!

Buio.

Il soldato sta finendo di indossare l'equipaggiamento per il viaggio che lo porterà insieme a Otello sulla luna.

SOLDATO: E daccussì sta storia finìu 'n tragedia… E quannu dicu storia sentu diri cuntu, che sempri a storia è cuntu, discursu, costruzioni. Pi chistu 'un pò chi essiri 'nvinzioni.

DESDEMONA: Volevo diventare
per te come la spada
o come il tuo pugnale
con cui sferrare quel colpo segreto
che nell'ora del pericolo estremo
assicura la vita.
Un'arma nelle tue mani.
Un'arma scintillante e fedele.
Come la lama che presto mi uccide…

OTELLO: Nessuna lama, solo mani, amore.
Adesso ti addormento
senza sangue, né tagli, né ferite.
Con le mie mani ti addormento, amore.

DESDEMONA: Ricordi il tempo delle
passeggiate?
Ci fermavamo quasi ad ogni passo
ad ascoltare come fa la notte
quando si calma il vento.
E sentivamo che lì dentro,
nel mondo all'improvviso silenzioso,
solo noi eravamo vivi,
solo noi guardavamo la luna.

OTELLO: Adesso dormi! Dormi! Dormi!
Dormi!

SOLDATO: E così sta storia finì in tragedia… E quando dico storia intendo racconto, che la storia è sempre un racconto, discorso, costruzione. Per questo non può che essere invenzione.

DESDEMONA: I wanted to be
    for you the sword
    or your dagger
    that inflicts that secret strike
    that in utmost danger
    insures life.
    A weapon in your hands.
    A shiny and faithful weapon.
    Like the blade that will soon kill me…

OTHELLO: No blade, just hands, love.
    Now I'll make you sleep
    With no blood, nor cuts, nor wounds.
    I'll make you sleep with my hands, love.

DESDEMONA: Do you remember our strolls?
    We used to stop at almost every step
    to listen to what the night does
    when the wind subsides.
    And we felt that there,
    in the suddenly silent world,
    we alone were alive,
    we alone looked at the moon.

Othello gets closer to his bride and chokes her until she dies.

OTHELLO: Now sleep! Sleep! Sleep! Sleep!

Darkness.

The soldier is gearing up for the journey that will take him and Othello on the moon.

SOLDIER: And so history ended in tragedy… and when I say history I mean tale, because history is always a story, a discourse, a fabrication. That's why it can only be invention.

Eppuru m'avissi piaciutu essiri amicu strittu d'Otello, avirici cunfidenza e aiutallo a nèsciri d'a cunfusioni. Ma 'un fu pussibili. E stu dispiaciri m'u portu cu mmia ogni notti quannu mi va curcu ntù lettu. Ma prima di salutarivi vi vulìa cuntari u 'nsonnu ca fici quarchi jornu narreri. U 'nsunnu stranu, unni iu cu Otello eramu amici e nni davamu di tu. S'avìa misu 'ntesta che vulìa jiri supra la luna, picchì dicìa ca supra la luna s'attrovanu tutti li cosi ca si pirderu supra a terra. E ddà vulìa jiri pi ricupirari u fazzulettu ca ci avìa arrialatu a Desdemona e chi certamenti s'attruvava ddancapu. E vulìa pigghiari puru l'ampolla cu li lacrimi e li suspiri 'i so' mugghieri. Iu ci dissi 'i priparàrisi cu l'abbitu di viaggiu, di tinìrisi leggiu, megghiu chi putìa…. e ci dissi 'i fàrisi truvari davanzi a la distesa d'a marina d'unni avissimu partutu cu l'ippugrifu.

Ai cincu 'i matina s'apprisintò Otello. Parìa vistutu 'i matrimoniu e iu m'arrabbiavu ca 'unn'era a giusta tinuta pi pàrtiri. Ma iddu mi dissi ca ci tinìa a essiri licanti pi st'avvintura. E daccussì partemmu, iddu assittatu beddu commudu 'ngroppa all'ippugrifu e iu annagghiatu pi lu coddu, tuttu sturtigghiatu. Accuminciammu a vulari, a vulari, a vulari. Auti ntù celu. Prima varcammu a sfera di lu focu e ancora cchiù autu… fino a quannu 'un vittimu… la luna! La luna! Accuminciammu a scìnniri, a scìnniri, alleggiu alleggiu, planannu, planannu, scinnennu… E quannu stàvamu pi attirrari — anzi pi allunari — all'ippugrifu si cci rumperu i freni e accussì jiemmu a sbattiri e 'ntappammu cu grannissimu scrusciu e dulurusu schiantu.

Eppure mi sarebbe piaciuto essere amico stretto di Otello, essere in confidenza e aiutarlo a uscire dalla confusione. Ma non fu possibile. E questo dispiacere me lo porto con me ogni notte quando vado a letto. Ma prima di salutarvi vi volevo raccontare un sogno che ho fatto qualche giorno fa. Un sogno strano, in cui io e Otello eravamo amici e ci davamo del tu. Si era messo in testa che voleva andare sulla luna, perché diceva che sulla luna si trovano tutte le cose che si perdono sulla terra. E voleva andare là per recuperare il fazzoletto che aveva regalato a Desdemona e che certamente si trovava lassù. E voleva prendere anche l'ampolla con le lacrime e i sospiri di sua moglie. Io gli ho detto di prepararsi col vestito da viaggio, di tenersi più leggero che potesse…. e gli ho detto di farsi trovare davanti alla distesa della marina da cui saremmo partiti con l'ippogrifo.

Alle cinque della mattina si è presentato Otello. Sembrava vestito da matrimonio e io mi sono arrabbiato perché non era la tenuta giusta per partire. Ma lui mi ha detto che ci teneva ad essere elegante per quest'avventura. E così siamo partiti, lui seduto bello comodo in groppa all'ippogrifo e io avvinghiato al collo, tutto storto. Abbiamo cominciato a volare, a volare, a volare. Alto nel cielo. Prima abbiamo varcato la sfera di fuoco e ancora più in alto… fino a quando non abbiam visto… la luna! La luna! Abbiamo cominciato a scendere, a scendere, piano piano, planando, planando, scendendo… E quando stavamo per atterrare — anzi per allunare — all'ippogrifo si sono rotti i freni e così siamo andati a sbattere e a tamponare con grandissimo rumore e doloroso schianto.

Yet, I would like to have been a close friend of Othello, had his ear and helped him get out of his confusion. But it wasn't possible. And this sorrow follows me every night when I go to bed. But before saying good-bye I would like to tell you about a dream I had a few days ago. A strange dream, where Othello and I were friends and we used the familiar 'thou.' He had got it into his head that he wanted to go on the moon because he said that on the moon are found all the things that get lost on earth. And he wanted to go there to recover the handkerchief that he had given to Desdemona and that, for sure, was up there. He also wanted to get the vial with his wife's tears and sighs. I told him to wear travelling clothes, the lightest he had… and I told him to be at the expanse of the marina from whence we would leave on the hyppogryph.

At five in the morning Othello came. He looked like a bridegroom and I got mad because that was not the right attire to leave. But he said that he wanted to be elegant for this adventure. So we left, he sitting comfortably on the hyppogryph's back, and I holding on to its neck, all crooked. Then we started to fly, to fly, to fly. High in the sky. First we flew across the fire sphere, then higher… until we saw… the moon! The moon! We started descending, descending, slowly, gliding, gliding, descending… and when we were about to land — rather, to moon land — the hyppogryph's brakes broke so we hit and crashed down with great noise and painful smash.

Un grosso fragore segnala che ha avuto luogo l'allunaggio. Le luci si accendono lentamente sulla superficie lunare. In scena c'è solo il soldato con una pesante ampolla in mano.

SOLDATO: Mancu u tempu di susìrinni e ripigghiàrinni di sta caduta supra a luna ca già si nni jiu Otello 'ncerca d'u fazzulettu. L'ampulla di li lacrimi e di li suspiri di Desdemona l'attruvò a primu corpu. M'a lassò a mmia e turnò a circari u fazzulettu luna luna. "Spiramu c'arriva subbitu" pinzava dintr'a me' testa. Purtroppu l'ippugrifu s'avìa fattu mali, s'avìa struppiatu e mi scantavu ca si 'un s'avissi arripigghiatu 'unn'avissimu pututu cchiù turnari a casa. 'Nfatti m'addunavu chi all'ippugrifu ci duleva forti l'ala: "E si 'un pò cchiù vulari?" dissi. "E si 'un pò cchiù purtari pisu? E si arristamu ccà e 'un putemu cchiù turnari â casa…?"

SOLDATO: Manco il tempo di alzarsi e riprendersi da sta caduta sulla luna che già Otello se n'era andato a cercare il fazzoletto. L'ampolla di lacrime e sospiri di Desdemona la trovò al primo colpo. La lasciò a me e tornò a cercare il fazzoletto sulla luna. "Speriamo che arrivi subito" pensavo nella mia testa. Purtroppo l'ippogrifo si era fatto male, si era storpiato e avevo paura che se non si fosse ripreso non avremmo potuto più tornare a casa. Infatti mi ero accorto che all'ippogrifo faceva molto male l'ala: "E se non può più volare?" dissi. "E se non può più portare peso? E se restiamo qui e non possiamo più tornare a casa?"

Arriva Otello correndo con un fazzoletto in mano. Zoppica vistosamente a causa dell'impatto rovinoso con la luna.

OTELLO: 'U truvai! 'U truvai! Eccu ch'attruvavu u fazzulettu …!

SOLDATO: Ma comu camini?

OTELLO: Mi struppiavu. Mi doli na 'nticchia a jamma. 'Un ta firi a purtari l'ippugrifu, 'un sì bravu pilota… E poi m'allurdavu tuttu u vistitu bonu.

OTELLO: L'ho trovato! L'ho trovato! Ecco che ho trovato il fazzoletto…!

SOLDATO: Ma come cammini?

OTELLO: Ho preso una storta. Mi fa un po' male la gamba. Non ce la fai a portare l'ippogrifo, non sei un bravo pilota… E poi mi sono sporcato tutto il vestito buono.

A big clang signals the moon landing. Lights slowly turn onto the lunar surface. On stage there is just the soldier holding a heavy vial.

SOLDIER: Not even the time to recover from this crash landing on the moon and Othello was already in search of the handkerchief. He found the vial with Desdemona's tears and sighs right away. He left it to me and went back to search for the handkerchief. "Let's hope he returns quickly," I thought. Unfortunately, the hyppogryph had hurt itself, it had got maimed and I was afraid that if it did not recover we would not be able to go back home. In fact, I noticed that its wing hurt: "And if it can't fly anymore?" I said. "And if it can't carry any weight? And if we are stuck here and can't go home?"

Othello arrives running, a handkerchief in hand. He limps visibly because of the impact during the moon landing.

OTHELLO: I found it! I found it! I found the handkerchief...!

SOLDIER: How art thou walking?

OTHELLO: I twisted my ankle. My leg hurts a bit. Thou canst not drive a hyppogryph, thou art not a good pilot... I also got my nice suit dirty.

SOLDATO: Ti l'avìa dittu 'i mittìriti còmmudu cu l'abbitu di viaggiu. Ma tu 'un mi vo' sèntiri mai. Ora ni nn'amu a gghiri. T'haiu a ddari na nutizia amara.

OTELLO: Chi succidìu?

SOLDATO: Si struppiò puru l'ippugrifu, si fici mali, ci doli l'ala e 'un pò purtari tròppu pisu. Sti cosi c'attruvasti sunnu troppu pisanti e ccà l'amu a lassari.

OTELLO: Ma tu sì pazzu. Doppu tuttu stu viaggiu 'un lassu nenti. Ma poi mi servunu sti cosi priziusi.

SOLDATO: Chi ci ha' ffari cu sti cosi?

OTELLO: Ci vogghiu cunzari 'nta stanza 'i lettu 'n altarinu chinu di ciuri a me' mugghieri. E chistu fazzulettu ricamatu e chista ampudda china d'i so' lacrimi sunnu 'mpurtantissimi relicui. Sta cosa l'haiu a ffari picchì m'haiu a ffari pirdunari ca l'ammazzavu senza mutivu.

SOLDATO: Ma picchì, si c'era mutivu 'un t'avissi pintutu d'avilla ammazzata? Amunì va', ca si fici tardu.

OTELLO: No. Si tu ti nni vo' jiri, vattinni. Tantu iu arrestu ccà picchì mi cuntaru ca l'anima di tutti i fimmini ammazzati ntà terra vennu a finìscinu ccà, supra a luna. E pirciò ora mi mettu a circari a me' mugghieri. Pò essiri ca chiamannula macari l'attrovu. Desdemona! Desdemona! Desdemona!

SOLDATO: Te l'avevo detto di metterti comodo con il vestito da viaggio. Ma tu non stai mai a sentire. Ora dobbiamo andare. Ti devo dare una brutta notizia.

OTELLO: Cos'è successo?

SOLDATO: Ha preso una storta anche l'ippogrifo, si è fatto male, gli fa male un'ala e non può portare troppo peso. Ste cose che hai trovato sono troppo pesanti e le dobbiamo lasciare.

OTELLO: Ma tu sei pazzo. Dopo tutto sto viaggio non lascio niente. Ma poi mi servono queste cose preziose.

SOLDATO: Cosa ci devi fare con ste cose?

OTELLO: Voglio allestire in camera da letto un altarino pieno di fiori per mia moglie. E questo fazzoletto ricamato e questa ampolla piena delle sue lacrime sono reliquie importantissime. Devo fare questa cosa perché mi devo far perdonare per averla ammazzata senza motivo.

SOLDATO: Ma perché, se ci fosse stato un motivo non ti saresti pentito di averla ammazzata? Andiamo va, che si è fatto tardi.

OTELLO: No. Se tu vuoi andare, vai. Tanto io resto qui perché mi hanno detto che le anime di tutte le donne ammazzate sulla terra vengono a finire qui, sulla luna. E perciò ora mi metto a cercare mia moglie. Può essere che se la chiamo magari la trovo. Desdemona! Desdemona! Desdemona!

Otello, come preso da febbre dissennata, chiama sua moglie urlando, correndo ad ampie falcate zoppicanti. Il soldato lo rincorre cercando di farlo ragionare.

OTELLO: Desdemona! Desdemona!

OTELLO: Desdemona! Desdemona!

SOLDIER: I told thee to wear comfortable clothes. Thou never listenest. Now we have to go. I have to give thee bad news.

OTHELLO: What happened?

SOLDIER: The hyppogryph twisted its ankle too, it's hurt, a wing hurts and it can't carry too much weight. These things thou didst find are too heavy and we need to leave them here.

OTHELLO: Thou art mad. After all this trouble I shalt not leave a thing. I need these precious things.

SOLDIER: What dost thou need them for?

OTHELLO: I want to put up an altar full of flowers for my wife in my bedroom. This embroidered handkerchief and this vial are very important relics. I have to do this to ask for forgiveness for killing her without a reason.

SOLDIER: Why, hadst thou had a reason thou would not have repented for killing her? We better go, it's late.

OTHELLO: No. If thou wantest to go, go. I'll stay here because they told me that the souls of all the women killed on earth end up here, on the moon. So now I'll start looking for my wife. Perchance, if I call her I will find her. Desdemona! Desdemona! Desdemona!

Othello, as if seized by a delirious fever, calls his wife screaming, running taking big lame steps. The soldier runs after him trying to make him reason.

OTHELLO: Desdemona! Desdemona!

SOLDATO: Ma chi fai? Ma chi curri? Sccc… zìttuti! Ma chi vinisti pi rumpiri lu magicu silenziu di la luna…? Amunì: comu 'nsemmula vinimmu, 'nsemmula ni nni turnamu a casa.
(strappando a Otello il fazzoletto)
E sti cosi 'i lassamu ccà.

OTELLO: Nonzi. U fazzulettu m'u portu. Si vo', lassu a giacca pi nun fari pisu. E puru l'ampolla cu li lacrimi e i suspiri.

SOLDATO: Ma chi dici, "a giacca"? Senza a giacca, ntà galassia c'u friddu chi c'è! Ma poi, iu dicu, stu fazzulettu tu l'arrialasti a idda. 'Unn'è 'u to'. E pirciò ha' essiri bravu a sapillu pèrdiri…

OTELLO: Ma allura 'unn'ha' caputu nenti. Iu 'unn'u vogghiu pi mmia, 'u vogghiu pi l'altarinu.

SOLDATO: Ma chi altarinu e altarinu! 'Unn'u capisti ca fu chistu u dannu? L'amuri 'unn'è cosa c'havi bisugnu d'altari o monumenti. Pi chistu 'nfuddisti. Picchì scanciasti a to' mugghieri pi na cosa troppu cilesti. Ma idda era na fimmina, na fimmina tirrena, bedda pi chistu, picchì 'mpricisa, 'mpirfetta, bedda pi chistu comu a luna… Havi natura tirrestri a luna… A vidi? È china di difetti e 'mpirfizioni. Havi la peddi ruvida e scrizziata. E chistu 'a fa cosa cuncreta, cosa viventi. Tu ti l'aspittavi forsi ca lu mantu candidu, la luci sublimi, tinevanu ammucciatu tuttu st'universu di macchie, spurgenzi, pirtusi, avvaddamenti… A luna è bedda e 'a putemu taliari picchì 'unn'havi a luci 'ncandiscenti di lu suli. A luna, a candida luna, è fatta di burruni e di crateri. Eppuru resta magica e lucenti…

SOLDATO: Ma che fai? Dove corri? Sccc… zitto! Ma sei venuto a rompere il magico silenzio della luna…? Andiamo: così come siamo venuti insieme, insieme torniamo a casa.
(strappando a Otello il fazzoletto)
E ste cose le lasciamo qui.

OTELLO: No. Il fazzoletto me lo porto. Se vuoi lascio la giacca per non fare peso. E pure l'ampolla con le lacrime e i sospiri.

SOLDATO: Ma che dici, "la giacca"? Senza la giacca, nella galassia col freddo che c'è! Ma poi, dico io, sto fazzoletto lo hai regalato a lei. Non è tuo. E perciò devi essere bravo a saperlo perdere…

OTELLO: Ma allora non hai capito niente. Io non lo voglio per me, lo voglio per l'altarino.

SOLDATO: Ma che altarino e altarino! Non l'hai capito che il danno è stato questo? L'amore non è una cosa che ha bisogno di altari o monumenti. Per questo sei impazzito. Perché hai scambiato tua moglie per una cosa troppo celeste. Ma lei era una donna, una donna terrestre, bella per questo, perché imprecisa, imperfetta, bella per questo, come la luna… La luna ha una natura terrestre… La vedi? È piena di difetti e imperfezioni. Ha la pelle ruvida e screziata. E questo la rende una cosa concreta, una cosa vivente. Tu ti aspettavi forse che il manto candido, la luce sublime, tenessero nascosto tutto st'universo di macchie, sporgenze, pertugi, avvallamenti… La luna è bella e la possiamo guardare perché non ha la luce incandescente del sole. La luna, la candida luna, è fatta di burroni e di crateri. Eppure resta magica e lucente…

SOLDIER: What dost thou do? Where dost thou run? Shush… quiet! Didst thou come to break the magical silence of the moon…? Let's go: we came together and we'll return home together. (*snatching the handkerchief from Othello*)
We'll leave these here.

OTHELLO: No. I'll bring the handkerchief. If thou insist I'll leave my jacket to be lighter. The vial with tears and sighs too.

SOLDIER: What dost thou say, "the jacket"? Without a jacket in the galaxy, as cold as it is! Thou gavest this handkerchief to her. It's not thine. Thou hast to be good and let go of it…

OTHELLO: Thou hast not understood, then. I don't want it for myself, I want it for the altar.

SOLDIER: What altar! Didst thou not understand that this was the problem? Love needeth no altars nor monuments. That's why thou didst go mad. Thou didst take thy wife for a celestial being. But she was a woman, an earthly woman, beautiful because flawed, imperfect, beautiful as the moon… the moon has a earthly nature… Thou seest her? She is full of defects and imperfections. She hath a rough and cracked skin. This maketh her a concrete, living thing. Did thou expect, perchance, that the white surface, the sublime light hid this whole universe of spots, ledges, nooks, crannies… the moon is beautiful and we can look at her because she doth not have the incandescent light of the sun. The moon, the white moon, is made of cliffs and crates. Yet, it is magical and shiny…

È chista a so' poesia: sta luci tenui. Si tu nasci arreri e trovi n'atra Desdemona, l'ha' pinzari comu a luna: bedda picchì ruvida e scabrusa. Va bbe'. Facemu d'accussì. Si mi dici quanti su' i fraguluni di stu fazzulettu, t'u lassu 'n manu e t'u porti â casa.

OTELLO: Ma certu c'u sacciu: quinnici!

SOLDATO (*contando con una certa suspance*): Nonzi! Quartordici! Sunnu quartordici li fraguluni… Tuttu stu dannu, tuttu stu schifiu pi stu fazzulettu e mancu sai com'è fattu…
(*getta via il fazzoletto*)
Amunì… Amuninni p'a casa… Lassalu ccà e partemu… Dammi a manuzza. Camina cu mmia. Talìa. Talìalu quantu è beddu l'universo. L'universo è beddu picchì è apertu. È liberu e continua a caminari… L'amuri è 'n celo stiddatu. Ah… u firmamentu… strazianti, miravigghiusa biddizza d'u firmamentu…

È questa la sua poesia: sta luce tenue. Se tu nasci di nuovo e trovi un'altra Desdemona, devi pensarla come la luna: bella perché ruvida e irregolare. Vabbe'. Facciamo così. Se mi dici quante sono le fragole su questo fazzoletto, te lo lascio in mano e te lo porti a casa.

OTELLO: Ma certo che lo so: quindici!

SOLDATO: (*contando con una certa suspense*): No! Quattordici! Sono quattordici le fragole… Tutto sto disastro, tutto sto macello per sto fazzoletto e non sai nemmeno com'è fatto…
(*getta via il fazzoletto*)
Andiamo… Andiamo a casa… Lascialo qui e partiamo… Dammi la mano. Cammina con me. Guarda. Guarda quanto è bello l'universo. L'universo è bello perché è aperto. È libero e continua a camminare… L'amore è un cielo stellato. Ah… il firmamento… straziante, meravigliosa bellezza del firmamento…

This is her poetry: this feeble light. If thou art born again and meet another Desdemona, thou must think her as the moon: beautiful because rough and irregular. Listen, let's do this. If thou canst tell how many strawberries are on this handkerchief I will let thee bring it home.

OTHELLO: Of course I know: fifteen!

SOLDIER (*counting with anticipation*): No! Fourteen! There are fourteen strawberries... All this damage, all this mess for a handkerchief and he doesn't even know how it is...
(*he throws away the handkerchief*)
Let's go... Let's go home... Leave it here and let's go... Hold my hand. Walk with me. Look. Look how beautiful the universe is. The universe is beautiful because it's open. It is free and it keeps going... Love is a starry sky. Ah... the firmament... excruciating, wonderful beauty of the firmament...

ABOUT THE AUTHOR

LUIGI LO CASCIO is a theatre and film actor, director, and writer. He was awarded the David di Donatello as Best Actor for his first film role in *I cento passi* (2000, directed by Marco Tullio Giordana, with whom he also worked in *La meglio gioventù*, *Sanguepazzo*, and *Romanzo di una strage*). Among other films, he starred in *Luce dei miei occhi* and *La vita che vorrei* (Giuseppe Piccioni), *Il più bel giorno della mia vita* and *La bestia nel cuore* (Cristina Comencini), *Buongiorno notte* (Marco Bellocchio), *Mare nero* (Roberta Torre), *Miracle at St. Anna* (Spike Lee), *Baarìa* (Giuseppe Tornatore), *Noi credevamo* (Mario Martone), and *Il capitale umano* (Paolo Virzì). His directorial film debut, *La città ideale*, which he also wrote and starred in, won the Best Italian Film award at the 69th Venice Film Festival. He wrote and directed several works for the theatre. *Otello* debuted in February 2014.

ABOUT THE TRANSLATOR

GLORIA PASTORINO is Full Professor of Italian and French at Fairleigh Dickinson University, where she also teaches English and World literature, drama, and film. Her publications include articles on Italian theatre, cinema and migration, Italian cinema, mafia and masculinity, *Beyond the Grave: Zombies and the Romero Legacy* (with Bruce Peabody; McFarland), and translations for American productions of plays by Dario Fo, Luigi Pirandello, Mariangela Gualtieri, Romeo Castellucci, Lella Costa, and Juan Mayorga.

CROSSINGS
AN INTERSECTION OF CULTURES

Crossings is dedicated to the publication of Italian-language literature and translations from Italian to English.

Rodolfo Di Biasio. *Wayfarers Four*. Translated by Justin Vitello.
   1998. ISBN 1-88419-17-9. Vol 1.

Isabella Morra. *Canzoniere: A Bilingual Edition*. Translated by Irene Musillo Mitchell.
   1998. ISBN 1-88419-18-6. Vol 2.

Nevio Spadone. *Lus*. Translated by Teresa Picarazzi.
   1999. ISBN 1-88419-22-4. Vol 3.

Flavia Pankiewicz. *American Eclipses*. Translated by Peter Carravetta.
   Introduction by Joseph Tusiani.
   1999. ISBN 1-88419-23-2. Vol 4.

Dacia Maraini. *Stowaway on Board*. Translated by Giovanna Bellesia and Victoria Offredi Poletto.
   2000. ISBN 1-88419-24-0. Vol 5.

Walter Valeri, editor. *Franca Rame: Woman on Stage*.
   2000. ISBN 1-88419-25-9. Vol 6.

Carmine Biagio Iannace. *The Discovery of America*. Translated by William Boelhower.
   2000. ISBN 1-88419-26-7. Vol 7.

Romeo Musa da Calice. *Luna sul salice*. Translated by Adelia V. Williams.
   2000. ISBN 1-88419-39-9. Vol 8.

Marco Paolini & Gabriele Vacis. *The Story of Vajont*. Translated by Thomas Simpson.
   2000. ISBN 1-88419-41-0. Vol 9.

Silvio Ramat. *Sharing A Trip: Selected Poems*. Translated by Emanuel di Pasquale.
   2001. ISBN 1-88419-43-7. Vol 10.

Raffaello Baldini. *Page Proof*. Edited by Daniele Benati. Translated by Adria Bernardi.
   2001. ISBN 1-88419-47-X. Vol 11.

Maura Del Serra. *Infinite Present*. Translated by Emanuel di Pasquale and Michael Palma.
   2002. ISBN 1-88419-52-6. Vol 12.

Dino Campana. *Canti Orfici*. Translated and Notes by Luigi Bonaffini.
   2003. ISBN 1-88419-56-9. Vol 13.

Roberto Bertoldo. *The Calvary of the Cranes*. Translated by Emanuel di Pasquale.
   2003. ISBN 1-88419-59-3. Vol 14.

Paolo Ruffilli. *Like It or Not*. Translated by Ruth Feldman and James Laughlin.
   2007. ISBN 1-88419-75-5. Vol 15.

Giuseppe Bonaviri. *Saracen Tales*. Translated by Barbara De Marco.
   2006. ISBN 1-88419-76-3. Vol 16.

Leonilde Frieri Ruberto. *Such Is Life*. Translated by Laura Ruberto. Introduction by Ilaria Serra. 2010. ISBN 978-1-59954-004-7. Vol 17.

Gina Lagorio. *Tosca the Cat Lady*. Translated by Martha King. 2009. ISBN 978-1-59954-002-3. Vol 18.

Marco Martinelli. *Rumore di acque*. Translated and edited by Thomas Simpson. 2014. ISBN 978-1-59954-066-5. Vol 19.

Emanuele Pettener. *A Season in Florida*. Translated by Thomas De Angelis. 2014. ISBN 978-1-59954-052-2. Vol 20.

Angelo Spina. *Il cucchiaio trafugato*. 2017. ISBN 978-1-59954-112-9. Vol 21.

Michela Zanarella. *Meditations in the Feminine*. Translated by Leanne Hoppe. 2017. ISBN 978-1-59954-110-5. Vol 22.

Francesco "Kento" Carlo. *Resistenza Rap*. Translated by Emma Gainsforth and Siân Gibby. 2017. ISBN 978-1-59954-112-9. Volume 23.

Kossi Komla-Ebri. *EMBAR-RACE-MENTS*. Translated by Marie Orton. 2019. ISBN 978-1-59954-124-2. Volume 24.

Angelo Spina. *Immagina la prossima mossa*. 2019. ISBN 978-1-59954-153-2. Volume 25.

CPSIA information can be obtained
at www.ICGtesting.com
Printed in the USA
BVHW011056250920
589625BV00006B/275